TRIAD

BY THE SAME AUTHOR

Novels

Angels in the Snow
The Kites of War
For Infamous Conduct
The Yermakov Transfer
Touch the Lion's Paw (filmed as Rough Cut)
Grand Slam
The Great Land
The St Peter's Plot
I, Said the Spy
Trance
The Red Dove
The Judas Code
The Golden Express
The Man Who Was Saturday
Vendetta
Chase

Autobiographies

The Sheltered Days
Don't Quote Me But
And I Quote
Unquote
Just Like the Blitz

Under the pseudonym Richard Falkirk

Blackstone
Blackstone's Fancy
Beau Blackstone
Blackstone and the Scourge of Europe
Blackstone Underground
Blackstone on Broadway
The Twisted Wire
The Chill Factor

TRIAD

by

Derek Lambert

HAMISH HAMILTON · LONDON

First published in Great Britain 1987
by Hamish Hamilton Ltd
27 Wrights Lane London W8 5TZ

Copyright © 1987 by Derek Lambert

British Library Cataloguing Publication Data
Lambert, Derek
Triad.
I.   Title
823'.914[F]   PR6062.A47

ISBN 0–241–12154–X

Typeset at The Spartan Press Ltd,
Lymington, Hants
Printed and bound in Great Britain by
Mackays of Chatham

For Ed Owen
in Madrid

ACKNOWLEDGEMENTS

Mike and Sybil Keats, without whose hospitality in Hong Kong the book would never have been written; Don Wise and Daphne for being there.

All the journalists who assisted me, in particular Emily Lau of the *Far Eastern Economic Review*, Zelda Cawthorne of the *South China Morning Post*, David Bonavia, who seems to know China as Lawrence once knew Arabia, Bert Okuley of UPI and John Ball.

Jackie Pullinger, the lady from South London whose resolute belief in God as a missionary in Kowloon, seeded the creation of her fictional counterpart, an American missionary who doubts.

Detective Superintendent John Norman of the Royal Hong Kong Police; Hari Bedi, of Exxon; Hu and Annie van Es and Russell Cawthorne of Golden Harvest films.

And all the kind people in Hong Kong who helped me at the beginning of this the last decade of a colonial epoch.

I must also offer thanks to Chief Superintendent Brian Merritt, head of the Serious and Organised Crime Group in Hong Kong, who, fortuitously for me, led a massive assault on a triad society in April '87, thus adding factual credence to the narrative. I have never met Mr. Merritt and my superintendent, Harry Price, is wholly imaginary.

AUTHOR'S NOTE

There will inevitably be mistakes in a novel about Hong Kong written by an outsider; for these I crave indulgence. Some apparent errors, however, are intended. There is, for instance, no 18G triad, although there are many others, and members of these societies rarely refer to their organisations as triads. For such variances I seek understanding.

'Triad activities are a menace in two main ways. As far as the general public is concerned, it is the gang activity, the threatening behaviour, the assaults, the intimidation and the blackmail that are most worrying. But triads are also deeply involved in organised crime: drugs, gambling, vice and protection rackets. Both areas need to be tackled.' – Fight Crime Committee Secretariat, Hong Kong, April 1986.

CHAPTER 1

The Chinese shoeshine boy, who was 62, assembled the implements of his trade with care. Tins of Kiwi polish, bowl of water, brushes, cloths, puffs of cotton wool and five packets of No. 4 heroin.

Then he settled on his haunches behind his worn footrest and gazed into the moving forest of legs and feet on the tourist shopping street in Kowloon on mainland Hong Kong.

The prospects for legitimate business looked promising: it had rained overnight but now a warm breeze funnelling down the street from Victoria Harbour was drying shoes but leaving a residue of splashed dust.

Without looking up the shoeshine boy, bare–chested with cropped grey hair, yellow eyes and a red and green dragon tattooed on one arm, identified the occupants of the shoes. Blunt-toed and sensible, American tourists – bad joss because they thought his trade was degrading; Italian-made loafers, wealthy Chinese – good joss because they weren't concerned about degradation as long as *they* didn't lose face; shabbily expensive, British – possibilities because they liked to place one foot on the pedestal as though it were the globe.

A shoe came to rest in front of him. Brown with cracks between the last lace and the pointed toe. Indian, Filipino, Portuguese from Macao . . . a sorry object worn by someone who could have neither the pride nor the money to want a shine. Unless. . . .

The shoeshine boy known as Red Eye Ng because of a red spot on one eyeball, picked up the plastic protectors which shielded

1

sock from polish and inserted his forefinger between leather and nylon. Not a cent.

A voice from above said in Cantonese: 'It is my shoes that need cleaning not my feet.'

Your shoes need burning, you piece of dogmeat, Red Eye Ng thought. A street vendor, perhaps, with a body-belt heavy with fake Rolex Oyster watches, or a pimp on his way to recruit a new girl. Red Eye Ng applied himself vigorously to the unworthy shoes; still he did not look up.

A five-dollar coin held between two long-nailed fingers entered his vision.

'Ten,' he said automatically. Once, according to street legend, a tourist had paid 50 Hong Kong dollars.

'Five is three too much,' said the voice. 'But I am generous today.'

Ayeeya, if you are generous then I am the God of Wealth!

The dragon on Red Eye Ng's arm writhed as he took the coin.

He replaced the brushes and polish, checked the concealed bags of heroin with the tips of his fingers – thieves would steal the fillings out of your teeth these days – and settled down again to study the passing footwear.

After a while his concentration faltered and he looked up at the floating faces of the *gweilos*, the foreigners, scavenging for bargains beneath the Cantonese signs on the broad reaches of Nathan Road. Cameras, videos, computers, calculators, jade, opal, ivory, silk. . . .

They always bargained but they always paid over the top and the shopkeepers smiled into their cash registers and thanked the gods for making the barbarians think they were smart.

A shoe as bright as a mirror descended onto the footrest. American Navy; Red Eye Ng wasn't fooled by civilian clothes. Three US warships had berthed yesterday greatly exciting the bar girls of Tsim Sha Tsui in Kowloon, and Wanchai on Hong Kong Island. The shoe didn't need shining but US sailors, who wore plastic footwear, liked posing for photographs; they also paid well, generously not stupidly.

Red Eye Ng had a sneaking regard for American sailors and

he glanced almost shyly at the owner of the beetle-bright shoe.

A black face bunched into a grin looked down. 'Hi, buddy, how you doin'?'

Red Eye Ng said he was doing fine but he didn't think the sailor understood.

'How much?'

'You name price.'

The sailor produced two HK ten-dollar bills and asked the other black: 'How much is that in real money?'

'Three, four bucks.'

'Okay?'

Red Eye Ng said it was okay and applied himself to the shoe while the second sailor took a picture with a new Pentax. Red Eye Ng hoped he hadn't paid too much for it.

He glanced at his watch. Ten forty-five am and still no requests for white powder. But he had consulted the calendar and the best hours for his day sign in this, the Year of the Ox in the Heavenly Stem Yi Earthly Branch Ch'ou, were 11 am to 1 pm.

Furthermore there were four auspicious stars on duty, five hours were good, three average and four evil. It was not a good day for honouring your ancestors or praying to the gods but it was propitious for installing a new bed and inviting the parents of many children to sleep in it, an inducement to the owners to have children although hardly applicable to a sixty-two-year-old grandfather. Two bad stars were on duty and it was inadvisable to show off; the day, therefore, was finely balanced between optimism and pessimism.

But when were the evil hours?

Red Eye Ng, a member of the 18G Triad Secret Society, glanced uneasily at two Chinese members of the Royal Hong Kong Police, crisply smart in their fawn uniforms. One of them was talking into a radio handset. Fifteen years ago this wouldn't have worried him: the triads had infiltrated the police so comprehensively that he would have been warned if he was under observation. But since the corruption scandals the force had been cleaned up and he couldn't rely on a tip-off.

3

He turned his head and inspected a mildewed block of offices, apartments and hostel rooms scabbed with advertising signs. Triads were entrenched there and from one window framed with ferns he noticed a flash of light. A weatherman with field glasses? Lord, he was nervous today. Red Eye Ng whose religious beliefs embraced Taoism, Confucianism and Buddhism wondered what he had done to offend the gods. Or encourage the devils.

He conferred with the shoeblack sitting on the sidewalk next to him.

'Bird Breast Choi, what sort of a day lies ahead for you?'

'A day of prosperity,' replied Bird Breast Choi who consulted a variety of diviners to assess the portents; and since, at the beginning of the new year, he had resorted to the Secret Book of Chu-Ko which relied on the number of strokes in your name, more than his fair share of soft-leathered shoes had alighted on his footrest.

But Bird Breast Choi whose chest looked as delicate as a sparrow's didn't make that much money: he didn't sell dope. Red Eye Ng felt no guilt about supplying heroin: he lived in the Walled City where addicts were as common as fleas in a dog pound and he knew that addicts had to have their fixes and therefore he was performing acts of mercy. Furthermore, being a triad under oath, he had no choice.

At present addicts were enjoying a respite: a big consignment had arrived from the Triangle and No. 3 heroin was selling at only HK $60 a gram. So why, Red Eye Ng, are you selling pure No. 4? In numerology three means long life, four death.

He said to Bird Breast Choi: 'This good fortune that will bless you today. . . . Will it touch others who labour with you?'

Bird Breast Choi folded his thin arms and said: 'If I were not honest with you, Red Eye Ng, the gods would frown on me so I must tell you that the prosperity is confined to me,' and Red Eye Ng thought: *Diu nei loh ma*, one day I will crush that matchstick chest of yours until your heart fills your throat.

He pointed at the two policemen: 'The currents of air have a lot on their minds today.'

4

'Small minds have to work busily, Red Eye Ng.'

Another flash of light from the mildewed block.

Red Eye Ng glanced at his watch again. 10.50. In ten minutes the best hours of the day would begin.

The light was probably a mirror, a girl brushing her hair in front of it. Red Eye Ng remembered a girl he had known in his youth who had brushed sparks from her long, blue-black hair.

The shoe that appeared on his pedestal was grey, pointed, with two buckles; the sock was also grey, almost transparent; the skin beneath white. The leather had been groomed with care but with cheap, instant-shine polish; the soles and heels had been repaired once with more haste than skill. The shoe of a flash European, with little time to spare. An expensive account middleman, Red Eye Ng decided, buying rhinestone blouses or cigarette lighters or computer games in bulk for resale in London, Berlin, Rome, Paris. . . .

He ran one finger between sock and shoe. The bill was folded twice. He palmed it. A red one, HK $100. He glanced up; loss of face but he had to be sure. From where he squatted he could see sandy hair in the nostrils, teeth stained yellow on the inside by tobacco tar, bristles on the underside of the close-shaved chin. Flushed cheeks, pin-point pupils, running nose . . . this *gweilo* was hooked.

Red Eye Ng slipped a protector and a small transparent bag of heroin inside the shoe and applied himself vigorously to the grey leather.

When he had finished the second shoe he pushed it away. It joined its companion on the sidewalk. Sometimes grateful addicts paid over the top for the actual shoeshine, sometimes they didn't pay at all. At moments like this it was loss of face to look up and question intentions.

The two shoes pointed at Red Eye Ng.

The voice of their owner reached him in passable Cantonese: 'I am a police officer. . . .'

It was 10.59.

*   *   *

5

Thoughts fluttered like moths inside Red Eye Ng's skull as he made his way through the geometric web of streets separating Nathan Road from the waterfront to the Yau Ma Tei entrance to the MTR, the underground railway.

Possibly wisdom would visit him when he sought guidance at the temple he frequented outside the Walled City but at the moment he could only perceive two alternatives: co-operate with the police and risk a triad execution, refuse to co-operate and spend the rest of his life in gaol.

Touts beckoned from girlie bars, tourists gawked, construction workers sitting on the sidewalk gobbled takeaway rice lunches, a street sleeper twitched in his dreams. Red Eye Ng saw none of this, only the face of the detective from the Organised Crime Bureau accompanying him in the jade market beneath the Gascoigne Road fly-over.

The detective had rubbed the rouge from his cheeks and blown his nose and the pupils of his eyes were slowly dilating as they threaded their way past the squatting salesmen and women haggling with tourists over the price of pendants, bangles, statues and talismans.

'The elixir of life,' remarked the detective pointing at green ornaments spread on the ground on white satin. 'The link between heaven and earth. Once upon a time the rich were buried in suits of jade.'

A threat? Red Eye Ng wasn't sure how to approach this *gweilo* who talked in angles. Was he a fiend or merely one of the innocents who flew from Britain to fight crime with Cantonese and recitations about Chinese customs? Why the jade market? Was he cunning enough to know that this wasn't 18G territory? He decided to test him.

'You are signing my death warrant,' he said, 'talking to me here.'

'Garbage,' said the detective briskly. 'I am new here. A businessman chasing the dragon and we are here to do business, you and me.'

Hope briefly warmed Red Eye Ng. Perhaps this current of air was a drug addict seeking a fix in the most devious of fashions.

6

He glanced at his face. It was surprisingly neat for a *gweilo* with a mole between the eyes which meant he rarely used his brain.

The detective said: 'In any case this is not 18G territory so no one will recognise you.'

So much for moles.

The detective stopped in front of two squatting jade dealers, each with one arm covered by a sheet of the *Oriental Daily*. His fawn trousers, Red Eye Ng noted, were creased like knives; his eyes and hair were pale. A neat, colourless fiend.

The detective pointed at the dealers. 'How much, I wonder?'

So he knew that beneath the newspapers they were shaking hands, moving their fingers to indicate prices before clinching a deal.

Red Eye Ng shrugged. How would he know? But he noted that the detective hadn't projected his knowledge, merely implied it. Gods, how devious was this one!

The detective said: 'Two weeks ago I was in London.'

Red Eye Ng waited for the next thrust.

They passed stalls of green, lavender and black jade from China, Australia, Taiwan, Burma. . . . Some tourists might buy pure jade, others relatively worthless serpentine or soapstone. The girl he had been thinking about earlier had drunk potions containing finely powdered jade to keep her long hair glossy.

'Soft, smooth and shining like kindness,' said the detective. 'Fine and strong like intelligence. . . .' He didn't add: 'Confucius.' Instead he said: 'Gerrard Street, London. Chinatown. That was my manor,' the last word incomprehensible in English.

Red Eye Ng inclined his head politely.

'The triads are taking over,' the detective said. 'And in New York, San Francisco, Amsterdam, Little Bourke Street in Melbourne. . . . That's why I'm here.'

A half-truth registered with Red Eye Ng but he said nothing.

'Officers like me have come here from all over the world to learn how to combat the gangs.'

'So how can I help you in your task?'

'By co-operating,' the detective said.

7

'I cannot do that. Surely you know the rules.'

'I want to know about organisation from No. 489, the Shan Chu, downwards to a humble 49 such as you. Methods of distribution. Rackets – prostitution, gambling, debt collecting, loan sharking, protection. . . .'

'I know nothing of these things,' Red Eye Ng protested.

'Membership, territories, relationship with other triads.'

Ayeeya, it is as though I haven't spoken. 'A humble 49 cannot possibly know such details.'

'I don't want you to disappoint your customers on Nathan Road; I want to see you there every morning selling white powder. . . . Let me know the current price, when there's a consignment due.'

And now the half-truth was expanding. How could such information help to fight the triads in London?

The detective said: 'To nail the leader in London I must know about the movements and habits of the leader here.'

So that is it, Red Eye Ng thought – this rotten mouth wants me to betray Kwan Tai. The whine of traffic on the flyover above was a dentist's drill.

'All 489s act differently,' he told the detective.

'His routine,' the detective said. 'When he meets the Grand Council, when he crosses the water . . as though he were crossing the river that divided London.'

Such cunning, helping me to save face by substituting London for Hong Kong. Betray Kwan Tai? Never. He must have shaken his head because the detective said pleasantly: 'There are alternatives. . . .'

'Then I must take them,' Red Eye Ng said, 'because although I would like to please you I cannot possibly do the things you ask.'

'You are getting old, Red Eye Ng.'

'We are all getting old from the moment we are born.'

'Sixty-two is not a great age but eighty-five. . . .'

'Eighty-five?' This angle was as sharp as a blade.

'The age you will be, Red Eye Ng, when you leave prison if you do not help me to overcome those devils in London.'

The detective bunched his fist and adjusted his fingers. Gods,

8

he was making the hand signal that a triad made to indicate he had been in jail.

Red Eye Ng stopped and gazed at a freckled European man bargaining over a jade carving of a dragon. I will never live to be eighty-five in Stanley or Shek Pik, he thought; after a few years they will move me to Ma Hang where they take the very old to die.

The European whose thighs were red beneath too-tight shorts said: 'I give you half,' winking at the fat girl beside him.

The woman behind the stall, her face as wrinkled as an autumn leaf, shook her head slowly and stared through the *gweilo* because now he didn't exist.

Red Eye Ng said: 'You are passing a death sentence on me.'

'One half,' the freckled European said, 'not a dollar, not a cent more.'

Several tourists had gathered beside the stall to observe how a deal should be struck. The European's smile was fierce now and his freckles moved with it.

The detective said: 'You have a choice.'

Such a choice. *I shall not disclose the secrets of the Hung Family, not even to my parents, brothers, or wife. I shall never disclose the secrets for money. I shall be killed by myriads of swords if I do so; I shall never betray my sworn brothers.*

He had taken the triad oath at the same time as Kwan Tai. But Kwan Tai had been born a Dragon, an emperor, dashing, wild, obstinate, whereas I was a Sheep, shy and withdrawn. And the Dragon had clawed his way to the leadership of the 18G while I was content with my lowly position. As a Sheep I fear and respect the Dragon and I cannot betray him.

'Put it this way,' the detective said, 'if you don't help me to overthrow those devils in London you will die in prison. You have my word on it.'

'And if I do help I will die at the hands of my brothers.'

'You are a secretive man, Red Eye Ng.' *Ah, he even knows I am a Sheep. What else does this rotten mouth know?* 'You are also clever. Is there any reason why your brothers should know you have helped me?'

9

The fat girl was urging the freckled *gweilo* to increase his offer. The smile on his face sickened. The vendor stared towards the land of her ancestors.

'You think a man such as Kwan Tai would not know?' Red Eye Ng asked. 'It is by knowing such things that he has been Shan Chu, our Dragon Head, for so long.'

Kwan Tai's name seemed to usher a new layer of thought into the detective's reasoning, a cloud across a clear moon. It was common knowledge that the authorities were trying to end the long reign of the triads, obvious that to do so they had to damp the fire of the Tiger who led the 18G.

I cannot be the instrument of Kwan Tai's destruction, he who was born in the same street as me in the Walled City, he who played with me in the alleyways while our fathers smoked foreign mud.

The detective said: 'It is not pleasant to die in Ma Hang.'

Not the death, the manner of it. The shame. This *gweilo* wasn't like so many others: he understood.

Freckle-face was shouting at the fat girl. His freckles danced angrily. Absorbed, the onlookers nodded and murmured. Freckle-face said: 'Half, no more,' and, arms crossed, stared at the vendor.

Still staring through him, the vendor pushed the carving across the stall with one hand and held out the other for the money. The *gweilo* blew air through pursed lips and winked grossly at the fat girl.

A part of Red Eye Ng applauded too because the carving was worth only a quarter of what Freckle Face had paid. If it was soapstone – and Freckle Face hadn't tried to find out by scratching it – then it was worth only a fraction.

'So tell me your thoughts,' the detective said, feeling the crease of one trouser leg and examining his finger as though he expected to find blood.

'The wings of my thoughts beat slowly today,' Red Eye Ng told him.

'They need a rest,' the detective said. 'Sleep well tonight, Red Eye Ng, and let me know tomorrow where their wings have

10

carried them. I will pass your pitch at the Hour of the Ox. If you have decided to help then touch the lobe of your right ear. If not. . . .'

Ma Hang! Red Eye Ng bought a tiny jade charm shaped like a peach for longevity and took it with him onto a northbound metro train.

Strap-hanging Chinese gazed incuriously at him sitting on the bright metal seat; two children ran squealing towards the head of the snake burrowing beneath the congestion of Kowloon towards the duck ponds and mountains of the New Territories.

Were all the eyes really so impersonal? Red Eye Ng glanced from one face to another. On the seat opposite two men slept, heads lolling. There were always exhausted Chinese on the Mass Transit Railway. Red Eye Ng tried to relax; instead he reflected that, if you were pursued, there was no escape inside the connecting segments of the snake; if you were trapped in its head or tail an assailant would wait until it slowed down before a station, slip a knife between your ribs and disappear with the crowds seeking the daylight.

He glanced again at the two passengers who had been asleep. The eyes of one of them, young and studious, a briefcase between his legs, were open, staring at him. It was often the case when people noticed the bloodspot in his eye; after all red was auspicious. But the young man had apparently been asleep and the weary didn't awake until the train slid into their stations. Red Eye Ng stood up and made his way casually along the length of the train stopping under an advertisement for toilet soap.

He glanced behind him. There was no sign of the young man. The strap-hangers reminded him of bats waiting for dusk.

He alighted at Lok Fu and walked south along Junction Road towards the Walled City. As he approached the squatting slums of his birthplace a little confidence returned: he would seek an audience with Kwan Tai and ask his advice. Teeth, gold, silver and white, grinned reassuringly at him from the shop windows of the illegal dentists on Tung Tau Chuen Road; he almost smiled back; instead he stroked the smooth surface of the jade peach in his pocket.

11

In a small temple hidden behind street stalls he lit a joss stick before the Goddess of Mercy who 'looks down and hears the cries of the world'. The flakes of his thoughts settled even more soothingly, an avenue in their midst leading to Kwan Tai. He stopped at a stall owned by another 49 and ate noodles and minced beef balls washed down with a carton of chrysanthemum tea.

Apartment blocks climbed above the stalls; the approaches to the Walled City seethed with humanity eddying around the berets of Tactical Unit police trying to stop refugees from Communist China finding sanctuary in the City. Serpent-faced airliners landing at the airport close by threatened to settle on the rooftops.

Red Eye Ng crossed the street and made his way along a narrow unmade path slippery from recent rain. On either side of him languished the ruins of shanty dwellings that had withstood a legion of typhoons but not the Government bulldozers. The sheet of corrugated iron to his left had been the roof of an opium den.

So elated was Red Eye Ng at the Goddess of Mercy's confirmation of his decision to consult Kwan Tai that, as he approached the public lavatory that had once been crowded with addicts shooting heroin and the corpses of those who had injected their last fix, he didn't notice the weatherman wearing a coolie hat get up from his stool at the entrance to the City and vanish into the gloom behind him.

Three minutes later Red Eye Ng was knocking at the door of his birthplace.

CHAPTER 2

The first thing that strikes the visitor to the Walled City of Kowloon is that it has no wall.

The walls were built in the 1840s by a group of Chinese who wanted to protect themselves against the barbaric British who, in 1841, had already grabbed the island of Hong Kong, Fragrant Harbour, as one of the spoils of the First Opium War. The gods advised them well because later the barbarians also *acquired* the mainland peninsula of Kowloon, Nine Dragons. But the Walled City wasn't included in the lease signed by Peking.

Chinese troops and a mandarin remained in the tiny, five-acre kingdom for a few months until they, too, were sent packing by the British.

But controversy about ownership, outside any general disagreement about the territory, lingered. As for the walls themselves, they survived until World War II when they were demolished by the Japanese invaders to extend the runway at Kai Tak airport.

Because of its disputed parentage the city has always remained a bastard. A stew which even today is not penetrated by police with enthusiasm.

It has a second name. Darkness.

From the outside it is a conspiracy of apartments, seedy and lofty, that from a distance look like cages and boxes piled on top of each other, their secrets contained by bars and shutters and dripping laundry. The true Darkness is within these barriers at ground level with a roof of cables, plastic, hardboard and sheet metal that forces a tall man to stoop and staunches the daylight.

13

The slimy alleys are lined with mousehole homes, stores and workshops.

Until recently prostitutes, children and grandmothers, solicited outside blue movie flea-pits, opium dens flourished and incumbent triads drew the blood of trespassers with fighting chains and hatchets.

Then electricity was installed. Police made occasional raids. The opium barons took to the hills of the New Territories separating Kowloon from China; the heroin dealers moved in; most of the whores moved downtown to Kowloon.

The squalor remained and so did the triads.

On the day of Red Eye Ng's encounter with the police the leader of the reigning triad, Kwan Tai, sat beside an altar on the third floor of an apartment block above the Darkness finding comfort from the ceremony in which he was a protagonist.

He enjoyed all the rituals, insisting against considerable opposition, that they be enacted to the full, because they were a legacy of the days when the triads possessed dignity and purpose. Before the societies had splintered, before street gangs had besmirched the name of Hung Mun, the true name of the triads implying a universal sect.

Before he grew old.

Kwan Tai, who was sixty-three, fled to Hong Kong from China in 1949 when the Communists drove the Nationalists – and their triad supporters – from the land. Men of Kwan Tai's age still supported the Nationalists on their offshore island, Taiwan; patriots of a lost cause, he supposed. But even if it was lost there was no reason why the 18G – born on the 18th day of the Fourth Moon, birthday of the Ruler of the Pole Star, in Guangzhou, better known to Westerners as Canton – should not retain its honour.

On the other side of the altar the Incense Master in white robe, long red scarf and head-band of a 489, began to intone:

'Two ancient trees on either side,

'Will bring stability to the nation. . . .'

A promotion ceremony. Kwan Tai remembered his own initiation nearly half a century ago in Canton. The intensity of

14

the thirty-six oaths reached him through the years. Loyalty to the 'sworn brothers' and help for their families, honesty within the triad. . . . *If I have supplied false details about myself for the purpose of joining the Hung family I shall be killed by five thunderbolts.*

Kwan Tai pressed the tips of his fingers together: his parents had been killed by the Communists and he had given himself the name by which he was now known. It meant God of War.

The Incense Master continued to intone beside the altar bearing two brass lamps – the ancient trees –, an incense pot, fruit, dates and flowers, glasses of tea and wine and three symbols of rank, Red Pole, Fan and Grass Sandal.

From being a humble 49 Kwan Tai had been promoted swiftly to Messenger, middleman between the Society and those who funded it, and then to a Red Pole, a warrior, proficient in the martial arts, renowned for the ruthlessness with which he fought rival societies and executed traitors within the 18G.

With such clandestine knowledge how could he fail to rise still further. Within twelve years of his initiation Kwan Tai was leader, Shan Chu, Dragon Head. He had stayed in command for thirty years and today he controlled 100,000 of the 300,000 triads in Hong Kong and legions more in Chinatown outposts all over the world. According to a government report there were fifty triad societies in Hong Kong. Kwan Tai acknowledged half a dozen of them, in particular the Yellow Pang.

The Incense Master was now worshipping the Hung family. Any minute now Kwan Tai, casually dressed in black trousers and white shirt because it was promotion, not initiation, would address the candidates. He had no idea what he was going to say.

Remember the old values? An honourable family permitted only to wreak vengeance on its enemies, to exploit only the weak and the corrupt?

Weak. . . . It is you who are weak now, Dragon Head. Sapped by the long years of power. Gods, how power finally devours itself!

Kwan Tai gazed at the candidates standing in groups of three facing the altar and wondered how they saw him. Despite the

15

needles of grey in his black hair and thick eyebrows, despite the knotting of the muscles on his pugilist's arms, the creases on his bull neck and the tentative meeting of chest and belly, despite all these did they still see strength? The Dragon breathing fire, the Emperor, impetuous, omnipotent, stubborn, zealous. . . .

Or did they notice the claws of doubt at the corners of his eyes? *See* the hesitancy of vision. *Hear* the question in his skull: can honour ever justify death?

And had it not been written that, unless he disciplines his passions, the Dragon will burn himself out and disappear in a puff of smoke?

Kwan Tai made a conventional speech, outlining the aims of the 18G, forgotten by so many, and lauded the candidates. But his words had not glinted with knives and he felt their disappointment.

What if they had known of the battle for his body on the one hand, his soul on the other?

The policeman, the current of air, they would understand.

The girl, a *gweilo* – never!

The Red Pole candidate knelt on a rush mat in front of the altar while the Incense Master intoned:

'With the support of our brethren and the permission of our President you are appointed to the office of Hung Kwan. You are required to be loyal, faithful and energetic in the service of the Hung Mun.'

The candidate replied: 'I shall obey your commands.'

The Incense Master tied a red band around the candidate's head, and hung a red sash over his right shoulder, tying it beneath his left arm.

Then Kwan Tai took a gold paper flower from the altar and handed it to the Incense Master who placed it in the head-band of the candidate who was Kwan Tai's son.

*   *   *

Red Eye Ng was waiting for Kwan Tai in the Darkness outside the hovel where a craftsman who made grotesque rubber masks

16

that were exported all over the world was preparing to shut up shop and sleep beside his nightmares. Water dripped from pythons of cables above the alley; a rat splashed through a puddle.

As Red Eye Ng approached Kwan Tai two bodyguards grabbed his arms and Dragon Head's son, now Warrior, slid his hand inside his jacket. Am I to be his first victim? Red Eye Ng wondered. What joss for him to save Dragon Head's life on his day of promotion.

Kwan Tai held up his hand. 'Let him go,' and to Red Eye Ng: 'What do you want, old friend?'

Red Eye Ng bowed, hands praying. 'I must speak to you privately, Dragon Head. The honour of Hung Mun is at stake,' he added craftily.

Kwan Tai's son, whose bold face was known to millions, said: 'You know full well, Red Eye Ng, that to be granted an audience with Dragon Head you must apply through the Vanguard.'

'That is true, Red Eye Ng, and for that you may be punished,' Kwan Tai said. 'But if our honour is truly at stake then I will listen to what you have to say. You will come across the water and we will take tea together.'

Red Eye Ng glanced at the features of the new Warrior, neater than his father's, thick eyebrows thinned as befits a star of Golden Harvest film studios. It was a secret.

In the back of the grey Nissan taking them through the Cross Harbour Tunnel from Kowloon to Hong Kong Island, Kwan Tai said: 'It is good to be alone with you, old friend.' He slumped in the seat and Red Eye Ng knew that he had allowed the power to flow from his body.

But even when it was relaxed Kwan Tai's wrestler's body was in better shape than that of Red Eye Ng whose belly had sagged towards his workplace, the sidewalk.

'I seek your counsel, Dragon Head.'

'Later, later.' Kwan Tai patted Red Eye Ng's knee. 'It is as though we had never gone our separate ways, you and I.'

'How could it have been otherwise? You are a Dragon, I am a Sheep.'

17

Red Eye Ng sat stiffly. He felt the pressure of the water above the tunnel, the squeezing of its walls. It was the first time he had travelled through the tunnel; he preferred the old Star ferries butting their way across the broad waters of the harbour channel swarming with junks, pilots, freighters, warships, hydrofoils, hovercraft, car ferries, sampans. . . . He liked to feel the breeze from the South China Sea on his face and he saw pirates on its distant waters.

'But we have both served the cause well, you and I, and our ancestors must be proud of us. The peace of Nirvana awaits us.' Kwan Tai's voice lacked the flints of confidence. 'But in this earthly passage we must expect power and wealth to fade to preserve the harmony of the universe.'

But not in Hang Man jail!

Red Eye Ng who had sought out Kwan Tai to receive succour not to administer it said: 'What I have to tell you, Dragon Head, affects us all.'

Kwan Tai said: 'We are not in the City of Willows now. So let this matter that grieves you so wait until the tea is between us. Do you remember the time in the Darkness when we drove the Yellow Pang from the streets?'

The scar that still ached where a sharpened rasp wielded by a Yellow Pang had entered his belly through his navel never let him forget. The fight when he had killed two invaders with his hatchet and strangled a third had established Kwan Tai as the legitimate candidate for the leadership of the 18G.

But, or so it seemed to Red Eye Ng, his old friend was now seeking strength from the past. What had happened to him?

The Nissan, driven by a 49, burst into the twilight at Causeway Bay. Lights in the skyscrapers reaching for the peaks of the island were multiplying; streets and flyovers ran with homeward traffic.

The 49 drove the Nissan to Kwan Tai's tea store in 18G territory in Wanchai as though he were pursued.

Red Eye Ng had entered the shop only once before. It was becalmed in time, history imprisoned in the coloured tins of tea on the wall shelves. Keemun Red, White Peony, Luk On black, rare yellows, green-red Cliff from Fujien and Chaozhou. Tea, one of the Seven Daily Necessities.

Kwan Tai led Red Eye Ng through the shop to his private chamber where he played mahjong, where opium had once been smoked. They sat at a black table inlaid with mother-of-pearl while Kwan Tai's servant poured mountain water into a brew cup of Keemin Red.

'He is good this one,' Kwan Tai said. 'He knows that water must not be boiled until it is dead: it must still have life when it reaches the leaf.' He rinsed lines from his face with the tips of his fingers. 'What would happen to us without tea?' he asked Red Eye Ng.

'I think,' Red Eye Ng said carefully, 'that we would die.'

He studied Dragon Head's profile. Nose of purpose, eyes of courage, ears of prosperity. And he saw him as a young man, face flat and strong, eyes hooded with wisdom, still carrying the banner of the Nationalists.

Why had the strokes of purpose wandered? Not surely because he suddenly acknowledged the People's Republic; that had been established for decades.

The level of the water in the brew cup fell, the servant snatched the lid, poured the russet infusion into the drinking cups and passed the lid to Kwan Tai. Kwan Tai inhaled and nodded almost sleepily.

The servant left them with their tea.

Kwan Tai held a mouthful in his mouth to alert his taste buds, swallowed, sighed. Then he said: 'I hear your thoughts, Red Eye Ng.'

Alarmed, Red Eye Ng said: 'Are you ready to hear what I have to say?'

Kwan Tai who manufactured proverbs said: 'Tea teaches you that age is youth.' Red Eye Ng to whom no one listened on this treacherous day waited. 'It is the tincture of the past and yet it glows with life. Look into your cup, Red Eye Ng.'

Red Eye Ng looked and saw the face of the detective.

'In age the mind glows while the body withers.'

He is trying to reassure himself, Red Eye Ng decided, and felt surer of himself. 'What of green tea, Kwan Tai?'

19

'It is callow not young; it hasn't acquired wisdom. It is strange, is it not, to reflect that the British barbarians once paid for their tea with opium?'

'Not strange for devils who think with two minds,' Red Eye Ng observed daringly.

'Opium and tea . . . a curious barter. But both drugs. Do you have any view on drugs, Red Eye Ng?'

Bewildered, Red Eye Ng said that he had none.

'You must have some. After all you provide the addicts with Miss White.'

Gods, where was the conversation leading? Red Eye Ng swallowed a mouthful of tea. He said: 'I help them in their need and I know that in the next life they will be born stronger.'

'I'm glad you feel that way,' Kwan Tai said. 'It is only *gweilos* who wield two-edged swords who condemn us. Gambling, money lending, debt collecting. . . . The *gweilos* indulge them all and help us to buy the drugs. *Ayeeya*, how they deceive themselves. And do they spurn the services of our girls, our Wanchai chickens?'

Red Eye Ng, astonished at this recital of the obvious, shook his head and wished he possessed the courage to ask the Dragon Head why suddenly he sought reassurance.

Steam from his tea wreathed Kwan Tai's face with questions. Red Eye Ng took the opportunity to tell him about his dilemma.

When he had finished Kwan Tai said: 'I'm glad you came to me. We will find an honourable solution.'

'The current of air said that if I don't co-operate I will spend the rest of my days in prison.'

'Then you must co-operate. Tell him what we want him to know.'

'Soon he will realise that I am giving him false information. What then?'

'We will think of something. Perhaps a little tea money will change hands. . . .'

'But those days are over.' Red Eye Ng was surprised to hear himself contradicting the Dragon Head.

'There is a pocket in every man's armour.'

20

Red Eye Ng wasn't so sure. Only the other day a pimp who had offered a policeman tea money had been charged with bribery.

'Or ,' Kwan Tai went on, regaining authority with every word, 'we might do a deal. Details of a heroin factory if the currents of air leave you alone.'

Am I that important? Red Eye Ng marvelled.

'A Yellow Pang factory,' Kwan Tai said. The webs at the corners of his eyes smiled.

*   *   *

After Red Eye Ng had departed Kwan Tai sat staring into the depths of his tea, peering, it seemed to him, through dynasties, Ch'ing, Ming, Yuan . . . to the birth of truth.

He had no doubt that the attempt to turn Red Eye Ng into a Little Horse was part of a plan devised by one man to destroy him.

But it was the girl who worried him more than the man.

*   *   *

Standing in the stern of the second-class deck of the late night ferry to Kowloon, Red Eye Ng felt happier than he had all day. Dragon Head's words still warmed him, he had drunk a delicious bowl of snake soup served with fried wheat flakes and lemon leaves and he had seen a flying fish dart from the water behind the wake of the ferry, surely good joss.

He gazed contentedly at the high-rise wall of lights shimmering and blinking on Hong Kong Island; he looked up at the starlit heavens from which the gods looked down; he peered into the dark waters where the devils lurked.

He hardly felt the sharpened umbrella-spoke as it slid between his ribs but he felt the flow of death inside him as it pierced his heart. As the two assailants helped him overboard he gazed into the dark waters but, just before he died, his body turned and he stared into the stars and beyond.

21

CHAPTER 3

The young woman was frightened.

I'm losing him, she thought looking at the sixteen-year-old boy lying behind screens on a camp bed in the burned-out factory in Kowloon where plastic flowers and fruit had once been made.

The boy's bones protruded through his grey skin, through the sheet covering him. His eyes and nose ran and from time to time his body jerked as though an electric current had passed through it.

Three weeks ago new flesh had begun to pad the bones of Li Ting who had been a drug addict, regressing from smoking heroin – chasing the dragon – to mainlining it into his veins until his parents had summoned the young woman to their hovel inside the Walled City.

'We have heard that you work miracles,' the old man with opium eyes had said in Cantonese.

'God works them,' Rachel Crown had said. 'Not me.'

'Can your God help our son?'

'Do you believe in God?'

'In many gods,' the old man said. 'Perhaps yours is one of them.'

In a corner of the minuscule room a joss stick burned in front of one of his gods.

'Where is your son?' she asked.

The old man pointed towards a blanket hanging from the ceiling. The boy lay behind it on a bed made from packing cases; his naked chest was wasted; his eyes were open and he was staring at a pitted wall where a small lizard pulsed. What did he see? A benign dragon? Rachel Crown who had been in the presence of many addicts knew that the boy was close to death.

She spoke to him but he didn't reply. His smile was skeletal. Soon the benign dragon would start to breathe fire.

She motioned to the old man, and to his wife who had so far remained as silent as her son. 'You must kneel and pray with me,' she told them.

They copied her as she knelt and made a spire of her hands. Then she prayed aloud to God to save his sick child.

The boy hadn't needed a fix the following day and that evening he, too, had prayed and afterwards he had eaten some rice and drunk tea and two days later he had been transferred to a home on the island of Cheung Chau where the sea and sky were broad and free.

Two months later Li Ting was back in the Walled City chasing the dragon in a hall where the owner provided the tin foil on which to heat the white powder over a flame and the cardboard funnels, often the shells of matchboxes, through which to inhale the fumes. Then he returned to the needle.

Why? Perhaps fellow triad youths had taken the ferry to Cheung Chau and taunted him; perhaps he had been forcibly injected; perhaps he hadn't found enough strength from God to resist withdrawal.

It was the last possibility that scared Rachel Crown as she looked down on the skin and bone that was Li Ting in the derelict factory that the Government had allowed her and her helpers to occupy until it began to build public apartment blocks on the site.

Was God selective? Did he favour only those who possessed the strength and the wisdom to follow him? Surely weakness is the most deserving of all causes.

When you doubt God all values waver. Most of all your own. Why had she journeyed from the tyre plants of Akron, Ohio, across the world to this teeming anachronism of colonial Britain? Couldn't she have been employed just as gainfully among drug addicts in the United States? Or was there an element of self-

23

indulgence in her crusade? After all, most good deeds are illuminated by a glow of self-satisfaction.

At moments like this, when she was confronted by failure, the possibility that everything she had achieved had been selfish obsessed Rachel Crown and she applied herself to hiding her doubts in public.

That was not difficult. Her hair was glossy black and cut according to fashion, her smile was instant and beguiling, her limbs were tanned and her attitude towards Christianity was sensible. Such was her sunny image that few noticed the questions that sometimes gathered around her eyes.

Li Ting who had been brought from the heroin den that morning stirred on the camp bed.

She held his hand, thinking how fragile were his bones, and asked him what had happened. His eyes focussed. 'I failed you.'

She wanted to say: 'You failed God,' but instead she told him: 'You haven't failed anyone, Li Ting, you haven't lost yet.'

His eyes regarded her from deep in their sockets. Such foolishness, they said. Both you and I know the journey is over. She had observed such fatalism before in the brief serenity before death.

She said: 'Shall we pray once more?' and his eyes said: 'If it makes you happy,' and again she wondered why God had let this happen. Why he had allowed Li Ting to be born in a slum if he was only to be allowed sixteen years of life.

Rachel Crown knew she had a lot to learn and at night in her cubicle in the factory that still smelled of burned plastic she read deep into The Bible for the answers that lay like pressed flowers between its pages.

'. . . help Li Ting in his agony.'

The trouble was that, instead of being terrified, Li Ting seemed quite happy to die.

Was she interfering with his destiny?

'Please God. . . .'

She frowned. She hadn't spoken. She peered at Li Ting's face. His lips were moving.

It was midday. At 5 pm Li Ting was still alive.

24

*   *   *

Doubts temporarily banished, Rachel made her way across the floor of the factory to the makeshift office where Detective Superintendent Harry Price of the Organised and Serious Crime Squad was waiting for her.

On one side of the floor reformed addicts were building plywood cubicles around punished army-surplus beds. They waved to her as she strode past. She waved back, enjoying their glossy health.

There were pools of water on the concrete surface and through holes in the roof she could see patches of blue sky. But the factory, burned out prior to a fraudulent insurance claim, was a Hilton compared with the previous premises, a cellar inside the Walled City and, later, two tin shacks between an abattoir and a methadone clinic off Waterloo Road.

Squatters had moved into the factory, scouts of the army of homeless in Hong Kong – illegal immigrants from China and Vietnamese refugees mostly – but they had been moved by the Housing Authority to sites in Tsuen Wan.

The Housing Authority had been at pains to emphasise to Rachel that the accommodation was only temporary; she had listened without committing herself; a deceit, perhaps, because as far as she was concerned it was permanent, but she thought God would condone it; God wasn't a pedant. Crown Property. . . . She smiled. There had been many such jokes in Akron. And how about the initials R. C. in a resolutely Protestant family? A member of her workforce, a young and prematurely balding Dutchman who was sweeping the floor, smiled back.

She turned into the corridor leading to her office wondering vaguely what this detective was like. She had met many policemen since she came to Hong Kong nine years ago, some helpful, some derisive, a few openly hostile, especially when she had helped to get an addict acquitted in court. What brand are you, Superintendent Harry Price?

She skirted a heap of melted plastic grapes and sunflowers with weeping petals and went into the office.

25

Price was reading her broadsheet. He stood up when she entered. He looked like a policeman, true enough, aggressively built, features groomed by observation of human frailty, but Rachel sensed that he had grown into the part. Often they were the worst, the policemen who had wanted to be farmers or architects. His hair was very black, wintered here and there with grey, his eyes blue; but when he offered a smile it didn't fit his face. He wore grey slacks and a blazer bearing a badge. Rachel wondered which club he belonged to because in Hong Kong your club was your bond.

They sat on opposite sides of the green metal desk salvaged from a rubbish tip and she said immediately: 'And what can I do for you, superintendent?' because in the past policemen seeking information about drug suppliers had wasted too much of her time with pleasantries.

'You don't believe in small talk, Miss Crown.' His voice, she decided, had been honed in London, but she often misplaced British accents.

'We don't have time for it here, Mr Price.' She smoothed the skirt of her white cotton dress against her thighs.

'You're very outspoken, you put me at a disadvantage.'

'A policeman at a disadvantage? Pull the other leg, Mr Price.'

'You don't like policemen?'

'They have a duty to perform.'

He clasped big hands together. 'I have a favour to ask.'

'My files? Where did my latest recruit get his last fix? A drug-related robbery as you call them. . . .'

'Routine inquiries . . . I abandoned those years ago.' He pressed tired-looking eyes with thumb and forefinger. 'You really don't like us, do you. Why? We both want to help addicts.'

'You want to lock them up, I want to free them,' Rachel said.

'We want to cure them, too.'

'Cold turkey? Torture. Does it ever work, superintendent?'

'It works,' Price said. 'Sometimes,' he said. 'With help.'

'Methadone?'

'It works,' Price said. 'If the patient wants it to.'

26

'You know something, Mr Price? I figure naivety is one of the greatest crimes in the world today. *If the patient wants it to.* . . . Have you ever chased the dragon?'

Price shook his head. She noticed that his clasped hands were fighting each other. A green and white Cathay Pacific jet dropped low over the tenements opposite the factory.

'Ever wanted to?'

'Never.'

'Ever thought what it's like to be tempted?'

A pause. Then: 'Perhaps.'

'Great. For a moment I thought you were too good for this world.'

He became aware of his hands and unclasped them. He was a safe waiting to be unlocked, she thought.

She said: 'I have known temptation. Just one fix to see what it's like. Ah, the excitement, superintendent. A glimpse of what enslaves men and women, kids. *Then* I can understand, help. Just one fix, mind you, because I am strong and I've seen what it does to the mind, the body. Well, maybe two, maybe three because I've got will power. *Had* will power. Then the needle sliding so easily into the vein and the peace that it brings. . . .'

Price said abruptly: 'You might impress your helpers with your melodramatics: you don't impress me.'

'Really?' She looked into his tired eyes. 'You don't believe in pleasantries either, do you? Surprising when you've come to me for help.'

A knock on the door. A nineteen-year-old Chinese who had been spending HK $100 a day on heroin came in carrying a tray bearing an earthenware teapot and two cups. His name was Wong Yan and he had been a triad.

'Tea's a drug,' Price said, taking a cup.

'How can I help you?'

Laughter reached them from the factory floor. A plump pigeon with cruel eyes peered in through the window. In one hour she had to preside at a prayer meeting inside the Walled City.

27

'Bear with me,' he said.

'I don't have much time.'

'To crush organised crime in Hong Kong and drug smuggling with it? I'm sure you have enough time for that, Miss Crown.'

'The Chinese say Clown.'

'Because that's what I aim to do. But to do it I have to have your co-operation.'

'Usually a euphemism for betrayal.'

Price said: 'As you know, crime in Hong Kong, on the island, in Kowloon and the New Territories is controlled by triads. There are probably about fifty societies, half a dozen wielding the power. And you must also know the Government is cracking down on them. The Fight Crime Committee . . .' Price opened his briefcase and produced a pale blue document. '. . . *Options for Changes in the Law and in the Administration of the Law to Counter the Triad Problem.* . . .'

'And the Independent Commission Against Corruption?'

'Below the belt, Miss Crown?'

'I'm sorry,' she said.

'You're talking about something that happened a long time ago.'

The corruption scandal that had stigmatised the Royal Hong Kong Police had occurred before she came to the territory.

'How can I help you?' she asked again.

'Which is the most powerful triad in Hong Kong? In the world?'

'The 18G?'

'With headquarters inside the Walled City?'

'A rhetorical question, superintendent?'

'Triad,' Price said, 'is an English word. It refers to the sides of a triangle representing the powers of Heaven, Earth and Man. The triads go back as far as the seventeenth century when they swore to overthrow the Ch'ing Dynasty. They first met in the Red Flower Pavilion and what happened? The sky turned red! A sunset probably, but it sealed the existence of the triads of the Hung, which as you know means red. They fought against the Ch'ing Dynasty, Tartars from the north, until the revolution in

28

1911. One year later Sun Yat Sen established the Republic of China and the triads had achieved their aim.'

Rachel Crown glanced at her wristwatch. 'I have to leave in fifteen minutes,' she said. 'I don't need a history lesson.'

'There is a point to it,' Price said. 'When Sun Yat Sen quit the war lords took over, and the triads, who no longer had a cause, fought for them and supported the Nationalist leader, Chiang-Kai-shek, when he came to power in 1927. Did you know Chiang-Kai-shek was a triad?'

Rachel said she didn't.

'A lot of triads became gangsters pure and simple – Shanghai was one of the first capitals of organised crime. Some remained intensely patriot and fought the invading Japanese. When the Communists seized power in 1949 Nationalist refugees swarmed into Hong Kong, triads among them. A lot of them forgot the Cause, some remembered. One of those who remembered was Kwan Tai.'

So that was it.

Rachel switched on the ceiling fan. Its blades blew away history.

Price leaned across the desk. 'I want him,' he said.

Rachel leaned back in her chair. 'So does God.'

'Which would God prefer, to save one soul or thousands of innocent lives?'

'One doesn't preclude the other,' Rachel said. She suspected she sounded pompous.

Her crusade to convert the leader of the 18G to Christianity had begun a year ago. She felt she was on the brink of success.

Price sipped his tea. The cup looked fragile in his thick fingers. Thick but not insensitive. He put down the cup gently as though he sometimes broke things unintentionally.

He said: 'The history lesson was to show that some triads still possess honour. They're mocked by some of the younger racketeers – feared too – but respected by the majority, even in rival societies. You see, Miss Crown, tradition and superstition are blood brothers in China and Hong Kong.'

29

'I know a little about the Chinese philosophy, superintendent.' Outside a star had materialised in the cooling sky.

'To many triads Kwan Tai is a god. Topple that god and you're poised to destroy the believers.'

'If pigs could fly,' Rachel said, looking at her watch again.

'You've got to believe me. We don't know how many active triads there are in Hong Kong, street gangs and splinter groups apart. Probably about 300,000. Of those at least 100,000 are 18G. Destroy the 18G and you've got the other triads on the run.'

Rachel said: 'Put Kwan Tai on trial and you've gotten yourself a martyr.'

'I don't think so.'

And Price explained why. The prosecution would strip him of all his charisma and catalogue the misery his society had caused: schoolgirls turned into prostitutes, teenagers ravaged by drugs, small businessmen ruined by loan sharks and debt collectors. . . .

'The whole truth and nothing but the truth, superintendent?'

'Not quite,' Price admitted. 'The 18G is big business. Overseas and here. But we don't want to glorify it.'

'Don't you think big business interests would stop you prosecuting Kwan Tai? Only last night on television Mrs Chan claimed that some triads were in the Queen's Honours List.'

'Mrs Chan doesn't always get things quite right.'

'Sorry to hark back to the past, superintendent, but it was Mrs Chan – Mrs Richards in those days – who forced the investigations into the police.'

Price said wearily: 'There have always been crooked cops; there always will be – set a thief to catch a thief. But don't condemn the whole force because of one or two scabs. Have you ever considered what life would be like without the police? It would be back to the dark ages, Miss Crown.'

Rachel switched on the light. Moths flew to the naked bulb. The unrelenting radiance stripped Price's face of its disguises; for a moment it was vulnerable, like a face divested of spectacles.

Another knock on the door. A woman's voice. 'It's 7.30.' Lilian Ridley. Occasionally Rachel found the English girl's total

30

commitment irritating. You had to question values. She called back: 'Five minutes.'

She said: 'Kwan Tai, God of War. Did you know that?' And when he nodded: 'Kwan Tai is a worried man. He's reached the age of doubt. He glimpses the end of the journey on earth and wants reassurance, faith. He wants to believe.'

'In God? What makes you think he's so different from the gods Kwan Tai already worships?'

'Read The Bible, superintendent.'

'Read Confucius, Miss Crown.' He paused. 'I've known a lot of villains who have decided to repent after a life of crime. Wonderful, isn't it. Rob, rape, kill, then kneel down, seek forgiveness and hop into the Kingdom of Heaven. Haven't you ever doubted the justice of that?'

Rachel, who had, said quickly: 'They have to be sincere,' and was relieved when Lilian Ridley, voice shrill with agitation, called out: 'It's 7.35, Rachel. They'll be waiting. . . .'

'A couple more minutes.'

'Are you all right in there?'

'I'm not under arrest. Am I?' to Price.

'I want Kwan Tai. I came to put my case. Not very convincingly perhaps – I would never have made a crooks' lawyer. But you must agree that the triads should be smashed.'

'Smashed? How about controlled? Supposing their most feared and respected leader became converted to Christianity. Started to preach love, peace. . . .'

'I admire your optimism, Miss Crown.'

'A lot of people sneered when God first called me to the Walled City. They said the triads ruled, they couldn't be broken. But there are a lot of ex-triads in this factory. Look around. If I can convert them I can convert Kwan Tai who is more intelligent than most of his followers. And if I convert him then there is no end to the possibilities.'

Price stood up. 'I came seeking help: I've failed.'

'You need my help, superintendent, I don't need yours.'

'Take a look at some of the addicts in the Nei Kwu Chau Treatment Centre.'

31

I've seen more addicts than you've had hot dinners.' She stood up. 'And I've cured a lot of them. Have you?'

His face seemed to tighten. As though, unwittingly, she had touched an exposed nerve.

She said intuitively: 'You're not being completely honest with me, are you, superintendent?'

'Good-night, Miss Crown. I'm sorry you couldn't help. But maybe you'll visit Kwan Tai in jail.'

She opened the door. Lilian Ridley stood in the shaft of light, face taut with worry.

*   *   *

A bold cockroach ran across The Bible on the table. Cigarette smoke from the congregation crammed into the tiny courtyard drifted into the night. Somewhere in the Darkness a cat that, when it was old, might be eaten to benefit the consumer's eyesight, cried.

'. . . God is love.' Eighteen Chinese stared at her intently. 'God is interesting, God is fun.'

She heard their breathing and their thoughts. Many doubted. Why not? When she had addressed her first prayer meeting inside the Walled City when she was twenty-three, she had been tormented by doubt. And had determined to fly back to New York the following day.

Why had she ever left Akron? In a way she blamed Quaker Oats.

*   *   *

Emil Kania, of Polish extraction, worked in the public relations department of Quaker Oats and spent weekends with his parents in Akron which is fuelled by Goodrich, Firestone, General Tires and Goodyear, lies thirty miles south of Cleveland and Lake Erie and boasts a Quaker Square in which shops have been opened in the renovated Quaker Oats Company factories.

Emil Kania also sold God. Sold him to Rachel Crown with a

32

verve that she had never connected with religion. The preachers she had listened to before had been intent on warning worshippers of the hell and perdition that lay ahead if they didn't carry out God's will. God was wrath, God was a misery. Not according to Emil Kania he wasn't. In small halls smelling of Lysol the young Pole who looked like a tennis star drew believers and non-believers to prayer, song and, yes, laughter. He also drew Rachel Crown to his bed.

Rachel, who had just graduated from Akron University, enjoyed making love to him but she didn't love him. What she liked was his physical presence, the touch of hard warm muscle and the smell of him, and the laughter inside him, and his easy relationship with God. Surely that was the way worship should be, casual without being different, sincere for all that, exciting even, and surely *their* approach to God shouldn't be restricted to Akron in the Buckeye State. He, assisted by Rachel, had done what they could here and it was time to preach liberated devotion elsewhere. Throughout the world . . . after all faith and good humour combined were infectious – they had proved that in Akron. When Emil pointed out that she had no qualifications she studied theology and its progeny; but to her it was a litany not a rhapsody; nevertheless she stuck with it.

Eighteen months later Emil persuaded a Missionary Society to enrol them – God's luck, everyone said, Quaker Oats' loss – and accepted a post in Hong Kong about which Rachel knew very little except that it was an over-populated outpost of the almost defunct British Empire where the Chinese worshipped a variety of gods and everyone worshipped Mammon.

Because he had family affairs to finalise Emil sent Rachel ahead. Six months later he had not joined her; after nine months she knew that he was never coming and she discovered to her mild surprise that she wasn't upset – she had found God. But it was no laughing matter.

*   *   *

She moved into the Walled City with a missionary, a Canadian.

33

On her first night she saw a triad who had trespassed on 18G territory mutilated with hatchets and fighting chains.

Saw a boy smoking heroin mixed with barbitone – 'To make it last longer,' the Canadian woman explained – heated over a lighted taper on a piece of tinfoil.

Slipped on excrement.

Saw old women and young girls soliciting.

Smelled opium.

Looked for the stars and saw only the makeshift roof that covered the Darkness.

She said to the Canadian whose name was Connie Saunders: 'Where are the police?'

'The currents of air don't come here often.'

'Currents of air?'

'Cantonese jargon for the fuzz.' Connie who was plain and fat punctuated her theatrical composure with slang and obscenities. 'When the British grabbed Hong Kong it was agreed that the old walled city should remain Chinese. Then Perfidious Albion reneged and the Chinese magistrate was never replaced by the Brits or the Chinese. And so five acres of Asia remained No Man's Land, the asshole of the world.'

'Are we in any danger?' she asked the unprepossessing woman recommended by the Salvation Army.

'You more than me. They've given up tangling with old Connie. Too much flesh. They can't afford to lose their knives in it.'

They passed a naked Chinese boy sitting in a stream of effluent.

Connie said abruptly: 'So when are you leaving?'

'What makes you think I am?'

'Why the hell would anyone want to stay?'

Connie ran a small mission in an apartment above the cellar where she lived. Two rooms had been knocked into a chapel; that evening a dozen Chinese prayed and sang, half of them drug addicts. Despite Connie's cheerfulness she conducted a stereotyped service. God's wrath again.

Afterwards Rachel asked: 'Do you cure many addicts?'

34

'I used to think I did. But the sods are great actors. They even act cold turkey to make you think they're trying. Give them money to buy food and they rush straight to a pusher for another fix.'

'Have you asked God to help them?'

'In the general sense, sure.'

Asked him to save the souls of poor miserable sinners, Rachel presumed. 'Individually?'

'Listen,' Connie said, 'I've been in this dump for eight bloody years. I reckon I've saved maybe a thousand souls. Don't come here wet behind the ears telling me what to do.'

'Saved?'

'Converted,' Connie said.

One month later Rachel had acquired enough money – a loan from her parents, savings from the meagre salary paid by the parent mission – to fly back to America. But by then it was too late: Connie was in an isolation hospital with cholera and she was poised to cure her first addict.

*   *   *

'. . . God is here with us now. He *is* going to help you.'

Not *wants* to!

The faces in the lighted courtyard stared at her unemotionally but Rachel knew she had imparted hope. After nine years you knew these things.

Sometimes visitors remarked that it was extraordinary that she had come to love the Walled City.

She didn't. She had hated it nearly a decade ago, still did.

*   *   *

After the meeting Rachel hurried back to the factory to see Li Ting. But he had died ten minutes before she got there.

CHAPTER 4

Kwan Tai believed that he was pursued by two people, the policeman and the girl. But he was wrong; there was a third.

At 6.30 on a May morning Lu Sun took his thoughts with him to Victoria Park, an unprepossessing oasis among the skyscrapers of Hong Kong Island.

It bore no comparison to the gracious parklands of his native Peking but Lu Sun found that its early morning tranquillity encouraged lucid reasoning. Indeed much of Hong Kong's future was shaped by Lu Sun between 6.30 and 7 in Victoria Park.

He carried with him a canary which welcomed the dawn from its cage and occasionally he acknowledged other fanciers taking their birds for a walk. Men and women shadow-boxed on the dew-wet grass; old men set up the first game of chequers.

You could hear the earth breathe.

Lu Sun, nominally a deputy with the New China News Agency, more exactly head of Chinese overseas intelligence in Hong Kong, glanced round to see if he was being followed. An academic precaution; it was the same Special Branch agent as yesterday, coolie hat, string vest, dark blue trousers, motheaten ears.

Lu Sun, as fragile almost as the canary, hung the cage on a tall hibiscus and sat on a bench to consider the case of Kwan Tai.

It had once been said that Hong Kong was ruled by the Jockey Club, the Jardine Matheson business moguls, the Hong Kong and Shanghai Bank and the Governor, in that order. The author of this wisdom had omitted one other participant, the triads.

In ten years Hong Kong's sovereignty would revert to China. To ease themselves into power Peking needed the triads. Just as Tokyo had needed them before the Japanese invasion in 1941.

Lu Sun put on his Taiwan-made spectacles, opened his briefcase and consulted the potted history of that period prepared by his assistant, Chen Chang.

The canary sang. On the balding grass opposite a middle-aged man practised shadow-boxing, *tai chi*, the slow and gentle art of self-defence that also relaxes the nerves and stimulates circulation.

The shadow-boxer swivelled slowly and, with ballet grace, executed *the catching of the peacock's tail*. Perhaps I should indulge, Lu Sun thought, beginning to read.

The Japanese had dispatched an agent to Hong Kong four years before they invaded to bribe and cajole the triads into co-operation. He was arrested by the British on the eve of the attack but the Japanese were partially successful in recruiting the triads.

The Japanese made one mistake: they divested the triad leaders of power because they feared their influence. We shall make no such mistake, Lu Sun decided.

He watched the shadow-boxer. *Tai chi* was introduced, according to legend, by a Taoist priest watching a fight between a bird and a snake. When the bird became weary of attack the snake uncoiled, struck its adversary and killed it with venom.

But we want Kwan Tai alive.

Lu Sun folded the résumé, replaced it in his briefcase, polished his spectacles. The Special Branch operative was absorbed with the game of chequers burgeoning beneath a banyan tree. He was Cantonese, cunning, rough with his tongue but fastidious with his palate. Lu Sun preferred the gangsters of Shanghai to the Cantonese. And he mourned the day he had been dispatched from the Institute of International Relations in the Fragrant Hills west of Peking to Hong Kong, the swollen appendix on China's belly. But if he subverted Kwan Tai he might receive the ultimate reward – retirement on the banks of the Yellow River, cradle of Chinese civilisation.

The shadow-boxer, now a White Stork, stretched his legs. The rising sun lit his teeth. It was 7.45.

How shall I approach Kwan Tai?

Stealthily.

Tai chi.

What are Kwan Tai's weaknesses? Lu Sun consulted the file on the leader of 18G.

Age? The universal weakness.

Lu Sun watched the dew drying in the gathering heat. Hong Kong's awakening yawn was growing stronger. A helicopter buzzed the Causeway Bay typhoon shelter; traffic swelled on Victoria Park Road.

If you accepted the information in the file Kwan Tai had no other weaknesses.

He was a Dragon.

The shadow-boxer *sought a needle at the bottom of the ocean.*

Lu Sun, dressed for the heat assembling for summer in a brown lightweight suit, turned the pages of the file. It wasn't fat, like those on prominent Hong Kong citizens, because triad leaders didn't publicise their activities.

What did emerge was Kwan Tai's loyalty to the Nationalist cause. Surely a man as wily as Kwan Tai must have accepted years ago that the Nationalists had been driven from the mainland to Taiwan forever.

What else? Honour, according to the file. A flexible commodity in Lu Sun's experience in intelligence.

How could a triad who trafficked in drugs be honourable? In China they had a simple solution to drug addiction: they executed the pushers. Result: a minimal narcotic problem. Lu Sun could never understand why Western countries didn't execute traffickers; exterminate the murderers, save the innocents.

But Peking's uncompromising attitude to crime presented Lu Sun with another problem. Triads who had remained in the People's Republic after Mao Tse-tung had assumed power in 1949 had been purged – twenty machine-gunned to death in Canton in one day. Such measures hardly helped Lu Sun to suborn Kwan Tai.

So how does a Communist approach an honourable, fervent anti-Communist?

The canary sang from its prison, notes like falling feathers. The chequers players finished a game and departed leaving the Special Branch shadow stranded in the sunlight.

Honour had to be the weakness.

Lu Sun turned to the last page of the file, in Mandarin for his benefit. A widower with one son.

One!

The lucidity of his thoughts expanded as the last moments of dawn tranquility withered. He replaced the file in his briefcase and stood up. The shadow waited.

Lu Sun started to walk. The canary fell silent.

*   *   *

China has no consul in Hong Kong because it does not acknowledge that the territory is British. Instead it has the New China News Agency.

And it was to the headquarters of the NCNA, an old black-glass hotel near Happy Valley Racecourse, that Lu Sun made his way that early summer morning already strumming with honest and dishonest endeavour.

In his austere second-floor office he tackled his intray with minimal interest. Party membership figures in Hong Kong – 3,722 with the latest arrivals at China Resources and the Bank of China; an analysis of Intelligence penetration into trade unions and commerce, by his earnest assistant.

Honour a weakness. What sort of reasoning is that?

He drank some tea, bought from Kwan Tai's store, and glanced at the résumé of yesterday's Hong Kong newspapers, two dailies in Chinese and two, the *South China Morning Post* and *The Hongkong Standard*, in English.

The *Post* carried an article about the New China News Agency comparing its hierarchy to a shadow cabinet during the transition to Chinese sovereignty in 1997 and the benign jurisdiction promised until at least 2047. Hardly surprising because after the

39

Sino-British deal had been struck the Agency had been remodelled – journalists moved to another building and ten new departments which sounded like government ministries installed in the old hotel.

Only one son.

Lu Sun buzzed his assistant.

Chen Chang, pudgy guardian of silent reproach, materialised in front of Lu Sun's desk. 'You called?'

Even his manner of speech was irritating. But it was his beliefs, sturdy but flexible, that really irked Lu Sun. He had been a Red Guard during Mao's Cultural Revolution, doubtless a sincere iconoclast, and was now a devout admirer of Deng.

Lu Sun held up the analysis of Communist penetration in Hong Kong. 'Who asked you to prepare this document, Chen Chang?'

'No one but my conscience, Lu Sun. I felt it would be of immeasurable value.'

'To whom?'

'To yourself, Lu Sun.'

'But I know everything contained in it.'

'But your diligence will be appreciated in Beijing; they will assume you instigated it.'

'You think it is not already?' asked Lu Sun who preferred the old name of the Chinese capital, Peking, City of Kings, to Beijing, City of the People. 'Tell me, do you think this interpretation of our influence in Hong Kong will influence its future?'

And what are the weaknesses of Kwan Tai's son?

'It takes many grains of rice to fill a bowl of wisdom.'

Mao or Chen?

'How do you see the future of Hong Kong, Chen Chang?'

Chen pressed his cocktail-sausage fingers together and gazed through the window at the new skyscrapers climbing the hillsides. How I hate this place, Lu Sun thought.

'I think the Sino-British agreement ratified on May 27, 1985, was a masterly example of . . .' Had he almost said compromise? ' . . . diplomatic initiative.'

It took a ratification to squeeze the empty eloquence from men such as Chen.

40

But what did he really think about Hong Kong? He was born in Canton a mere 150 kilometres away on the banks of the Pearl River and therefore more possessive about the territory than Chinese in the north.

But what foolishness it would be if we did change our policy and overran the financial capital of Asia, the world's biggest exporter of clothes, toys, radios . . . third largest gold market, container port and air cargo base, host to forty-four of the world's top fifty banks . . . all here on China's doorstep for her convenience. Financed and marshalled by *gweilos*. And not a Russian in sight. Lu Sun smiled.

Chen said: 'May I share the joke, Lu Sun?'

'You may not.' All jokes were mysteries to Chen Chang. Lu Sun handed him the file on Kwan Tai. 'You are responsible for this?'

'Not personally.'

'I think so,' Lu Sun said taking off his spectacles and placing them gently on the functional desk. 'Triads are your responsibility, are they not?'

'Overall, yes. Not individually.'

'Overall,' Lu Sun said pointing at the file, 'there seem to be some grains missing in this particular bowl of wisdom.'

Chen Chang thumbed the pages. 'It is not easy to gather material on a man such as Kwan Tai.'

'It should be: we have enough Little Horses inside the triads. More than the police.'

'They're all gangsters together,' Chen said.

'And we need them. If we are to control the destiny of Hong Kong we need the triads.' Lu Sun noticed his reflection in one of the lenses of his spectacles; a miniature of ageing benevolence. 'Do you know what is missing from the dossier? An omission so obvious that it should take a bow?'

Chen Chang riffled the pages more urgently.

Lu Sun stood up and walked to the window, stared at the green hills and saw Hong Kong as it was in 1841 when the British seized it, a huddle of tranquil buildings populated by '7,800 smugglers, stonecutters and vagabonds'.

41

I am the past and that is *my* weakness. His soul reached back to the age of Darkness and Light, to the god Pan Ku who took 18,000 years to carve the universe, whose head was the mountains, eyes the sun and moon, breath the wind, flesh and blood the soil and rivers, sweat the rain, bone marrow jade, semen pearls. . . .

And we are the parasites who feed on his body.

Such mystical nonsense. But when an uncle died in Peking during the Cultural Revolution Lu Sun and other relatives secretly burned paper cars and clothes, even a rocking chair, to provide his spirit with creature comforts, and bank notes drawn on the Bank of Hell to appease the agents of the devil. If the Red Guards had discovered them indulging in such degenerate practices they would have been shot.

A Communist and a mystic. Contradictions surely. Perhaps the answers would be conveyed to him in the autumn of his earthly life in the City of the Kings. After all he had been born on the sixth day of the sixth month, a double ration of prosperity, his soul the beneficiary.

'Well?' He turned to Chen Chang.

'There are, of course, several omissions and I will tax the individual responsible –'

'You are responsible, Chen Chang.'

Chen Chang's eyes reproached him for the unwarranted reprimand. 'Then I beg forgiveness.'

'But you don't know what for.'

'I accept your judgement.'

Lord, what a crawling toad! 'So we know that Dragon Head has a weakness, *heya*?'

'His age?'

'He is the same age as me. I do not think you are destined for high office in the diplomatic corps.'

'A thousand pardons. . . .'

I am committing the unforgivable, Lu Sun admonished himself: I am making him lose face.

He said abruptly: 'His son.'

Chen Chang accepted the compromise. 'Only one.' He blinked, the flutter of eyelids quick in his slow face.

42

'Your alacrity does you credit. One son, what a delicate responsibility. It makes Dragon Head vulnerable,' Lu Sun said. 'So now you know what is missing from the file?'

'His son's weakness?'

'Precisely. Vanity? He is an actor.'

'A star.'

'Conceit is a beginning,' Lu Sun said. 'The handle of the lever that will topple him. What else . . . white powder? Many triads become slaves themselves.' Lu Sun stared at a painting of Sun Yat Sen, father of the People's Republic. 'Who do we have at the film studios?'

'I will make inquiries.'

He should have known. Too much time studying Party doctrinaire, too little applying himself to practical matters.

Lu Sun said: 'Within the hour, Chen Chang.'

He turned in his swivel chair and studied the green hills. The past stirred.

'You may go,' he said over his shoulder.

He turned again and regarded the back of his departing assistant.

He envied him.

He believed.

CHAPTER 5

The corpse spilled over the slab.

'Are you sure?' Price asked.

It was difficult to see how anyone could be – the body was grey, bloated by the gases it had manufactured, and decomposing.

'Reasonably,' Sandilands told him.

There were no dental records, of course: if Red Eye Ng had ever had toothache he would have visited one of the illegal dentists on Tung Tau Chuen Road. His eyes had been taken by fish or crabs, his face was blubber.

Sandilands said: 'Red Eye Ng has been missing for two weeks. This,' pointing at the cadaver in the Kowloon morgue, 'has been in the water for about two weeks. Right?' He turned to the pathologist, small and cheerful with a monk's fringe of hair.

'Give or take a day. They float in ten days. This was found in a creek by a fisherman and it could have been floating for some time.'

'Cause of death?' Price asked.

'Don't make jokes, it's too early in the morning.' The pathologist grinned.

'His build,' Sandilands continued, 'is about right, too. Torso sturdy, legs thin from a lifetime of squatting on the pavement. And there's a tattoo left on his arm. Can we go?' He pressed his hand against his surgical mask.

On the Star ferry taking them back to Hong Kong Island they gulped sea-fresh air.

44

The channel churned with ships, sunlight gilding the tight-clustered high-rises on the island found a pivot at the golden tooth of the Far East Finance Centre, sea birds glided above the ferry, the *Shining Star*. Price rarely took the MTR or tunnel: he preferred his seven minutes of escape on the ferries that plied mainland and island as regularly as heartbeats.

He watched another Star Ferry pushing past in the opposite direction, gouging a silver and gold wake. He turned to Sandilands on the bench seat beside him. 'Not much doubt why Red Eye Ng was killed,' he said.

'Not much. He was seen talking to me.'

'Pity.'

More. An important Little Horse in the plan to smash Kwan Tai and the 18G. Red Eye Ng, crony of Kwan Tai, one of the busiest pushers in Kowloon, would have been one of the first to know when a big shipment was due to arrive. Intercept the consignment, bust Kwan Tai with information supplied by a whole ranch of little horses . . . Kwan Tai would have lost face, the 18G would have been ridiculed. Gang warfare. Balkanisation of the triads, the Chinese Mafia. One decisive sweep by the police . . . a pestilence exterminated forever.

Steady, Harry. Don't let your personal crusade overwhelm reason.

He said: 'Do you think Dragon Head authorised the murder?'

Sandilands said he didn't. Sandilands . . . how well some names fitted their owners. Shrewd, neat, sandy.

'Why should he? Red Eye Ng probably told him I had approached him.'

'To eliminate a weakness?'

'Kwan Tai has a soft spot for old friends.'

The breeze took their words with it towards the South China Sea. Tourists on this the first-class deck clicked their cameras; Chinese looked through them; you had to admire the Chinese who hadn't the slightest doubt about their superiority over *gweilos*.

'Who then?'

45

Price had never been totally convinced about the wisdom of dispatching a newly-arrived officer ignorant of Hong Kong's elaborate crime strata into the ranks of informers. But his Cantonese was almost perfect – better than mine – and his IQ was formidable and he wouldn't be recognised. . . .

But he had been.

'We'll never know. Oath number five.'

I shall not disclose the secrets . . . I shall be killed by myriads of swords if I do.

Price had seen an initiation ceremony performed by Chinese actors on information supplied by members of breakaway triad societies arrested during the 1967 riots fermented by Mao's Red Guards.

Candidates bared their left shoulders to signify defiance of government, intoned symbolism, drank a cocktail of cockerel's blood, wine, cinnabar and sugar. At one stage a triad officer tapped each recruit on the back of the neck with a sword and asked: 'Which is harder, the sword or your neck?' to which they replied: 'My neck,' meaning, Price was told, that even under threat of death they wouldn't disclose triad secrets.

The ceremony conducted by an Incense Master and a Vanguard, both in robes, had lasted for hours.

Price said: 'Someone recognised you.'

'Maybe I just look like a policeman.'

'No,' Price said truthfully, 'you don't.'

But I do. Twenty years' service, an indelible stamp.

A row of schoolgirls in blue uniforms giggled as a gangling tourist weighted with cameras snapped them. Then he photographed the signs BEWARE OF PICKPOCKETS and NO SPITTING. An old Chinese man beside Price, unable to retain the evil in his throat any longer, spat.

'I reckon someone in London tipped off the 18G that you were on your way,' Price said.

'Anyway, I'm blown,' Sandilands said.

'If you weren't we wouldn't be together now.'

'The 18G are strong in London,' Sandilands said. 'In Gerrard Street, around that area.'

46

'And one day China will rule the world,' Price said. 'More than a billion people. A quarter of the world's population. . . . The sleeping giant has been awoken.' He watched a Chinese woman stern-paddling a sampan towards a motorised junk; when he had first come to Hong Kong twelve years ago junks in full sail had plied the channel, now they were rare, tourist attractions. He said: 'It wasn't my idea to bring you here.'

'Good. It was a lousy idea. Do I have to go back to London?'

'No way, you're a good cop and you know about triads. And your Cantonese. . . .'

'Learned ordering Chinese takeaways,' Sandilands said. 'They also fry the best fish-and-chips.'

'Is nothing sacred?'

'So if I'm staying, my wife and kids. . . .'

'I'll arrange it,' Price said.

'You're not. . . .'

'I was,' Price said, seeing his wife and son emerge from immigration at Kai Tak airport all those years ago. 'You're a marked man, of course.'

'Aren't we all?'

The ferry, churning dead fish and debris, approached the quayside.

'I wonder where Red Eye Ng bought it,' Sandilands said.

'Here?'

'I killed him, I suppose,' Sandilands said.

'Don't waste any sleep over it. He was a mass murderer. Every drug-pusher is.'

'They don't see it that way.'

'I don't give a fuck how they see it,' Price said.

'Arms dealers are mass murderers.'

'You don't have to buy guns?'

'You don't have to –'

'Yes, you do,' Price said. 'If you're hooked you do. It isn't difficult to corrupt the young, you know,' aware that Sandilands was looking at him quizzically. 'Did you know that some of the bastards forcibly inject kids to make them addicts?'

Sandilands didn't reply.

I'm breaking the rule he learned in England, Price thought. *Stay impersonal.*

The ferry chafed the quayside.

'So how are you going to replace Red Eye Ng?' Sandilands asked as they followed the passengers swarming up the covered causeway to the waterfront.

'There are plenty of candidates.'

'Was he that important?'

'You can never put a value on a grass. Circumstances, fear, envy. . . . A row with his wife could make him come across. I've got twenty informants who could shop Kwan Tai. Maybe one of them will; maybe Red Eye Ng would have been that one. That's how important he was.'

He guided Sandilands towards the taxi pick-up point. The queue snaked back upon itself: the evening stampede was under way.

'All 18G?'

'You know better than that,' Price said. 'Other triads too. Splinter groups, street gangs, hoods who are jealous of the genuine societies. Jealous of Kwan Tai. If we get a break – a tip-off about a big consignment – then they will provide the nails for his coffin. There's nothing like small-time gangsters to help you bust a Godfather,' Price said. 'They think small. Put the bastard away, they think, and we'll be able to move in. Fat chance,' Price said.

'Which leaves the tip-off. . . .'

'I've got a few contacts inside 18G. . . .'

'Red Eye Ng would have been good,' Sandilands said, the breeze coming off the harbour, barely disturbing his thin hair.

'The best. I could do with another like him.'

They joined the taxi queue. In front of them a European girl with mauve hair shaved above the ears, behind them a Thai with a Filipina whore.

They climbed into a red, air-conditioned taxi. Price told the driver to take them to police headquarters on Arsenal Street.

He said: 'What do you fancy at the races at Happy Valley tonight?'

'Dragon Head,' Sandilands said. 'In the third.'

Sandilands left the taxi at Arsenal Street and Price told the driver to take him to his home in Pokfulam. As the taxi climbed the highway to the suburb on the west flank of the island Price telephoned the apartment in case the Chinese girl who cooked and cleaned was there. He let it ring several times, each note lighting an empty corner of the apartment, then cradled the receiver on the back seat beside the driver. The voice of the woman radio dispatcher filled the taxi with Cantonese.

He stopped the taxi before it reached the apartment in Bisney Road and paid off the driver. Beyond, the silk-screen sea, hump-backed with some of Hong Kong's 236 islands, losing itself in the mists and peaks of Lantau, the biggest of them. Beneath, the terraces of a cemetry, site chosen by a geomancer, student of the elements, earth, water, air and fire. . . . It faced water, prosperity, and so the contented dead would promote the fortunes of their living progeny.

Some apartments near Price's sported mirrors to deflect neglected and restless spirits from the graveyard. Perhaps I should have installed one, Price thought.

He stared at the ranks of the dead, so revered that, years after the burial, the bones were exhumed, cleaned and placed in an urn on the hillside. In three months' time the Festival of the Hungry Ghosts would be observed and offerings would be burned to appease the neglected spirits hellbent on spreading misery.

Price's skin prickled. His mother would have told him that someone had walked over his grave. Or over the graves of Frank and all those who had been killed by drugs. . . .

Price continued to stare at the graves and, beyond them, the islands floating in time. Young voices reached him from wasted lives, telling him that he had until the Festival of the Hungry Ghosts to break Kwan Tai. . . .

Premonition? Superstition? Christ, what's happening to me?

He heard the telephone ringing in the empty apartment.

He hailed another taxi and told the driver to take him back to the gaudy heart of Hong Kong.

49

*   *   *

Who would come up with the tip-off?

Price left the venerable blue and white police station on the corner of Old Bailey Street and walked past the curio shops in Hollywood Road where, occasionally, you could buy a genuine antique.

An informant inside the Golden Triangle – Burma, Thailand and Laos? Price shook his head: the grass would also tip off the triads and the consignment, raw opium, morphine or heroin, would be dumped in the backwaters of the Pearl River near the island of Lintin, Solitary Nail, to be retrieved later.

He walked down the steps of Ladder Street to the flea market in Cat Street. The evening had thickened, warm, damp and smoky, and the street-sellers had settled behind toothless sewing machines, old Mao badges, blind televisions, leaking oil lamps, punctured kettles. . . . Jangling noise pushed the daylight into hiding; the air smelled of cooking oil and mildew.

No, he would contact informants inside Hong Kong. A little horse working in a heroin factory in the New Territories, a weatherman on one of the islands, Lantau or Lamma or Cheung Chau or a cargo handler at the airport or harbour.

But not an informant doubling for Customs and Excise. In one year their narcotics operatives had seized 48 kilos of heroin, 90 heroin base, 33 opium, 144 cannabis and 1,300 offenders had been charged. An impressive haul but totally inadequate: Hong Kong was still addled with dope.

What was needed instead of a series of small operations was one big bust. Mine. Vengeance?

Price turned into a small street where, beside a trader revitalising bed springs, one of his informants sold brushes. Hair brushes, clothes, boot. . . . His covered stall was a hedgehog turned inside out.

Price murmured: 'Where were you born?' and the vendor replied: 'Beneath the peach tree.' So he had nothing.

Near Queen's Road he stopped at a restaurant for some *dim sum*, little hearts, the Chinese snacks normally eaten in the morning and at lunchtime. He ate steamed shrimp dumplings, deep-fried bean curd roll filled with pork, shrimp and oyster sauce and hot custard tart.

Across the street, above potted ferns black in the dusk, laundry fluttered on a wrought-iron balcony.

According to the latest statistics from the Central Registry of Drug Abuse the price of No. 3 heroin had risen to HK $25,000 a kilo. Which meant it was short on the streets. Which meant that a big shipment was due soon.

He said in English to the sleek waiter who was counting the baskets of food he had eaten: 'Is there any white coconut?'

'Supplies in the kitchen are very short.'

'When are you getting more?'

'Sorry, no wholesale available.'

Price paid his bill and walked into the night. He wandered into Bonham Strand, past snake and medicine stores selling rhinoceros horn and dried sea horses and deer's antlers and ginseng to encourage flagging virility and herbs to cure all maladies. He bought a pack of Mild Sevens at a stall and, in Cantonese, asked: 'How much for a real smoke these days?'

Cannabis had recently become more popular among the youths of Hong Kong; soon it would be the lethal crack.

'I don't know, master.'

'Find out,' Price said. 'And the latest price for white powder.'

'I don't –'

'Find out,' Price said.

What upset Price was the casual acceptance of drug abuse by responsible citizens. He blamed the middle-aged liberals who were scared that commonsense would be confused with senility.

He took a cab through streets festooned with neon signs in Cantonese to Wanchai and went into a topless bar. A girl wearing a green silk dress slashed to the hip joined him at the bar and said: 'You sailor boy?'

'Do I look like one?'

'You buy me drink?' snapping her fingers at the barmaid.

Price watched the barmaid with the small bare breasts pour her a glass of green liquid and ordered a beer for himself.

'You very handsome man,' she said. 'I get vibes.'

'You can take pills for that.'

'I get feeling. . . .' She rubbed her thigh.

'What's your name, Suzie Wong?'

'Maisie,' she said. 'You buy Maisie another drink?'

Price ordered another.

'You very generous man,' she said, sipping the drink. 'I think I like you very, very much.'

'And I like you Maisie.'

A handful of British servicemen in civilian clothes came into the bar. Girls in split skirts fluttered around them. Pimps watched from the kaleidoscope of spinning lights. Two girls with skinny breasts danced on a small floor, skimpy panties pulled into their pubes.

Price knew the history of the bar. It had refused to pay triad protection so the water sprinklers had been switched on overnight flooding it. The management was now paying.

He said: 'Where do you come from, Maisie?'

'Many years ago Canton.'

'Not so many years ago. When did you arrive in Hong Kong?'

Around 1962, he guessed. When the exodus of refugees from China escaping hunger – many of the 'useless mouths' encouraged to flee by Peking – had reached unmanageable proportions and barbed wire barriers had been erected to stop them.

'I can't remember.'

'Nineteen sixty-two, three?'

'That *is* many years.'

A lifetime if you were still young, he supposed. Perhaps Maisie had been a baby carried on the back of her mother slipping illegally across the border with the New Territories one dark night.

A baby. At what age had she become hooked? She wouldn't remain young much longer.

Music, Western pop splintered by Cantonese punctuation, assaulted them.

The barmaid said: 'Another drink?' And poured one.

Price said: 'When did you have your last fix?'

Her eyes, barometers of addiction, stared at him.

'I know,' Price said.

She searched in her rhinestone evening bag for cigarettes, produced a pack of Double Happiness and lit one with a shaking hand. Her bare arms were thin; her face, framed by black polished hair, sculptured with the hollows of a hunger that could never be satisfied.

She reminded him of a girl he had seen in Kowloon courtroom. She lived in a heap of shacks on a hillside; her father was chasing the dragon and by the age of twelve she was following him. By the age of eighteen she was an addict, the rest of her short life sacrificed to the needle.

Why? If you shared a leaking box on a hillside with five members of your family you knew the answer.

Not, perhaps, if you lived nearby in a trim Mid-Level house or above the shacks in an aloof home on the Peak. But Fifth Avenue led from Bloomingdales to Harlem and Park Lane wasn't that far from a squat in Notting Hill Gate.

And in Hong Kong the Government *was* pushing up towering blocks of public flats, 50,000 in one year. The difference with Hong Kong was that people were treated as cargoes. Thirty thousand British and Americans, 8,000 Australians, 7,000 Canadians . . . five and a half million Chinese.

But cargo manifests had little impact on a Vietnamese refugee in Hong Kong imprisoned behind barbed wire in a closed camp earning HK $10 a day to strip and clean machine bearings to be recycled to the US.

Statistics, Price thought, were smug.

He said to the girl: 'How much did the white powder cost you yesterday, Maisie?'

'I don't chase dragon.'

Price switched to Cantonese; the girl looked surprised. 'So what do you do, inhale it through a matchbox top, play the mouth-organ?'

'Are you –'

'Yes,' Price told her, 'I'm a current of air. And I know you buy

53

white powder and no, I'm not going to take you to court before the enemy and no, I'm not going to fornicate with you as a reward for not arresting you and yes, I would like some help.' Price sipped his San Miguel.

The girl looked at the two pimps, almost certainly 18G triads. The bar had recently been the scene of a territorial battle between the 18G and another society. One dead, two with the tendons of their shoulder-blades severed, 18G the victors.

Two American sailors in tropical whites came in. 'Excuse me,' the girl said, 'I must entertain them.'

Price held her arm, felt the bone beneath the flesh. 'Another drink,' he said to the barmaid and to the girl: 'What was the price of the powder of dreams yesterday?'

'I told you –'

'I don't want to take you in front of a magistrate. . . .'

The girl reverted to Wanchai chicken English. 'You kind man. I think I love you, no shit.'

Price wanted to touch the hollows in her cheeks. In a couple of years she would be fellating customers in a fishball stall.

She held up the glass of green tea. 'Me get drunk as a cat.'

'How much did you pay?'

'Seventy Hong Kong,' she said, glancing at the pimps who had sauntered closer.

Seventy HK dollars. So the street price was rocketing, supplies shorter than he had thought. There *would* be a big shipment soon. But supposing Narcotics or Customs got to it first. . . .

He told the girl he would pay her a lot of money if she heard anything about a consignment, and palmed a match folder on which he had written his 'phone number.

'The last two figures,' he told her in Cantonese, 'are round the wrong way. How much?' he asked the barmaid.

On the other side of the dance floor, faces mottled by spinning lights, an American sailor and a British serviceman were fighting over a Wanchai chicken who was applying lipstick while they swung punches.

'A hundred HK,' the barmaid said, eyes on the fight.

He gave Maisie HK $20 for herself.

'You kind man,' she said. She placed her hand on his knee. 'You come back my place later?'

He shook his head. 'Can you remember a *gweilo* name?'

'Your name?'

The American sailor swung his fist into a wall mirror smashing it; the British serviceman fell across a table. The bouncers moved in while the two girls picked the combatants' pockets.

'Remember this name,' Price said. 'Remember it well. Even if you don't telephone the barbarian,' pointing at himself, 'telephone this lady.' Price spoke softly. 'Rachel Crown.'

*   *   *

They came at him with Kung Fu kicks but he was ready for them. His readiness and his knowledge of martial arts nonplussed them. But not for long. How many of them were there? Price, adopting the Main Horse Stance, peered into the doorway from which the two pimps had emerged onto the pavement. A foot struck out, low and strong, a Front Kick, the heel the hammer. Price had seen corpses that had been kicked to death by bare feet.

Protecting his Centre Line, he blocked the kick with his arm. Economy of movement; hands and feet, acting instinctively. Now, with one opponent flustered, the Centre Punch, the only fist blow taught in Ving Tsun. Knuckles into neck. A cry like wind through splintered bamboo. A variation of the Centre Punch, side of the hand a blade, towards the second pimp's belly but he was already switching from block to attack, wheeling Price round, kicking the back of his knee. As he turned a Centre Punch came at him. Grab and strike, his opponent's punching power weakened. Price slapped aside another Centre Punch, and struck at the armpit. Crowds veering away from the fight under red, blue and white neon. A police siren braying. They moved towards him from three compass points. Hands and feet killing tools. Price covered his centre line. A foot caught him in the groin. Flames of pain sprung upwards . . . the blade of a hand on his neck. . . . He forgot Ving Tsun and aimed a Hendon Police College punch, felt a nose split. . . . Then he was on the pavement and the kicks were hooves in a stampeding herd of cattle. Suddenly, peace, aching and flowing. He looked up into a pair of milky blue eyes framed by a beard and thick ropes of brown hair.

CHAPTER 6

Rachel Crown knelt in the makeshift chapel in the derelict factory and prayed: 'Oh God, why did you let him die?'

Why cure Li Ting and then let him die?

He had been dead for nearly a month but, although death was a habit among addicts, she still grieved. She had been God's instrument of deliverence and she had failed. Therefore God had failed. . . .

Blasphemy in the judgement of the gloomy preachers from whom she had fled, the magistrates of religion who plucked wrath and reproach from The Bible – and hurled them at crowded congregations. If they were to be believed God was an ogre who only welcomed the faithful to heaven, making grudging allowances for penitents.

What about those who were born evil? What chance did they have?

No, God was understanding, God was fun. So why did he let Li Ting die? Because he is fallible! Why not? *God created man in his own image.* . . . And Man was most certainly fallible. Wasn't a vulnerable God more worthy of love than an omnipotent deity?

Rachel smiled at the Cross on the altar, made from packing cases, and squeezed some of the doubt from her praying hands.

In the office two young Chinese, both former addicts, wearing vests and blue shorts, tawny skins glossy, eyes clear, greeted her in English.

She put her arms round their shoulders. 'Good morning, Fleet

57

Foot Yan, good morning, Hard Knuckle Xu.' Before the Darkness had claimed them Yan had been a promising footballer, Xu a boxer.

Lilian Ridley said anxiously: 'Fleet Foot Yan is mending mattresses, Hard Knuckle Xu is working on the holes in the roof. Is that all right, Rachel?'

The daughter of a wealthy butcher in England who supplied county families with meat, she was uncertain and pale as though the slaughter-house had bled her.

'That's fine, Lilian. You've got your priorities right. Somewhere for the boys to sleep and keep dry when the typhoon season starts. Off you go,' releasing the two Chinese.

She sat at her desk. 'Any other problems?' Everything was a problem for Lilian.

'These.' She handed Rachel two bills, electricity and building materials. 'Shall I pay them?'

'How? There's no money in the bank.'

Lilian's hand went to her mouth and Rachel thought: 'I needn't have been so abrupt.' The girl made her act perversely. She said: 'Don't worry, God always provides.'

Which was true. Whenever funds were needed to maintain the burned-out factory or the rehabilitation homes at Lantau, or Hong Kong Island, or to feed the fifty occupants and ten full-time staff money materialised from somewhere.

The 'phone rang. The voice of bureaucracy, male. 'As we told you at the time your tenure of the factory is temporary.'

'You mean you've sold out to a developer?'

'I don't think you realise, Miss Crown, just how charitable Her Majesty's government has been?'

'Which developer?' Rachel asked. 'How high is the block going to be? How many millions have they paid?'

'You're being unreasonable. In fact the site is scheduled for public housing apartments.'

'What's wrong with the New Territories?'

'We cannot continue to spoil the countryside. . . .'

'You haven't done a bad job so far,' which was unfair: the great clusters of skyscrapers were necessarily ugly.

The voice of bureaucracy said: 'I've telephoned to remind you that your tenure isn't forever. . . .'

'And?'

'You owe –'

'We'll pay. . . .'

'And to say that we are in no hurry. . . .' Breath inhaled abruptly. ' . . . I admire what you're doing, Miss Crown.'

Rachel grinned at the receiver. 'You're very kind. . . .'

'But –'

'I know. . . .'

'You see, the Department feels that the erection of public housing apartments is essential.'

'And who's to say they're wrong?'

God? How did he reconcile the construction of homes for the homeless with the retention of a derelict site to save a few souls? Miserable sinners. . . . The holy anger of the preachers of her youth echoed down the years.

'Are you still there, Miss Crown?'

'I'm here,' Rachel said.

'You see the Department thinks it is more important to accommodate the homeless.'

'You're right, of course,' Rachel said.

And so am I. The lives of Hard Knuckle Xu and Fleet Foot Yan are important.

She said: 'Build your apartments in the New Territories and to hell with the environment.'

What had environment ever done for Xu or Yan?

She cradled the receiver and said to Lilian who was tearing at a receding fingernail with her teeth: 'Don't worry, God will provide.'

'Where will we go?' Lilian asked.

'Go? We shan't go anywhere.'

'Maybe housing *is* more important. I went to a shanty settlement the other day. Human beings shouldn't have to live like that. . . .'

'Human beings shouldn't have to live the way Hard Knuckle Xu and Fleet Foot Yan were living.' Rachel leaned across the desk and touched the girl's hand. 'God found this place for us. God will find homes for the homeless.'

But he's taking his time about it, a part of her thought. Because they believed in other gods? God cured the addicts from the Walled City, from the tenements of Kowloon, but only when they believed.

'We must have faith,' she said to Lilian and herself. She held the girl's hand. 'Let us pray.' They closed their eyes and conviction flowed back.

They were interrupted by a knock on the door; the Dutchman came in with the post. Pleas for help, accommodation. A couple of abusive letters, one obscene. Tracts from other missions. A postcard from her mother on vacation in California. Statistics from the Central Registry of Drug Abuse – known number of addicts 37,000. In fact more like 100,000. A report from the Society for the Aid and Rehabilitation of Drug Abusers. Did you abuse a drug? Surely the reverse. Bills. . . .

She placed the bills, pink, blue, white, in the pending tray. They filled it. Lilian stared at them as though they were alive.

Why had she come from the countryside of Gloucestershire which she described so lyrically to this? Rachel stared through the window at an apartment block. Six to a room in some of them. In one which she had visited a senile grandmother and a retarded child roped to a bed.

'Why did you come here?' she asked Lilian.

'Because God called me.' She looked at Rachel in surprise.

'To Hong Kong?'

Lilian nodded miserably. 'Have I failed him?'

'Of course not,' Rachel said irritably. 'I was merely wondering how we were all guided to the Fragrant Harbour. God didn't actually say Hong Kong, did he?'

'I went to church one Sunday and the vicar preached a sermon about missionaries in third world countries and I prayed and I heard God urging me to go out into the world and over lunch – a side of beef, always meat . . .' she grimaced. ' . . . over lunch my father talked about Hong Kong – he came here in the Army after the Japanese surrendered – and then I knew where God wanted me to go: he had found a way of telling me. How did God call you to Hong Kong, Rachel?' Her smudged eyes sought the reassurance of sharing.

'Through Quaker Oats,' Rachel said and laughed. 'Cheer up, Lily. You're doing fine. Now let's figure out a way to get some funds.'

'I thought God –'

'Sometimes he needs a cheer leader.'

One of the Chinese who had just returned from four months' treatment at the home in Lantau brought coffee. He was twenty years old and his name was Peter – he didn't know his family names and in any case Rachel had long since abandoned the subtleties of Chinese nomenclature – and after four years chasing the dragon he had been cured.

'Thank you, Peter.'

'Don't mention it,' his English improving every day.

She remembered him during the first ten days of treatment when no medication had been allowed, only God's strength. After five days she had feared they were going to lose him but they had prayed and he had survived.

They sipped their coffee. Airliners dipped low over the tenements. The 'phone rang intermittently. Visitors called. The sheaf of bills stirred in the breeze from the ceiling fan.

Lilian worried her nails.

God held back from providing.

Rachel picked up the *South China Morning Post*. TRIAD GANG WAR BREWING.

She stood up smiling. 'Cowper was right,' she said. 'Sometimes God moves in mysterious ways.'

*   *   *

Kwan Tai was worried.

About the newspaper prediction that triad gang warfare was imminent – he knew nothing about any such threat.

About the anti-triad crusade mounted by the Government's

Fight Crime Committee with branches in all the nineteen districts of Hong Kong.

About a fall in profits from prostitution, drug trafficking, gambling, loan-sharking and protection.

About the discovery of Red Eye Ng's body. Who had killed him?

About Rachel Crown.

In the room behind the tea store he sat on a rattan chair and prepared a pipe to settle the worries. He lit tobacco with a joss stick and inserted it, burning, into a tube protruding from a can attached to the broad, four-foot-long pipe. Nursing the pipe on his lap, he inhaled smoke, purified by water at the base of the pipe, and blinked slowly.

He reminded himself of an old cat sitting in the sunshine.

When he was younger such worries wouldn't have nagged. He contemplated a black-and-white photograph of himself after he had been made Red Pole. Crisp black hair and menacing eyebrows and a wrestler's torso. How they had feared him with his knowledge of *wushu*, the martial arts.

Kwan Tai drew deeply on his pipe.

He had studied shadow-boxing, weaponry – spear, cudgel and sword and scimitar, and attacking combat. Kicks, crouches, punches, turns, leaps . . . but his speciality had always been *shoubo*, wrestling, which had come into its own in the Han Dynasty.

An old cat. . . . What did they do with old cats in Hong Kong? Killed them and ate them to improve their eyesight!

Kwan Tai shook himself free from the past and applied himself to the worries. Time enough to dwell in the past when his No. 1 son, his only son, became Dragon Head.

How long would that be? Five years? Eight maybe? Kwan Tai decided to embark upon a regular diet of ginseng to sustain him.

Falling profits. Loan-sharking. The losses there had a ready explanation: two businessmen who had lost fortunes at an illegal 18G casino in Kowloon had borrowed the money, repayable at 500 per cent, to pay their debts and taken the next Cathay Pacific flight to San Francisco. Kwan Tai made a note on the report prepared by the 18G's adviser, White Paper Fan, to instruct the Ghost Shadows in San Francisco to execute them.

Their treachery, of course, also explained the dent in gambling income. What angered Kwan Tai about gambling in Hong Kong was the hypocrisy of the Government: it sanctioned betting on the tote at the two horse racing tracks and took its cut, but outlawed private bookmakers. Although he had to admit that illegal bookmaking was probably more profitable than legal –syndicates backing a rigged winner didn't want the odds on the tote to fall, a giveaway to all the other punters.

Kwan Tai sucked sweet smoke and pencilled instructions to the No. 438 in charge of gambling to concoct false tip-offs to the syndicates and to reinforce security in the bookmaking apartments overlooking Happy Valley racetrack on Hong Kong Island and Sha Tin on the mainland in case they were suspected.

Monopolies . . . no complaints there. Building, transport, services to squatter areas and markets within 18G territory were consistent sources of income.

Drugs. . . . Well, Miss White was thin on the ground right now, and the price was rocketing but that didn't compensate for mass sales. A temporary recession: a big consignment was due shortly.

Protection. . . . Obviously more punishments needed to be inflicted, more severe than the flooding by sprinklers of the topless bar in Wanchai that had refused to pay.

Kwan Tai picked up the separate report on the Wanchai bar. They were paying up punctually now. He read a footnote. One of the Wanchai chickens had been observed talking to a police officer. So? She had probably mistaken him for a tourist looking for sex and had, quite rightly, plied him with drinks and promises. Ah, these *gweilo* trippers, brains in their pricks.

Harry Price.

Kwan Tai stopped smoking.

Head of Organised and Serious Crime.

Gunning for the 18G. Gunning for me.

Kwan Tai read on. The girl had been questioned – Kwan Tai

interpreted that as beaten up – and had confessed that Price had tried to make her an informant.

Gods, that dog's turd. . . . And what had happened to him? He had been *dealt with*. Piss on the authors of snake talk. Dealt with – allowed to escape! However, you didn't kill or cripple a detective superintendent who had sworn to destroy the 18G.

The girl, Kwan Tai read, had subsequently been beaten with bamboo canes and deprived of the money with which to buy her next fix – a far worse punishment than the beating.

Kwan Tai pencilled another note beside Price's name.

The anti-triad campaign launched by the Fight Crime Committee. . . . The campaigners were becoming a menace, *according to White Paper Fan*.

This time Kwan Tai didn't write anything. Instead he made a mental note to call on an illustrious triad high in Hong Kong society.

Which left Red Eye Ng and Rachel Crown.

Who had killed the old shoe-shine boy? If it was 18G then it was an act of defiance because everyone knows I wouldn't have ordered the execution of my old friend from the Darkness. He came to me and I offered him Dragon wisdom and still he died.

You will be avenged, old friend. . . .

Rachel Crown. Kwan Tai drew on his pipe but the tobacco had gone out. An omen? In a way she was the biggest threat: she was doubt.

The intercom buzzed. One of the counter-boys said: 'Rachel Crown is here to see you.'

Gods!

Kwan Tai got up to escape through the emergency exit. Lose face to a woman, a *gweilo*?

He sat down again.

'Show her in,' he said.

*   *   *

For a barbarian, Kwan Tai had to admit, she was good to look at. Black careless hair, tanned limbs, firm breasts pushing at her

64

blue blouse. It was customary to deride the big jugs of Western women but secretly Kwan Tai had never harboured strong objections. His gaze lingered in their foothills, his imagination carried him to their heights. He wished he was wearing something more elegant than a cotton singlet and black varnished trousers.

But this woman, he reminded himself, is dangerous. She works miracles. She is eloquent about her God and she makes my spirit stir restlessly.

He smiled at her. 'Tea?' If she asks for coffee she will lose face and I will be a happier man.

'Do you have a Keemum Red? Or Iron Goddess perhaps?'

Ayeeya! 'Of course. How pleasant to meet a foreigner who understands tea.' He summoned his servant on the intercom. 'I was once invited to an Englishman's home in the Mid-Levels and he put little bags of tea in cold cups and poured hot water on them.'

'A barbarian!'

'Indeed. Has it occurred to you that Hong Kong would not exist if it wasn't for tea? The British paid for their tea with opium and when the Chinese said no more foreign mud they took up arms against the Dragon Emperor and when they had humiliated him they took the Fragrant Harbour as a prize.'

'Just like a lump of sugar for their tea.'

'Sugar and milk in tea. Don't upset the gods,' Kwan Tai said, and immediately wished he hadn't.

'I know of only one god, Kwan Tai.'

'*Ayeeya!* Spare me your illustrious words today, Miss Crown, my head is full of woe.'

'Which is why you should pray to the Lord Jesus.'

And now in almost perfect Cantonese she will prove why I should! All those servants of the white powder whom her god has cured. Addicts helplessly enslaved. Recently her Lord Jesus had cured an old whore whose skin had been needle-pricked like a pin-cushion. Impossible. Except that I witnessed it.

Yu Fat served the tea smiling hatred at Rachel Crown. He

had worked for Kwan Tai for twenty years and he was an authority on all subjects, particularly those about which he knew nothing.

Rachel Crown sipped her tea appreciatively. She put down her cup and, when Yu Fat had left, laughed. Such laughter, wind chimes in the breeze. Kwan Tai sipped his tea and waited for the sermon.

She said: 'Don't worry, Kwan Tai, today you will have to take aspirin for your woes.'

Still Kwan Tai waited.

'I have brought you a present.' She laid a package wrapped in paper printed with pink and red roses on the table. 'Well, not exactly a present. I want you to pay me for it.'

Kwan Tai looked at her in astonishment. 'But I don't know what's in the package.'

'Trust me, Kwan Tai?'

'How much?' he asked cautiously.

'Ten thousand Hong Kong.'

Kwan Tai relaxed. A squeeze. As simple and dishonourable as that. 'That's a lot of money. One thousand five hundred American dollars. . . .'

'You will not be disappointed.'

But a part of him already was.

'Very well,' another part of him celebrating because she had lost face.

He opened the wall safe, took out ten yellow bills and handed them to her. 'My pleasure,' he said in English, distancing himself from her.

'Thank you, Kwan Tai,' in Cantonese. 'Rest assured it will be put to good use.'

Kwan Tai bowed.

When she had gone he opened the package. It contained a Bible.

CHAPTER 7

The fight was staged in the sunlit garden of a Spanish-style house behind the factory blocks, godowns and shophouses of industrial Kowloon.

Barehand against broadsword.

The barehand fighter whose stage name was Michael Lo fought with the concentration and patience that his father, Kwan Tai, had taught him. Normally he stuck to the script but occasionally, if his opponent was displaying too much expertise in front of the cameras, he taught him a swift lesson.

And this antagonist *was* swaggering, probably because Crystal Lam was watching them. He wore a bright red singlet and white trousers and in one hand he carried a shield bearing the face of a dragon, a gift to cameramen. Michael Lo wore jeans and a combat jacket.

The broadsword cut the air above Michael Lo's head. Time for a salutory lesson, you son of a whore. Michael Lo embarked on a combination of kicks. High empty step, beat step, flying kick, flash palm in crouch step. The swordsman, caught in the chest by his left foot, staggered back, almost dropped his sword.

Michael Lo, crouching, noticed the director, angry, wanting to call 'Cut', but hesitating because the combination had been perfect; the cameras continued to roll; the swordsman advanced wanting to kill.

The broadsword is like a fierce tiger; the sword is like a gust of wind. . . . My hands and my feet, Michael Lo thought, are fierce tigers with gusts of wind behind them.

The sword swept back; the dragon snarled. The garden was quiet except for the song of a bird. Technicians and assistants were all aware that the actors weren't acting anymore.

His opponent feinted, jumped, cut. This time Michael Lo got him with a combination of outward leg swing and bow step. The swordsman sprawled.

Michael glanced round to see how Crystal Lam had reacted but the star from Shanghai had walked away to talk to a trendy assistant director. Her place on the wall beside a mossy pond had been taken by a girl wearing a badge BRUCE LEE LIVES.

The director, a chain-smoker with silky, silvering hair, said; 'What the hell was all that about?'

Michael Lo said: 'The prick was trying to upstage me.' Sometimes he preferred the American slang he had learned when he was studying at Columbia University in New York and acting in Los Angeles but he always thought in Cantonese.

'I know, I was going to cut.'

'So why didn't you when you knew you had lost control?' And when the director didn't reply immediately: 'Because it was too fucking good, that's why. Terrific. Better than anything any fight director ever arranged,' glancing at the assistant director talking to Crystal Lam.

'Don't ever try and pull a stunt like that again, Michael.'

'Piss in your ear,' Michael Lo said, and walked towards the girl wearing the badge. The director was a paper tiger and he knew it. Michael Lo was the new star of the studio; Michael Lo was the Warrior of the 18G; Michael Lo was the son of Kwan Tai. Although the fact that Dragon Head was his father was not the threat it had once been – the Dragon was losing his fire.

'So Bruce Lee still lives?'

'In someone else, perhaps?' the girl said. Her black hair had been freshly coiffured in an old-fashioned style and her face bore an expression of purity that could have been mistaken for naivety. She reminded him of a photograph he had seen of Lin Dai, the star who had died from an overdose of drugs in 1964.

'Isn't that a little fanciful?' Intriguing though.

Michael Lo had never denied that, to an extent, he had based his career on the San Francisco-born Kung Fu actor who had taught martials arts to Lee Marvin, Steve McQueen and James Coburn. He had followed his career in print and on the screen, his small-time roles in Hollywood, his discovery by Raymond Chow of Golden Harvest in Hong Kong. *The Big Boss*, *Fists of Fury*, *Enter the Dragon*, *Game of Death* . . . his own death while he was making it. In a beautiful actress's bed, alone. Cause never satisfactorily explained. Burial on a hillside in the Evergreen State of Washington.

On the plane the coffin had been inexplicably damaged and many Chinese believed that his spirit had never been laid to rest. Could it have been passed on? Publicly Michael Lo never made any concession to superstition; privately he neither believed nor disbelieved. After all the beliefs of the Chinese were no more preposterous than the beliefs of *gweilos*.

'No,' the girl said, 'I saw him today. In you.'

Michael Lo examined her. Her innocence was so transparent that she was probably a slut. He looked round to see if Crystal Lam was listening but she was still deep in conversation with the assistant director. Twice Michael Lo had asked Crystal for a date, twice he had been turned down.

'That's very flattering.' But understandable as he had modelled himself on Lee. Or could the restless spirit have found another soul to prolong the legend?

'What's your name?' he asked.

'Maria da Graça Wong,' she told him.

'From Macau?'

She lowered her face as though it was an admission of unmentionable depravity.

On the other side of the scuffed lawn the technicians were loading their lights into a van and the photographers were immobilising their cameras.

Across the pond Crystal Lam and the assistant director were on the point of parting. Crystal Lam, wearing a dark blue cheong-sam for her part as Michael Lo's aristocratic mentor, subsequent lover – Peking had only allowed her to film in Hong Kong provided capitalist decadence was given an airing – was

69

retiring into haughtiness, delicately-boned face tightening beneath severely styled hair.

Michael Lo called out to her but she affected not to hear. He turned to Maria da Graça Wong. To see such innocence dissipate as he entered her would be some consolation.

'So you want to get into movies?' he asked.

She looked at him in surprise. 'Of course not,' she said. 'I'm Crystal Lam's personal assistant.'

*   *   *

Michael Lo sailed to the small island of Cheung Chau, seven and a half miles from Hong Kong Island, on his white motor yacht. The other five 18G rebels went by ferry or motor junk.

Alone, Michael walked along the waterfront, past pans of spitting clams, crustacea, leopard-spotted eels and snouting fish on his left and shophouses hung with breeze-rippled banners on his right. He wore dark glasses and a blue peaked cap but even so people looked back at him, suspecting that they knew him.

He paused outside a store selling shell necklaces and carved cork ornaments. His face stared at him from a poster advertising his latest film, *Shadow Boxer*. The artist had contrived a daunting blend of cruelty and humour, but to Michael Lo the bold stamp of his father's features was unmistakable.

A thin-chested boy asked for his autograph. He signed the grubby exercise book and hurried away through the crowds, 3,500 living on this microchip of land known as Dumb-bell – another five thousand boat people on the junks in the harbour – and not a single car among them.

He paused again outside Pak Tai Temple. The Supreme Emperor of the Dark Heaven beckoned him and he entered the gloomy portals of the single-storey shrine. Two martial gods, Thousand Li Eye and Favourable Wind Ear, flanking the emperor's effigy regarded him sardonically. The American in him was amused, the Chinese in him gave a guide HK $100 to appease the monarch and his generals. He strolled through dark, incense-smelling chambers, past a photograph of Princess

Margaret who had visited the temple in 1966, past the thousand-year-old sword retrieved from the sea by fishermen a hundred years ago, and emerged into the hot June sunshine.

A few weeks earlier, towards the end of the fourth lunar month, he had attended the Bun Festival when bamboo towers seventy feet high were covered with pink and white buns, offerings to the unappeased dead, among them pirates whose mutilated bodies were found on the island in 1880, and to Pak Tai for protecting them from plague and pestilence. He had watched a procession – lion and stick dancers, banner-bearers, percussion bands, tableaux bearing children apparently floating in air, in fact suspended by wires – and afterwards had accepted a pink bun from a Taoist priest to bring him luck.

He was glad as he mounted the steps of a new apartment block overlooking the crowded harbour that he had eaten that bun. Stupid, admonished the graduate of Columbia University. Why tempt fate? replied the grandchild of the Darkness.

The other members of the breakaway committee were sitting round a black table inlaid with mother-of-pearl drinking tea or brandy. All of them ranking officials, Vanguard, White Fan, Grass Sandal . . . all their numbers divisible by the magic 3.

A joss stick burned in a small shrine in one corner of the room, its smoke joining the patterns from the triads' cigarettes. Silk tapestries hung on the walls, a chandelier made tears of the sunlight; the parquet flooring creaked as Michael Lo made his way to the head of the table.

He spread his notes and began to speak.

'We are here today, distinguished elder brothers, to discuss the bleeding from the veins of the most illustrious member of the Hung family. We are here to find ways to staunch those wounds so that the Gods may once again look down upon us with favour.'

'How do you know they don't do so now?' asked Grass Sandal.

Michael Lo considered him. A stolid, shaven-headed contradiction of the romantic legend in which the First Five Ancestors had escaped from a punitive force of soldiers in a sandal which turned into a boat.

71

'Perhaps,' Michael Lo said, 'Grass Sandal would permit me to finish without interruption in the interests of the Society. Then, still in the interests of the 18G, he will be permitted to question what I have in all humility presented to you.'

'Humility? A Red Pole?' Grass Sandal sipped his brandy. 'Pray continue, Warrior, but spare us your eloquence – we are not on a film set.'

How old was Grass Sandal? Michael Lo was acutely aware that among the rebels there might be a triad loyal to the old guard.

He said: 'I am indebted to Grass Sandal; he possesses the wisdom of the years. But it is surely apparent to all of us here today that our singleness of purpose has been thrown to the winds. What better example of this waywardness of the spirit than the case of Red Eye Ng. Thanks to information supplied by Bird Breast Choi he was seen walking in the jade market with a current of air and yet his execution was not ordered. It was left to us. . . .'

To me on my first day as Warrior. An immediate strike to underline my authority. Although a Red Pole, a 426, was not second in seniority to a Shan Chu he invariably succeeded him because he controlled the triad fighting machine.

Beware, Grass Sandal.

'If Red Eye Ng had not been executed that night he would have betrayed us,' Michael Lo said. He sipped tea from his father's store while Grass Sandal tipped the brandy bottle. 'So you see we must make our decisions as sharp as the blade of the Sword of Loyalty and,' looking at Grass Sandal, 'as forceful as a blow from a fighting chain.'

The Vanguard, a 438, said: 'Your father once had those qualities, Red Pole.'

As far as Michael Lo knew Vanguard was firmly behind him. But, of course, he was a 15, the sum of 4, 3 and 8. Reliable like the magic square in which all lines add up to 15.

4	9	2
3	5	7
8	1	6

'Indeed he did and we should honour him but for the sake of the Hung family we must persuade him that, like the powers of the Manchus, like the powers of the British colonialists, his powers have waned.'

'I am afraid that is true, Red Pole.'

From a bowl across the room beneath a jade figurine a goldfish ogled Michael Lo.

He drank tea and watched three flakes of leaf pursuing each other in the cup like autumn leaves in a slow breeze.

He said: 'Our first priority is the Yellow Pang,' eliminating some of the flowers from his speech to appease Grass Sandal. 'Because of the weakness within our society they are getting ideas above their station.' He consulted his notes. 'Last Friday they tried to squeeze several of our clients in the central market on Hong Kong Island. Taxi drivers within our territory have also reported threats.'

'Small-time operators, Red Pole,' Grass Sandal said, rubbing his bald head with the flat of his hand.

'They have set up an American lodge within our limits in Pell Street in Manhattan and only yesterday they raided a factory making white powder near Fan Ling in the New Territories. Small time, Grass Sandal?'

'They have always been jealous of our initiative,' Grass Sandal said but his tone admitted that he had lost face.

Encouraged, Michael Lo elaborated. What was needed among the triads was more unity. Unity, that was, under the command of 18G. With that in mind he proposed a meeting with the leaders of the Yellow Pang. 'If we merged then we would be the stone on which all blades would be blunted.'

'And the heart of the stone?' asked Vanguard, a long-faced Cantonese with two long-haired moles on his face.

'Need you ask, Vanguard?'

'But what if they don't wish to merge?' asked White Fan, a young duck farmer who spoke in questions.

'What do you think, White Fan?'

'War?'

'Someone has to achieve supremacy if the triads are to

73

continue to manipulate the thrones of power.'

'But I thought,' Grass Sandal said, a crease appearing on his scalp, 'that you had implied that, although *our veins are bleeding*, we are still supreme.'

'We are supreme,' Michael Lo said quickly. 'As long as some of those among us do not interpret threats as small-time operations.'

'This meeting,' said Vanguard. 'When will it be arranged?'

Michael Lo stared at each of them in turn. Then he said: 'It has been arranged.'

A breeze made fragile music in the chandelier. A helicopter clattered. Time swung on a trapeze.

Finally White Fan said: 'Where?' and Grass Sandal asked: 'When?' and Michael Lo said: 'Trust me.'

The goldfish blew a bubble.

Grass Sandal who was the menace but not necessarily the ears of the old guard, if, that was, those ears were listening, rolled brandy in his mouth as though it were a pellet and asked if Michael Lo had considered consulting his father before making such a controversial decision.

'Does not your very presence here today indicate that we have committed ourselves to controversy?' Michael Lo asked.

'Of course.' He ironed the frown on his scalp with his hand. 'But I for one would like to think that your father had been consulted. And if he rejected the plan then. . . .' Grass Sandal spoke with his fingers.

'I will speak with my father,' Michael Lo said. 'And I shall suggest that it is time for him to seek a pillow for his achievements.'

It was then that one of the two rebels, both 438s, who had so far remained silent brought Rachel Crown into the debate.

One of them, scarred and blunt-faced, said: 'It has come to our notice that Dragon Head has been consorting with a *gweilo* woman who is attempting to lead him into the temple of her god.'

Michael Lo who knew about Rachel Crown said: 'Because he meets this woman who prays with tongues does not mean that he meets her god.'

74

'Why consort with her at all, Red Pole? She cures the long-suffering addicts, so that they no longer pay us money for Miss White.' And the second 438, delicately vicious with the lobe of one ear missing said: 'We think you should talk to Dragon Head about this woman.'

'Very well, if the meeting so wishes it, but will it matter when Kwan Tai is no longer our leader?'

'It will matter,' said the first 438. 'Kwan Tai will still be a legend and legends must not lose their lustre, *heya*?'

Michael Lo, wanting to escape the thrall of his father, said: 'Then it is agreed that I shall approach the Yellow Pang? And that if they do not agree with our proposals we should take other measures?'

They spoke with their fingers: it was agreed.

'I suggest we meet here again, two weeks from today in the fifth lunar month.'

They filed out of the room past the goldfish which, like the pink bun, was supposed to bring luck.

*   *   *

The following day Michael Lo supervised the installation of a blue movie circuit. It was an idea he had brought back from Los Angeles: the film was transmitted from a video through a series of boosters to a cinema a mile or so away. If the cinema was raided a weatherman with a bleeper warned the transmitter who packed up his equipment at his leisure.

Then he drove his Jaguar to the Spanish-style house in Kowloon where he was to play a love scene with Crystal Lam. He was greeted by Maria da Graça Wong with a message from her mistress: the scene was to be played without physical contact.

Michael Lo grinned: a somewhat different interpretation of love from the scenes in the cinema he had just left. He told Maria da Graça Wong: 'Tell your mistress I am relieved,' wondering why Crystal Lam, an experienced actress who had played many love scenes unmoved by physical contact with other actors,

75

should suddenly become so particular. Was she more aware of him than she cared to admit?

But there was physical contact as they stood beside the fountain in the patio. He took her hand in his, improving the script, and she didn't withdraw it and when he looked at her face he saw that she was gazing at some invisible and distant object.

When the shooting was finished for the day he told her he was giving a party that evening at his apartment on Hong Kong Island and asked her if she would honour him with her presence. She told him that it so happened that she would be near the Peak that evening and yes, she would drop by for a few minutes.

*　　*　　*

That evening Crystal Lam called the headquarters of the New China News Agency and told Lu Sun: 'It has begun.'

CHAPTER 8

The girl's back and buttocks were striped with weals; one eye gleamed pink, her cheeks were bruised; one of her front teeth was missing. And she was in drug withdrawal, limbs jerking, nose weeping, facial muscles twitching.

Looking at her lying on a camp bed in a corner of the factory floor Rachel Crown was again visited by doubt. How many young people were at this moment being drawn into drug reliance while I and God cure one? She was assailed by the isolation of her endeavour, a doctor curing one soldier of dysentery on a battlefield of corpses.

The trembling of the girl's lips fragmented her Cantonese. 'A little white powder . . . just a little . . .'

Rachel shook her head. What do I look like from the bed? A grotesque matron with starched skin, part of a nightmare that has flowed into daylight. 'I'm sorry,' she said, 'that's not the way we do it here.' How trite; how callous the regrets must sound to the suffering girl.

'I will pray for you,' she said. 'And others will pray. And you must pray with us.' To her gods? What good had they ever done her?

'I have money. . . .'

Rachel called Lilian Ridley who was worrying on the far side of the floor. Lilian's hand flew to her mouth. 'We must tell the police.'

'First we must tell God.'

'And then the police?'

'What good will they do? Probation, methadone clinic . . . chasing the dragon again within a month.'

77

'Whoever did this to her must be punished.'

Rachel said: 'Lily, we are not in rural Gloucestershire. What's your name?' she asked the girl on the bed.

'Maisie.' Pin-point pupils stared at her.

'Very well, Maisie, I am going to kneel at your bedside and pray to the Lord Jesus.' She knelt and motioned to Lilian to do the same. 'Do you know who he is?'

'One of your gods?'

'There is only one.'

A paroxysm of shuddering.

Rachel laid her hand on one of the girl's arms. 'The Lord Jesus, God that is, loves you. He loves all Mankind,' she said, although occasionally she wished she could offer proof. 'Pray to him and he will help cure you.'

Did the girl wonder why he wouldn't help her unless she prayed?

Maisie said: 'Just a little powder. . . .'

Before praying Rachel asked the girl: 'Who gave you my name?' and the girl told her: 'A policeman,' and then faith pushed aside doubt and as, eyes closed, Rachel prayed aloud she felt that faith flow from her into the girl.

When she opened her eyes the girl was sleeping.

*   *   *

Rachel said into the old black telephone: 'I called to thank you for Maisie.'

Price said: 'How did you know it was me?'

'She described you. In English. "Black-haired, very handsome no shit."'

'All customers in Wanchai are handsome-no-shit. But if you don't pay them you're a cheap-time-Charlie.'

'Or worse. I've lived in the Walled City, superintendent, and anyway I merely called to say thank you for your faith. Coming from a policeman that's quite something.'

She heard him clear his throat. Then: 'I'm glad you called,

78

Miss Crown. As a matter of fact I was going to call you. I wondered if we could meet. . . .'

'Why?' To ask her to stop preaching to Kwan Tai?

'There's something I want to discuss with you.'

She hesitated. Perhaps he wanted to send her more addicts? 'When?'

'How about today?' Price cleared his throat again. 'Sometimes I take a walk around the Park. I wondered. . . .'

Rachel who was taking the MTR to Hong Kong Island to visit the rehabilitation home there said: 'Midday, at the Peak tram terminus,' and hung up.

On her way out of the factory she stopped beside Maisie's bed. The girl was shivering; she said her head was filled with pain. Rachel told Lilian to pray with her.

God, she said silently as she walked into the heat, we mustn't lose this one.

*   *   *

The Peak tram, a cable-hauled funicular, designed by a Scot and opened in 1888, climbs the 1.4 kilometres to Victoria Gap in eight minutes and, negotiating in places a gradient of one in two, is said to be the steepest ascent of its kind in the world. Despite its precipitous passage its safety record is unblemished.

As the green tramcar stopped at an intermediate station Rachel glanced at Price sitting beside her. It was his misfortune to look so much like a policeman, an impression reinforced by a blazer and grey flannels. But she still felt that he had grown into the role. Such things happened. Kids acted macho to stay with the gang and became macho. Price's face was smudged with fading bruises.

She said: 'So, superintendent, what do you want?'

'Later,' he said. 'Look.'

The harbour, seventeen square miles of it, lay crimped far below. Ships pushing arrows, motionless from this height. Toy bricks of thrusting high-rise vulnerable to a giant's fist. Across the creased channel the congested cement-blocks of Kowloon.

Beyond them the duck farms and fish ponds of the New Territories, beyond them the moss-green hills of China.

'Four hundred square miles of Britain,' he said. 'Four million square miles of China. How did you imagine Hong Kong would be before you came here?'

'A packed congregation,' she said.

They walked along Harlech Road which, with Lugard Road, made a triangle around Victoria Peak. Stunted evergreen forest swept down to Pokfulam and its reservoir and the sea, sumac, wax tree and Chinese hackberry woven into it. To their right a waterfall sought the ocean. Keep-fitters, Japanese mostly, swung and jumped at the exercise halts.

The air sweated.

Price pointed at a shrub with oval, spiny leaves. 'Wild kumquat. Crush the leaves and they smell like oranges.'

'A policeman knows about such things?'

'An escape hatch.'

'Why did you become a policeman?' she asked.

He said: 'We're all packaged, aren't we? When you're young you accept the wrapping.' He pointed at an Indian jogging. 'Hindu, shopkeeper, marriage arranged. . . . He had a choice but he never realised it.'

'Let me guess, your father was a cop. Superintendent?'

'No,' Price said. 'Sergeant. It was me he wanted to become superintendent.'

'He got his wish, I guess.'

'Not really. There was only one police force as far as he was concerned, the Met. But I met a girl from Hong Kong and some of the packaging worked loose.'

A fat European, flesh bouncing beneath his singlet, jogged past, paused to survey an exercise halt, shook his head and jogged on.

Price pointed at a shrub with small pink blossoms. 'Mountain sesame.'

'Somehow I didn't figure you were married,' Rachel said. 'Stupid, I guess. But you have a bachelor look about you.'

'Untidy?'

'No, self-sufficient. . . .'

'My wife left me,' Price said.

They came to a picnic area. Long-tailed kites flown by Chinese children chased each other in the sky.

She said: 'Why did you send the girl to me? You could have sent her to one of the official agencies, SARDA maybe.'

'A Wanchai chicken? They don't take kindly to officialdom. And I didn't want to take her to court. How is she?' he asked.

'We prayed for her.'

'And?'

'She's better.'

They began to retrace their footsteps. Two finely-muscled blacks jogged past.

'I believe you,' Price said, 'but I don't understand.'

'You must come to one of our meetings.'

'I'm not a good Christian, Miss Crown.'

'We can change that.'

'One thing bothers me about missionaries. What right do you have to change people's faith? Judaism, Buddhism, Islamism. . . . Aren't they just as credible as Christianity?'

'All I can tell you is that I believe.'

'So do they, in their gods.'

'Burning Bank of Hell money? The God of Wealth who rode a black tiger and threw pearls like grenades? The Kitchen God burned in the Chinese New Year to report to heaven on the family – and soused in wine to make sure the report is favourable? The geomancer looking for the dragon spirits?'

Price said: 'The Immaculate Conception? Christ walking on water? Rising from the dead? A priest exorcising evil spirits? And what about those loaves and fishes. . . .'

'The Bible teaches through allegories.'

'And you never doubt?'

'All the time,' she said, as a mauve butterfly as big as her hand fluttered past.

Fat drops of rain fell releasing dusty scents.

'You're very honest,' Price said, taking her arm.

'You, too, for a policeman.'

'We don't all beat the truth out of suspects with rubber truncheons.' He steered her out of the rain into the cafeteria opposite the tram terminal. 'Most cops do a good job,' he said, guiding her towards a table. Rain hammered on the concrete terrace outside and bounced through the open door.

They ordered Chinese beer brewed in the People's Republic.

'Assault,' he said. 'Riots, theft, accidents. . . . Who do you call? The police. And yet everyone knocks them.'

'They did have a bad name in Hong Kong.'

'That was a long time ago. A few bent cops.' Price sipped his beer; a sudden wind from the sea blew rain into the restaurant. 'But I'm not only talking about Hong Kong. London, New York, you name it: everyone bad-mouths the police. Kids are brought up to hate them. It's sad,' Price said.

'Are *you* completely honest? I mean surely you have to be a little dishonest to trap a criminal.'

'I try to be honest,' Price said.

She looked at him over the rim of her glass. 'Why did you want to meet me?'

A waiter closed the door; water slid underneath.

'I want your help.'

'To stop trying to convert Kwan Tai? You asked me that before. The answer's still no.'

'You must be close to a man to convert him.'

'He gets closer to God.'

'He must confide in you.'

'Sometimes. What do you want, his soul?'

'I want to save innocent kids,' Price said. He looked at the tongue of water licking a leg of the table. 'You can help me. Question Kwan Tai. Find out when the next shipment of drugs is due. Where. . . .'

She finished her beer. 'I have to get back,' she said. 'Maisie. . . .'

'We could save a lot of Maisies.'

She stood up. 'I didn't realise it was so late. See you in church, superintendent.'

82

She opened the door and walked into the rain.

*   *   *

In Wanchai Price talked to the street sleeper, an Indian half-caste, who had saved him from the Kung Fu attack.

The street sleeper sat up on his mattress, his home a few yards from a jeweller's shop stuffed with gold watches, pulled at the ropes of his matted hair and regarded Price with diseased eyes.

Price asked him about the current street price of heroin. About HK $70, the street sleeper told him. So a consignment was due any time.

The street sleeper said: 'Midnight tomorrow. Aberdeen,' lay down and closed his milky-blue eyes.

CHAPTER 9

Although the apartment was dead it contained capsules of life. Voices, fragrances.

The indoor plants which she had over-watered, drowning the roots. 'Let's have an early night. . . .' Waiting for him in the double bed that sighed when they had made love.

A book on the territory's fauna and flora. 'To the best dad in the world, Frank.' Before rugby and cricket and girls had elbowed aside nature study.

Price opened the drinks cabinet, poured himself a Scotch and added iced water from the fridge. 'Let's go down to the club tonight.' She was Hong Kong society but she had never made him feel out of place.

The second Scotch sometimes encouraged the hope that she might return from Rome; the third extinguished it.

Tonight only one drink, the street sleeper's message fuelling him. He paced the L-shaped living room furnished from Vietnam, Thailand and London.

Three times he had been poised to jump the 18G as they unloaded a shipment of drugs; each time they had been warned off. Their informants could be anywhere – Organised Crime, Narcotics, Communications, Marine, Customs; all he could do was minimise the number of officers involved.

He spread a map of Hong Kong Island on the dining table and prodded Aberdeen, facing south not far from Pokfulam, with his finger. Factories and high-rise packing the shoreline; across the harbour the junk-building of Ap Lei Chau, the power station – one of its five towering chimneys allegedly a dummy because

84

four meant death. And the Aberdeen the tourists knew, the channel accommodating three floating restaurants, red, green and gold hulks blazing with fairy lights, and the congestion of vessels accommodating five and a half thousand boat people.

A smuggler's paradise. With one disadvantage: it was the headquarters of the marine police whose patrol launches intercepted snakeheads ferrying illegal immigrants from China, and drug-runners. But that, of course, would make it appear an unlikely location to land narcotics.

Which was presumably why they had chosen it. *If* they had. The word of a street sleeper? Could he take it seriously? They were all enigmas, not beggars, not necessarily addicts or alcoholics, just outcasts with their own dreamy codes of morals. Which was probably why the street sleeper in Wanchai had been outraged by the attack on Price – three against one. In his youth he must have been a formidable Kung Fu fighter. Perhaps he had also been a drug addict, his motive for tipping off Price about Aberdeen. Street sleepers heard whispers because, like lamp-posts, they were unconsidered fixtures, and the Chinese in the Hong Kong police used a few of them as informants. Nevertheless a tip from one was a slender reason to mount an antinarcotics operation.

I need more proof, Price thought.

He picked up the 'phone and called Boyce. 'Can't it wait?' Boyce said.

'In the Chinese garden,' Price said. 'By the statue. In half an hour.'

Price drove his Nissan along Pokfulam Road and Shek Pai Wan Road and parked it off Aberdeen Old Main Street. He walked past a pawn shop and a bank; figures flitted past; the stars were thick in the sky.

Boyce, a detective inspector and Organised Crime's Aberdeen specialist, was waiting beside the statue depicting the bat wings of old-fashioned junks. He wore his career scars even in profile, broken nose, boxer's eyebrow; he had looked after Price when he had arrived from London and he was due to retire in six months.

'A street sleeper?' Boyce rinsed sweat from his forehead with his hand. 'You dragged me away from't dinner on the word of layabout minus a brick up top?' His North Country vowels snapped angrily.

'They hear things, Charlie. You know that.'

'So does my dog. He's crazy too.'

'We can't afford to ignore it.'

'We?'

'You know what it means to me.'

'Aye, I know.' The vowels softened. 'But this is a war not a vendetta. You can't go after 18G on a derelict's tip.'

'That's why I want you to ask around. It's your manor.'

'Was when you came here,' Boyce remarked. He began to walk. 'Things haven't changed much, have they. Not for me leastways.'

'You were too good, Charlie. They couldn't afford to have you shifted: you know every villain in Aberdeen.'

They reached Tse Kee fishball stall and the Chinese wedding factory, then retraced their footsteps.

Price said: 'I won't move unless you call.'

'I'll get some of my Chinese lads to ask around.'

Price touched his shoulder. 'Call soon, Charlie.'

Back in his apartment he made coffee and began to plan. One of the new $8 million high-speed launches, selected men from Organised Crime. . . . Price knew he should consult heads of other bureaux but their sons hadn't been killed by drugs supplied by 18G.

He opened the door of Frank's bedroom. The past lay undisturbed. A Polaroid snap of Frank holding a fish he had caught at Lamma. A bruised cricket bat. A photograph of a Chinese girl at Hong Kong University. The Hong Kong seven-a-side rugby team, a girl pop star with pink, punk hair. A movie poster for *Ghandi* . . . a life.

Frank had been eighteen.

Price closed the door. He drank some coffee. Sat down on the sofa. Waited.

*   *   *

The husk of the cargo on the old motorised junk chugging down the estuary of the Pearl River was Chinese culinary delicacies. Dragon's crystals from the inside of a Siberian fish, snake and chicken soup, dried egg yolks, eggs aged in black mud and bird's nest soup made from the saliva with which swallows along the South China coast glued together their nests.

The kernel was heroin.

Grade four, ninety-two per cent pure, manufactured in a laboratory in the Golden Triangle.

From the dispatch point half a mile inside Thailand the heroin, refined from opium reaped from the pretty white poppy *Papaver Somniferum*, had been driven south, drivers circumventing Border Patrol Police, US Drug Enforcement agents and other perils, to the capital, Bangkok.

From Bangkok, City of Angels, it had been transported by a number of vessels around the coasts of Cambodia, Vietnam and South China to the offshore island of Hainan. There the various cargoes had been replaced by dried fish which had been transported, concealing the heroin, up the Pearl River into the belly of the People's Republic of China.

In the muddy waters dividing the city of Canton the fish had been replaced by the delicacies, normal cargo for Hong Kong. And one which would not arouse the suspicion of Hong Kong customs because why would anyone deal in narcotics in China when the penalty was a bullet in the back of the head?

So the junk proceeded at a leisurely pace towards the mouth of the estuary of the Pearl River, with its twin guardians, the tiny Portuguese outpost of Macau and Hong Kong.

At the wheel stood the skipper, Golden Mouth Lang, a Kowloon snakehead who smuggled illegal immigrants into Hong Kong from China and four times a year turned his hand to drugs. Beside him stood a weatherman keeping watch for patrol boats; if one approached the junk the bags of heroin, weighted with lead, would be discharged through a specially constructed hatch just below the water-line to be recovered later by divers.

The broad waters of the estuary were busy with craft. Junks, rusty cargo ships, tankers, strings of barges, sampans. The weatherman scrutinised them all in case the marine police or customs officers were being devious: three weeks earlier a Yellow Pang junk loaded with raw opium to be refined in the New Territories had been boarded from a lighter.

Golden Mouth Lang, a podgy Cantonese, said to the weatherman: 'What will you be doing this time tomorrow when your pockets are heavy with yellows and reds?' Misty sunlight found the gold teeth in his mouth.

The weatherman, young and sharply handsome, said: 'I shall be drinking cognac and bedding two girls from Sydney, Australia.'

'*Gweilos* or little sisters from Chinatown?' asked Golden Mouth Lang who had long since lost sight of his stalk beneath his belly; and, with this loss of vision, loss of appetite.

'Barbarian whores,' the weatherman told him, glancing at the near shore where water buffalo toiled in the paddy fields. 'They are curious about our size. And what will you be doing, Golden Mouth Lang?'

'Restocking my fish ponds.' He spun the wheel to avoid a sampan paddled by a fist-shaking crone. 'Do you prefer these *gweilos* with big jugs?'

The weatherman grinned. 'Sometimes I prefer meat dumplings to spare ribs. But only occasionally. If I had to spend the rest of my days with one woman –'

'Gods forbid,' Golden Mouth Lang said.

'It would be with a Cantonese. So delicate, so warm, so willing.' He frowned. 'Or a Thai. . . .'

Golden Mouth Lang said: 'I used to find that the Shanghai girls knew a trick or two. Tell me,' his voice sly, 'is it true what they say about European girls?'

'Look!' The weatherman pointed at a pagoda leaning into the mist near Lotus Mountain. A mirror flashed from its pinnacle.

Forgetting the possible physical peculiarities of Western woman, reading the mirrored message, Golden Mouth Lang swore in Cantonese with an inventive fluency that was a revelation to the weatherman.

*   *   *

The call came at 10.33 the following morning, a Sunday.

Boyce said: 'Street sleeper confirmed.' And later from a temporarily unoccupied high-rise apartment overlooking Aberdeen: 'At midnight, over there,' pointing at one of the clusters of junks, as thick as aphids, where the boat people lived in the harbour which was also a typhoon shelter.

'Any particular boat?'

Boyce handed Price a pair of field-glasses. 'On the corner of the cluster, opposite the cemetery. Kids all over the deck; couple of old men playing mahjong, sampan lady shouting at them.'

'Got it,' Price said. His thoughts were handfuls of confetti. 'Any idea how much?'

'Dope? According to my information 470 kilos.'

'Jesus! That's more than all the seizures for last year.'

Boyce who enjoyed statistics said: 'Four hundred and sixty-seven kilos to be precise. . . . Have you told Narcotics?' and when Price shook his head: 'Don't you think you should?' and when Price didn't reply: 'Not to mention the Commissioner?'

'We went over this last night,' Price said. 'Four hundred and seventy kilos. . . . How many lives could that ruin?'

'Or terminate. Bloody bastards,' Boyce said, North Country flints in his voice. 'But I still think you should –'

'Triads,' Price said 'rely on informants. You know that, Charlie. The fewer people who know the better.'

He stared out to sea. Towards Lamma where Frank had caught that fish. His chest ached.

Boyce said: 'I hope to Christ you bust them. If not –'

'What are you going to do when you retire, Charlie?' seeking composure in Boyce's future.

'Buy cottage on't edge of Moors. Breed pigeons. . . . It's Kwan Tai you really want to bust, isn't it?'

89

'You know it is, Charlie. Now that his son is Red Pole, Warrior, I thought –'

'Not far out,' Boyce said. 'He'll be down there,' pointing at the junks flying laundry like flags, 'when the skag arrives. Get son, get father. . . .'

'An only son. . . .'

'Do you ever hear anything from Jane these days?'

'Not a thing.' Price scanned the sea and the basking islands. 'Why Aberdeen, Charlie?'

'Because they don't have to process this load in the New Territories. It's No. 4.' Boyce tapped the side of his ridged nose.

The confetti began to settle in Price's skull. 'Charlie,' Price said, 'I've got a great idea – let's go and have a beer.'

'Best bloody idea so far today,' Boyce said.

And over a couple of San Miguels in the red and gold hulk of the Jumbo floating restaurant already filling with tourists Price told Boyce what they had to do that night.

*   *   *

11.50. Sea silvered with moonlight. Ships' engines pulsing. Aberdeen a dark backdrop punctured by pinheads of light. Stars smeared.

'Chinatown my Chinatown. . . .' The music from a West End show he had seen as a kid accompanied Price's thoughts as he waited in the idling sampan. Officers from Organised Crime loyal to Price hid on the shore, on walla-walla boats, on a pleasure junk ostensibly anchored for degenerate revellers.

Triads caught bang to rights as they unloaded Miss White. . . . Kwan Tai and his son blinded by the glare of white beams. Photographed.

'One move and you're dead. . . .'

Steady.

11.55.

The pulse of an engine growing louder.

A flashlight from one of the blocks this side of the five fingers of the power station on Ap Lei Chau Island.

The old junk, skirting West Rock, following a ferry route, swung into the harbour.

Golden Mouth Lang eased back the throttle and said: 'Gods, we made it. I should never have doubted – it is the time of the Star of Five Riches.'

'You believe in all that rubbish?' asked the weatherman who had been a Red Guard during the Cultural Revolution.

'So do you,' Golden Mouth Lang said, 'although you don't admit it.' With one foot he touched the canvas bag containing clothes and food and a copy of *T'ung Shu, the Book of Myriad Things* which in itself brought good luck.

They passed a navigation light to their starboard. Beyond it the beams of cars beading Shek Pai Wan Road. To their port the power station. The harbour was a nest of lights.

A shooting star passed overhead and died. *Ayeeha!* Golden Mouth Lang glanced at the weatherman: his hands were clasped in prayer.

*   *   *

The junk finally anchored. Price flashed his torch twice. The sampan moved towards the junk. The pleasure junk and the walla-walla boat moved in. Two detectives took up positions on the line of moored junks, the obvious escape route.

Still Price waited. If Boyce was right Kwan Tai's son, Michael Lo, would board the old junk as soon as it berthed. A dingy with an outboard came alongside. A figure began to climb a rope ladder hanging from the hull. Price focussed his field-glasses. Michael Lo.

Price gave it another three minutes: he wanted them delving gleefully into their cargo, pulling out the bags of powdered loot which would be paid for in suffering and death.

He could feel the beat of his heart.

Another flash with the torch.

The searchlight from the pleasure junk froze figures in white light.

Price shouted through a hailer: 'Stay right where you are, we're coming on board.'

One of the crew made for the cabin.

Price fired a shot into the air.

The other vessels closed in; the two detectives on the line of junks ran forward.

Pistol in hand, Price climbed the rope ladder.

The plastic packages of white powder were on the deck.

Michael Lo said: 'Good evening, superintendent, to what do we owe the pleasure?'

Price took a penknife from his pocket and plunged it into one of the bags. Powder spilled onto the floor.

'Flour,' Michael Lo said. 'Self-raising as a matter of fact.'

Price tasted the powder. Flour.

'Take some,' Michael Lo said, 'your wife could bake you a nice cake with that.'

Price turned and climbed down the rope ladder to the sampan waiting in the dark water below.

CHAPTER 10

The People's Republic of China and the British Crown Colony of Hong Kong face each other across the main road of the fishing village of Shatoukok at the foot of the green hills of the New Territories.

Kwan Tai and his son, Michael Lo, faced each other in the courtyard of an apartment block, also used as an illegal casino, on the British side of the road, Chinese Village Street.

'So he lost face.' Michael Lo conducted his anger with his hands. 'So?'

'His teeth have been drawn. Perhaps he will lose his job,' Kwan Tai suggested.

'Your mind is in the heavens,' the Cantonese in Michael Lo said. Bullshit, the American in him thought. 'Price is the best policeman in the Hong Kong police force. They can't afford to replace him. And even if they did, even if they put him out to grass, he would continue his crusade.'

'I can understand that,' Kwan Tai said. 'I would feel the same if I lost my son to the white powder. But he was weak: you are a tiger. One snarl and the powder would be blown to the winds.'

'*Ayeeha*, such words. You have always used them well, my father. But once they were the sheath containing the sword. Now they are the sword and it has grown blunt.'

In the corner of the courtyard, crowded with potted chrysanthemums and anaemic roses, a large black and yellow spider took cover while a bluebottle buzzed its web as big as a lace curtain. The spiders were said to eat small bats.

Michael Lo got up from the table where they were drinking tea and walked to the mildewed wall surrounding the court-yard. Over the top he could see the main street divided down the middle by small cement pyramids – the border between Communism and Capitalism considered with much applica-tion by the world's China watchers, disregarded by the vill-agers who crossed and recrossed it as casually as tourists cros-sing Nathan Road. But only because the village was in the restricted border zone from which, theoretically, there was no escape. Michael Lo thought: Soon, as leader of the 18G, leader perhaps of all the triads, I shall have to decide how to tackle the Communists in 1997. Fight, as I shall continue to fight the *gweilos*, or take over the reigns of power on the Communists' behalf?

He watched a Hong Kong policeman patrolling on the Hong Kong side of the street; on the other side, in front of a row of five-storey offices, a member of the No. 6 People's Armed Police patrolled; they waved at each other.

Mist smoked in from the sea wrapping scarves round the hills.

His father's voice reached him, words lozenges of reproach. ' . . . words, not fists. Break his mind not his face. And in any case I have not yet finished with Mr Price. Tomorrow I shall climb to the Mid-Levels to speak to one of our representatives in high places, the Banker. One word can be stronger than two bullets, my son.'

Cars on Chinese Village Street overtook each other. Com-munists and Capitalists. All Japanese.

The spider trembled as the bluebottle brushed its web.

'There are some other matters to discuss,' Michael Lo said, sitting down and drinking his lukewarm tea. 'We must take action against the Yellow Pang.'

'We?'

'I am Red Pole.'

'And decisions are taken by the committee.'

'First we must negotiate with them,' Michael Lo said, not looking at his father, 'and then if they refuse to co-operate we should strike.'

94

'And demean ourselves? There are many ways of losing face. One is to shoot an insect with a cannon.'

'The Yellow Pang have grown strong, father. Your eyes are blinded by the glories of the past. Wiser counsels than myself believe they want to take over all 18G territory.'

'Ah, the stories in the *gweilo* newspapers. What wiser counsels?' Kwan Tai asked, staring at his son, retired muscles tautening beneath his vest.

'The Incense Master,' Michael Lo said, naming one of the officials who had refused to oppose Kwan Tai.

'Then the smoke of joss sticks has addled his brain.'

'One other matter,' Michael Lo said. He looked across the table and saw his father as a young man and resolved that he would never weaken and said as swiftly as a patient swallowing unpleasant medicine: 'Rachel Crown.'

'What of her?' His father stood up, squat and broad; even now Michael Lo wouldn't relish a fight with him. 'What business is she of yours?'

'It has come to our notice –'

'Our? We? Who are these confidants?'

'Well-wishers,' Michael Lo said swiftly, 'who do not think that it becomes the leader of 18G to entertain a *gweilo* woman who worships a foreign god and cures the slaves to Miss White who help finance the Society.'

Now it was all said he wanted to leave as quickly as possible.

'Then tell these well-wishers,' Kwan Tai said, 'that *whoever* Dragon Head entertains is his own business. And tell them this, if they want to advise me about my well-being let them come and use their tongues in front of me. And tell them this, "May all their family's property be ruined",' the worst curse of all.

'Not threats, father. . . .'

'Tell them.'

'Very well,' said Michael Lo who had no intention of relaying Kwan Tai's message because, at the sound of Rachel Crown's name, his father's words had suddenly been joined by sinews.

He walked to the rusted gate of the courtyard, turned and bowed. I may have to reassert my authority, he thought. By killing Price who would continue to threaten 18G until he was dead.

In the corner of the courtyard the spider pounced on the bluebottle and began to bind the wriggling body.

*   *   *

The Banker lived modestly by the standards of some of Hong Kong's Chinese tycoons. A house in the Mid-Levels beneath the Peak, a weekend retreat on one of the islands, a pleasure junk, a Rolls Royce with a lucky number plate for which he had paid an extra HK $500,000.

Although he was banker to the 18G none of his income derived from banking. He was shipping, real estate, finance, jade and opal, fast food, casinos outside the territory.

Currently, like most of the affluent businessmen in Hong Kong, he was hedging his bets for 1997. Establishing members of his family abroad so that, if Peking changed its mind about free enterprise, he would have an outlet. Sadly this involved breaking up families: to establish residency you had to stay in a country for several years. The Banker's eldest son had been in Los Angeles for three years, No. 2 son in London for eighteen months.

Although it was unlikely that Peking would impose any currency restrictions – it would rely then as now on Hong Kong as its clearing house – the Banker was also moving capital into Tokyo, Zurich, New York and London.

Such were the rarefied levels at which the Banker operated that, if the truth be told, he would have preferred to sever his connections with the 18G. But years ago when he was begging in the gutters of the Walled City he had taken the 36 oaths and become a No. 49, four times 9 being 36. Oath No. 11: I will take good care of sworn brothers entrusted to my keeping. Penalty for failure: death by five thunderbolts.

Kwan Tai, standing at the window of the Banker's comfortable but scarcely opulent living room overlooking crowded waters and frantic high-rise, debated whether to remind the

96

Banker about his obligation. Hopefully it wouldn't be necessary but, since he had been honoured by the Queen for his contribution to the territory's welfare, his attitude had been . . . elevated.

Kwan Tai strolled round the room decorated in faded golds and russets and ran his finger along the patina of dust on the grand piano in the corner that had about it a neglected air as though it hadn't been played since it had been installed. He struck a yellow-tooth key; the note lingered, imprisoned in the room until the Banker, opening the door, released it.

One of the Banker's daughters, as fragile as a butterfly, served tea and departed prettily.

'It is good to see you, Dragon Head,' the Banker said.

Like the note of music the lie lingered.

'And you, Fifty Per Cent Hoi,' reminding the Banker of his early days as a sidewalk moneylender and, indirectly, of his oaths. 'I see you have been attracting the bold eye of publicity.'

'I have no idea what you are talking about,' the Banker said, sharpening his Cantonese with European objectivity.

But his expression was bland. It had never changed as far as Kwan Tai could remember. Gentle wonderment beneath hair that had been grey since he was twenty. Even now there were no pouches of decadence beneath his eyes; it was a face that recognised fallibility in everyone except himself.

'You must surely have watched television, Fifty Per Cent Hoi. You must have heard the infamous allegations by the honourable lady member of the Urban Council. Triad members in high places who have been honoured by the Queen. . . .'

'I am not the only occupant of high office who has been honoured by Her Majesty.'

'Nor the only triad,' Kwan Tai conceded. 'But surely one of the most eminent.'

The Banker, wearing a blue mohair suit, lit a cigarette and smoked it delicately, blowing small puffs of smoke like a woman who does not really enjoy the habit. He watched one such puff dissipate in the sunlight and said: 'Your society, Dragon Head, it has also been attracting unwelcome attention of late.'

97

Kwan Tai, wearing a fawn jacket and an open-neck white silk shirt for the Mid-Levels, said: 'The break-away groups, Fifty Per Cent Hoi. Street gangs, kids . . . nothing to do with the Hung family.'

'Triad influence in the schools. . . .' The Banker picked up copies of the *South China Morning Post* and *The Hongkong Standard* and tossed them on the ornamental table separating him from Kwan Tai. 'Kids, drugs . . . surely not the sort of publicity that glorifies the honourable history of the 18G,' touching a nerve-ending.

'Exaggerated,' Kwan Tai said. And, remembering that he had not ascended the Mid-Levels to be lectured: 'We need your help from the heights.'

'Price?'

'Your perception does you credit.'

'I sometimes wonder, Dragon Head, why you didn't attempt to ascend those heights with me.'

'Because they were never built for me,' Kwan Tai said. 'My treasure chest lies in the foothills.'

'More illustrious than mine, Kwan Tai?'

Kwan Tai considered the question. He had no idea what the answer was, only that he ruled whereas the Banker negotiated.

He told the Banker: 'Price has lost face. But to a *gweilo* that is not a disaster. . . . He may survive.'

'And you want me to make sure he doesn't?'

'You ascend from Mid-Levels to high levels. . . .'

'I will have words.'

'Because it is time,' Kwan Tai continued, 'that Superintendent Price ended his long and honourable career with the Royal Hong Kong Police. There are many appointments awaiting such a man in security. In Britain,' he added. 'See to it,' he said.

The Banker lit another cigarette and puffed it distastefully. His daughter removed the tray, favouring them with fragile smiles. The July heat penetrated the window and died in the air-conditioning.

Finally the Banker said: 'Did it ever occur to you, Dragon Head, that a humble 49 could achieve a great eminence outside the 18G?'

Kwan Tai said immediately: 'Only if it allows him to.' And: 'Has it ever occurred to you that the 18G could break you and your No. 1 and 2 sons and your ventures in Los Angeles and Tokyo and London any time we want to. When did you last visit the Walled City, Fifty Per Cent Hoi?'

'Many years ago, Dragon Head. Only a fool returns to a cesspit.'

'Like white powder,' Kwan Tai said, 'there are several grades of shit. You are now No. 1, *heya*?'

'And you, Dragon Head?'

'No. 4,' Kwan Tai said. 'Pure.'

The Banker glanced at his watch. 'Is there anything else, Dragon Head? I have an appointment at my club. . . .'

'Which one? Hong Kong? American? FCC?' Kwan Tai who belonged only to the 18G knew that these days membership of clubs depended on means rather than birthright.

'All of them,' the Banker said.

'What do you charge these days?'

'Charge, Kwan Tai?'

'On loans from your finance house.'

'Do you want a loan, Kwan Tai?'

'A hundred per cent, two hundred. . . .' The 18G sometimes charged one thousand per cent.

'With respect, Dragon Head, it is none of your business.'

'You have made loans in high places, have you not, Fifty Per Cent Hoi?'

'I really must go. After the meeting at the club a round of golf at Deepwater Bay. So if there's nothing more. . . .'

'You could call in those loans when the repayment dates expire.'

'I prefer to take the interest.'

'Call them in if the debtors don't agree to relieve the pressure on the triads from the Fight Crime Committee, the ICAC. . . .'

'Independent Commission Against Corruption. . . . Isn't that something of a joke in Hong Kong? The colony was founded on corruption and it's prospered ever since. In any case, what is the difference between corruption and business practice?'

99

'You should know,' Kwan Tai told him.

'Bribery, graft . . . words invented by losers. What is so wrong with a gift, an inducement? A ten million dollar contract with an invisible 500,000 on top. A new Jaguar, a crate of Courvoisier. . . . So what? A job gets done, unemployment is kept down – something like 3 per cent, I believe – and the territory thrives. May the gods save us from self-appointed censors. How many unemployed are there in Britain?'

'Yes or no, Fifty Per Cent Hoi?'

'I cannot talk to business associates with a threatening tongue.'

Kwan Tai sighed. He walked to the window and looked across the garden blooming with hibiscus and bougainvillaea, across the water and the hills to the great land where the triads had been born in time of dire need.

He said softly: 'I don't have to remind you of your oaths, Fifty Per Cent Hoi. . . .'

The Banker said: 'I will see what I can do about the superintendent of police. . . .'

'The eleventh oath. . . .'

'And now I really –'

'Where is the junk on which you take your pleasures moored?'

The smooth skin tightened across the Banker's forehead. 'In the bay opposite the British spy school. Why?' massaging his forehead with the tips of his small fingers.

'There is a cemetery behind the school, I believe.' Kwan Tai moved swiftly towards the door; always better to leave first. 'I hope the mirrors on your junk are positioned to deflect the restless spirits, Fifty Per Cent Hoi.'

He closed the door gently behind him.

*   *   *

Kwan Tai told the white-gloved driver of the taxi to take him back to his origins. Back to the Darkness.

As the car descended to the lower levels he saw his spirit floating. Pulled one way by the policeman. Another way by the girl. And now in a third direction by my son.

War with the Yellow Pang. What dangerous nonsense. The trouble was that the boy was a tiger, impatient and reckless, suspicious and quick-tempered. But sincere, affectionate. . . . Kwan Tai smiled fondly. My only son is truly a tiger.

It has come to our notice –

Whose?

Kwan Tai's spirit convulsed.

And what had he meant about Price?

His spirit was joined by Red Eye Ng's. Who had authorised his death?

Kwan Tai closed his eyes as the taxi plunged into the tunnel beneath the harbour and the floating spirits.

In fifteen minutes it stopped beside the bulldozed shacks outside the Walled City. He saw the weatherman on the far side of the muddy track signal his arrival.

The dark corridors of his childhood closed upon him and it was almost with relief that he found Rachel Crown waiting for him outside the hovel where he had been born.

* * *

In the morning Maisie had been fine. Her withdrawal symptoms had been contained and she had reached the phase where she had to decide whether to stay with the mission or return to her home.

If she returned home, a two-room apartment occupied by six members of her family, then she would probably return to the topless bar in Wanchai, her pimp and drugs. Hopefully she would be persuaded by cured addicts now working for the mission to stay; to complete the treatment, to help others, to work, to belong.

Rachel had noticed several patients talking to her in the rehabilitation centre on Hong Kong Island. Her black hair, now cut in a fringe, was polished, her bruises had faded; the only evidence of the beating she had received was the gap in her teeth which evoked for Rachel the age of innocence the girl had never known.

The ex-addicts had gathered round her in a rest room beneath slow-turning fans pleading with her to stay. The girl had looked bewildered because people who cared were still strangers. Rachel prayed and, as she did so, a forty-year-old Chinese prostitute who had been found dying in a doorway outside the Darkness put her arm round Maisie's shoulder and told her about her life. 'Do you know when it began?' Maisie shook her head. 'Six months ago. Do you know when yours started?' and Maisie said: 'Now?' and the woman smiled and hugged her and Maisie said: 'Then I'd like to stay, if I may,' looking at Rachel who said: 'Forever if you like.'

Forever had lasted five hours. At 3 pm Rachel had received a 'phone call in the factory: two Chinese had come for Maisie. One had carried a dagger with a six-inch blade perforated with two patterns parallel with the blade. A triad knife.

'I want you to order them to hand her back,' Rachel Crown told Kwan Tai as they sat opposite each other in the cabin where Kwan Tai had been born. Close the shutters and they would be packed in a box, she thought. In another cabin across the alley a gaunt Chinese was making bootlaces.

She suspected that Kwan Tai felt he had lost face: had assumed she was in pursuit of his soul not the body of some little Wanchai hooker.

She admired his recovery. 'Why don't we pray to my gods for her safe return?'

'You know I can't do that,' Rachel said.

'Then sadly the chances that she will escape are remote.'

Rachel stared at him. She had already prayed to Jesus. If Maisie was handed back then that surely was the prayer that would have been answered. So it is not blasphemous to pray to heathen gods.

Tomorrow, July 3, was her birthday. The feast day of St Thomas the Doubter.

'Then let us pray,' Rachel said.

'But how will I know to whom you are praying?' Kwan Tai stood up. 'Come with me just the same.'

He led her past the street of grinning teeth to a small temple.

In the gloom she saw a benign red and gold god staring at her through wavering stems of joss smoke.

She clasped her hands and closed her eyes. Kwan Tai said: 'Pray with tongue.' She prayed aloud: 'Please send Maisie back.'

Outside the temple Kwan Tai handed her a beaker of bamboo slivers, each numbered. She shook the container until one fell out. No. 27. Kwan Tai selected a scrap of paper bearing the number and handed it to a soothsayer.

The soothsayer said: 'The lady with the black hair will have much luck today and much wealth tomorrow.'

As they walked along the street of smiles Rachel said: 'Numbers don't influence us, Dragon Head.'

'Friday the thirteenth?'

He went into a bookshop and came out carrying a package.

'Why doubt?' he asked as they thrust their way through the crowds to the MTR station. 'The evidence is all around us.'

'Do numbers heal?'

'Maybe numbers kill.'

At the mouth of the station Kwan Tai handed her the package. 'May the gods smile upon you on your birthday, Rachel Crown.'

'How did you know?'

'July the third. An auspicious number.'

He bowed and vanished in the crowds.

She opened the package. It was a red book, *T'ung Shu*, the ancient Chinese almanac. Even possession of it was reputed to bring luck.

When she got back to the factory she made a 'phone call to Hong Kong Island: Maisie had returned.

*   *   *

That evening the body of a blue-eyed street sleeper wrapped in plastic was found floating in Tai Tam reservoir and in the bay opposite the British spy school a pleasure junk belonging to a prominent Chinese businessman was burned to a shell.

CHAPTER 11

The canary sang, notes like drops of dew, as Lu San read his newspaper. It was dawn and already the air was moist and warm. Opposite him on the grass in Victoria Park an old woman exercised gently, *taijiquan*, shadow-boxing for the aged. Behind her a teenage girl in a blue track suit was a snake, one cupped hand a serpentine head poised to strike.

Lu Sun studied the paper, the pro-Peking *Ming Pao*, owned by Kung Fu novelist Louis Cha, intently. A lot of space was occupied by a story about Price's abortive coup at Aberdeen. The article disclosed that Price's son had died from a drug overdose and suggested that personal involvement had distorted his judgement. Lu Sun couldn't understand how, with such loss of face, Price could remain in the police, but *gweilo* pride was often inverted.

What the report did was emphasis triad power. Obviously Price's original information had been correct; obviously an informant had tipped off the 18G. Lu Sun replaced the newspaper in his briefcase and took out Crystal Lam's report on Michael Lo. He certainly had a weakness – one of the most common frailties of the Chinese character. One that even I possess.

Holding the report in his autumn-leaf hands, fragile body already recoiling from the latent heat, Lu Sun glanced down the path. The Special Branch agent, still wearing his coolie hat, was sitting on a bench eating noodles from a cardboard carton, as inconspicuous as a dog in a cattery.

The canary stopped singing and hopped up and down its

perch in its cage hanging between the red trumpet blossoms of the hibiscus.

SUBJECT: (stage name) MICHAEL LO, SON OF TRIAD (18G) LEADER KWAN TAI KNOWN AS DRAGON HEAD

AGE: 26

TRIAD RANK: RED POLE (WARRIOR)

NATIONALITY: CHINESE

PASSPORT: OCCUPIED TERRITORY OF HONG KONG

CHARACTER DEFECTS: MASCULINE VANITY ENCOURAGED BY ACQUIESCENT GIRLS SEEKING CAREERS IN MOTION PICTURES. (WEAKNESS SO COMMONPLACE AMONG CAUCASIAN MALES THAT ONLY MINIMAL IMPORTANCE IS ATTACHED TO IT.) AFTER SEVERAL OVERTURES BY SUBJECT A RELATIONSHIP WAS ESTABLISHED.

Ayeeha, what sort of relationship? It would be like bedding a computer.

AND A FRAILTY OF GREAT POTENTIAL VALUE TO THE OPERATION SURFACED. MICHAEL LO IS A COMPULSIVE GAMBLER.

The weakness that I understand. How much does he owe? Lu Sun wondered.

He didn't bother re-reading the rest of the report. He replaced it in his briefcase and enjoyed a few more minutes in the past that these days beckoned more and more enticingly; then he unhooked the cage from the hibiscus and, with the canary singing sweetly once more, made his way back to the headquarters of the New China News Agency followed by the shadow in the coolie hat.

*   *   *

Rachel Crown read the report of Price's humiliation in the *South China Morning Post*.

She telephoned him at home that evening.

105

She said: 'I'm sorry, I didn't know.'

'About Frank? Not many people did. He died in England.'

'Then how –'

'Someone tipped off the Chinese press,' Price said.

She pictured his apartment. A crypt.

'He died in England,' Price said, 'as a result of drugs supplied in Hong Kong.'

I could have helped him, she thought. God could have helped him.

'What will you do now?' she asked.

'Carry on, of course. Even if I'm sacked.'

'Will you be?'

'I'm seeing the Commissioner tomorrow.'

She told him about Maisie.

'And she's okay?'

'They forced her to inject herself again. I thought maybe you'd like to see her . . . . I thought we could go together.'

He said he would like that.

*　　*　　*

The Commissioner who was military-crisp with tufted eyebrows and a long-service tan had never been able to reconcile law enforcement with dishonesty inside the police.

He told Price to sit down and offered him a cigarette from a worn silver case bearing a coat of arms. When Price refused he lit a cigarette theatrically, tapping both ends, and inhaled without apparent pleasure. The Queen disapproved from a photograph on the wall of the comfortable office.

'Dreadful habit,' he said, words emerging in small gusts of smoke. 'Kills more people than any narcotic. Did you ever smoke, Harry?'

'Fifteen years ago, sir. Then they put up the price again and I thought, 'Why pay good money for something that's damaging your health?'

'Very sensible. I'm too old a dog.'

106

You weren't fifteen years ago, Price thought, waiting for the pleasantries to conclude.

The Commissioner picked up copies of yesterday's English language dailies. Tapped the front pages with one finger. 'A bad business,' he said.

'Every operation can't be successful. One in three is good.'

'Not every failure is plastered all over the Press,' the Commissioner observed, tightening the knot of a military-striped tie.

'The triads leaked it.'

'As indeed they might: it was a considerable victory for them.'

'Face. . . . They attach a lot of importance to it.'

'So do we,' the Commissioner said, 'in our own way. We're the laughing stock; we can't afford that, not after what's gone before.'

'Corruption? That was a long time ago. Maybe we should publicise some of our victories. . . .'

'Maybe we should.' The Commissioner studied his cigarette with distaste. 'Maybe we should. Especially when we make the triads lose face.'

'Or break them.'

The Commissioner glanced at the Queen, ground out his cigarette. 'Break them? Aren't you a little over-ambitious, Harry?'

'I don't think so, sir. Organised crime can always be disorganised provided there's no one on the take.'

The Commissioner, disregarding such a reprehensible suggestion, said: 'I thought you should know that approaches have been made through the . . . eh . . . higher echelons of Hong Kong Society. . . .'

'What sort of approaches, sir?'

'From influential –'

'What sort of approaches, sir?'

The Commissioner considered the platoon of cigarettes in his case, met Royal disapproval and snapped shut his silver case. 'Can't you guess? You're not that stupid. They want you sacked. For incompetence,' he added.

'They, whoever they may be, have a point.'

'And they want pressure on the triads, Fight Crime Committee, all that sort of thing, relaxed.'

Price said: 'Organised crime has always survived through influence in high places. Might I ask who, sir?'

The Commissioner said: 'A pleasure junk was set on fire recently. . . .'

'It figures,' Price said.

The Commissioner moved a photograph of his wife on his desk to field the Royal disapproval. 'Harry, why didn't you share your information?'

'The usual reasons, sir.'

'Narcotics, Customs . . . me?'

Price was silent.

The Commissioner said: 'These people who want you sacked say you're conducting a personal vendetta. That your judgement has been distorted. What do you say to that?'

'That's for you to decide, sir.'

'I think they're right!' Rain tapped the windows and slid into rivulets. 'You know my feelings about Frank. But however tragic his death was you can't let it interfere with your duty. With the future of other kids who might become drug addicts. If you had consulted other departments this consignment of heroin might have been confiscated and 18G operatives caught red-handed.'

'It's a possibility,' Price said.

'Is that all you've got to say?'

'I'm sorry,' Price said.

'I should transfer you.' The Commissioner finally defied Royalty and lit his second cigarette with an old-fashioned, liquid-fuelled lighter. '*Would* except that I don't like being leaned on.'

Rain machine-gunned the window.

The Commissioner, words smoke signals, said: 'I want the 18G as much as you do, Harry. Work with me not against me.'

Price stood up. 'Thank you, sir. There's just one thing.' He opened his briefcase and took out the documents impeaching Boyce – photocopies of his Andorra bank account, share certificates, deeds of a house in Glamorgan, valuations of antique jade and gold coins – and HK $300,000 found by detectives inside door panels in his modest home.

He said: 'If it hadn't been for Boyce we would have got heroin instead of flour.'

The Commissioner considered the evidence. Then he said: 'Your vigilance is to be commended.' But his voice was drained of compassion.

*   *   *

Michael Lo met the three leaders of the Yellow Pang in a tea house in the western sector of Hong Kong Island's commercial sprawl surrounded by shophouses selling dried shrimps, snake, squid, jellyfish and mushrooms, melon and lotus seeds, tangerine peel and bean curd.

They drank several pots of Black Dragon while they exchanged pleasantries. On the fifth pot Michael Lo said: 'Well, elder brothers of one of the two most illustrious branches of the Hung family, I think you know why we are here today.'

The Leader, the Vanguard and the Red Pole seated at a round table in the bare, second-floor parlour regarded him impassively. The long and shrewd face of the Leader, the 439, was adorned with a greying moustache that lapped the corners of his mouth; the Red Pole was flat-faced, middle-aged, defensively aggressive; the Vanguard was bland and uncommunicative.

In the centre of the table stood the three teacups that would be used to seal the decision of the meeting. If the 439 agreed to Michael Lo's suggestions he would drink one cup of tea: if he wanted war he would drink all three.

The 439 said: 'Before you proceed, Red Pole, I should like to know why your honourable leader is not present.' The silken tassels of his moustache trembled with his words.

'I think you know, Shan Chu.'

'Nevertheless I think you should set our minds at rest.'

And your bodies if I have my way, Michael Lo thought, saying: 'He regrets that he cannot be present' – he was probably with the missionary bitch – 'but for reasons of health he is resting in the New Territories. But I as his Warrior, as his son, have his blessing to confer with you.'

109

The detours of such negotiations still confounded the American in Michael Lo. Both he and the Yellow Pang leaders knew that Kwan Tai had not been consulted.

'Please convey to him our commiserations,' the Leader said. He nodded at his Red Pole. 'I believe you have something to say before your opposite number honours us with his doubtless persuasive address.'

The Red Pole, twenty years older than Michael Lo and sour with the disparity, said: 'Members of our society are bewildered at the way the affair of the current of air named Price has been handled. He was made to lose face, certainly, and that was amusing. Flour instead of white powder. . . . But he has not been dismissed, he has not even been transferred. He is still as well placed as he was before to continue his campaign against our societies.'

'So what is bewildering you, Red Pole? I am not the Commissioner of the Royal Hong Kong Police.'

'What is bewildering us is why he remains alive.'

'It should not be bewildering you,' Michael Lo said, 'because it is none of your business.'

'Ah, there, regrettably you are wrong,' the Leader said. 'What concerns 18G concerns us.' His yellowing eyes regarded Michael Lo steadily. 'What do you think?' turning to the Vanguard.

'I agree.' The Vanguard smiled plumply.

'Which brings us,' the Leader said, 'to the reason for this meeting.'

Michael Lo, aware that he was being out-manoeuvred, was abrupt. 'What I suggest, what we suggest,' he corrected himself, 'is a merger between our two societies. That way we can fight the campaigns being waged against us with a common purpose.'

The parlour was a coffin. Dust hovered in a shaft of sunlight. The Leader lit a Mild Seven and blew coils of smoke into it.

The abruptness, too, had been a mistake. Michael Lo determined not to break the silence. Finally the Vanguard spoke. 'But *we* are fighting the campaigns.' He smiled benignly at Michael Lo.

The Red Pole said: 'And *we* are expanding. In Yau Ma Tei, Mong Kok, Wanchai. . . . In fact we have helped you by moving into areas that you have allowed to lapse.'

'We are grateful for that help,' Michael Lo said. 'It gave us the opportunity to test our fighting strength and chase you out.'

In fact the strength of the Yellow Pang was its fighting wings commanded by their Red Pole. Four of them, each fifty strong, trained in martial arts and fighting with chains, daggers and axes. Under Kwan Tai's leadership the military wings of the 18G had grown slack. No longer.

The Red Pole said: 'I am pleased that we could be of service,' smiling for the first time. 'I am sure we shall be able to test your fighting strength many more times: it *is* sorely in need of practice.' He picked up a sheet of paper. 'I wonder how your finances compare with ours. The Yellow Pang, you see, is prospering. Gambling, prostitution. . . . Our protection service has never been better. We are expanding our control over home decorating and the fish market operation is proceeding satisfactorily. And we are now working with the Yakusa in Japan. Do you have connections there?' he asked Michael Lo, knowing that he didn't.

'Why split your takings with the Japanese mafia?'

'Why split them with the Ghost Shadows of America? Why split them with us?' the Red Pole asked.

Why indeed, rotten mouth? Michael Lo thought. The farce had to be enacted for the sake of the elders in the 18G.

The Leader said: 'And let us not forget that little matter of 4 million Hong Kong dollars.

Shaken, Michael Lo said: 'Let the teacups speak.'

They all looked at the Leader. He smoothed the drooping tips of his moustache with his fingers. The Vanguard poured tea in the three cups.

The Leader leaned across the table and drank from the middle cup.

He sat back, tasting the tea.

One cup – peace.

Ayeeha!

The Leader leaned forward and in rapid succession drained the other two cups.

Michael Lo bowed to the three officials who returned the bows. They left without speaking.

War.

*   *   *

Michael Lo spent his rage in bed with Crystal Lam.

But, as usual, he experienced none of the domination that accompanied sex with other girls. She aroused him with delicate but detached touches; she *permitted* his intimacies; when she reached a climax her passion was remote. But when he entered her the eroticism was so acute that he cried out as though in pain.

Normally after they made love – sometimes twice because her effect upon him was such that he was too quick the first time – she left the bed immediately and dressed unconcernedly as though she were alone. At such times Michael Lo was a voyeur spying on her small, firm breasts, the fine glossy hair of her pubis.

Today she lingered beside him, one hand absently stroking his chest as he lay on the bed in his apartment.

After a while she said: 'When this movie is finished I shall return to Shanghai. Where will you go?'

'To America,' he said. 'For some advanced coaching in Kung Fu from Master Moy Yat in New York. And then to Hollywood.' He spoke in English because his Mandarin and her Cantonese, unless scripted, were equally bad.

'Another Bruce Lee?' She treated martial arts with levity and he had ceased explaining that, although Kung Fu provided the means to kill, it was the perfection of technique that mattered.

'Why not?'

'If that's what you want. . . .' She dismissed the mystique and graces of the martial arts which he had once learned in the One Buddha Hall in Shaolin Monastery with a delicate shrug.

'I wondered,' her lingering mood making him bold, 'whether you would like to accompany me to America.'

'I've been there many times,' she said. 'But, well, it's a possibility. I have many friends in Los Angeles,' she said, divesting him of his initiative. Her hand slid down his stomach to his groin. 'Do you know what I'd really like?'

He had no idea.

'To take a hydrofoil to Macau. To stay in a pousada looking across the water to China. To eat Portuguese food. To visit a casino.'

'That can be arranged,' Michael Lo said, puzzled. 'Haven't you been there before?'

'Never. I'm always working – Beijing, Shanghai, Hong Kong, Hollywood. I'd like to rest in Macau.'

'Macau,' Michael Lo said as his penis began to harden, 'is lechery, robbery, treachery, gambling, drunkenness, brawling, wrangling, cheating, killing and other similar vices. At least it was in the eighteenth century according to a Franciscan friar. We'll find out,' he said as her warm, dry hand made him fully erect.

'I admire gamblers,' she said, sitting astride him. 'Do you owe very much? It takes courage to gamble when you owe a lot of money.'

'I owe a lot,' he said. 'About 500,000 US dollars.'

'Then you will have to play for high stakes,' she said.

She inserted his penis and began to ride him hard.

CHAPTER 12

By the end of July the shortage of heroin in Hong Kong was acute. The street price for a fix had risen to HK $150 and most of the available powder was mixed with additives.

The shortage was caused by Price's abortive operation – the heroin jettisoned in the Pearl River had been recovered by divers employed by People's Republic Customs and Excise – and a Narcotics Bureau raid on a refinery in the New Territories following a report by a Hakka duck farmer that the air around an oyster-drying plant smelled of vinegar.

The territory's methadone clinics were full, rehabilitation agencies such as SARDA were extended, Rachel Crown's factory was overcrowded, magistrates were overworked as drug-orientated crimes increased.

Police and customs listened for a whisper of the next drop.

Drug smugglers plotted new runs.

Addicts sweated, ached and screamed.

But Maisie prospered.

And one sweating day when clouds were steaming low over the hills Price accompanied Rachel to the rehabilitation centre on Hong Kong Island to take her to Lantau for the next phase of her cure.

They caught the 8.15 am ferry to Silvermine Bay and then hired a taxi to take them through the misty mountains of Hong Kong's largest island – Broken Head in Cantonese, better known as Big Island Mountain – to the little town of Tai O.

Maisie sat between them in the back of the cab.

As they drove through the creased mountains, past rose

114

myrtle and wild honeysuckle, Rachel told Price about Maisie's second deliverence.

'From the pimps who tried to kill me in Wanchai?'

'They injected her with more heroin; then they brought her back to the home.'

'Guided by God?'

'And Kwan Tai.'

'So you do use him?'

'I sought his help,' Rachel said.

'But not –'

'I'm sorry about your son.'

Price patted Maisie's shoulder and pointed at a rose myrtle shrub. 'Dark red memories in Cantonese,' he said to Rachel. 'You can make jelly from the fruit in the autumn.'

'You got to know about these things from Frank?'

'Or the other way round. I was a country boy, really. Guildford, just outside London. Box Hill, Colley Hill, the River Mole. . . .'

'It sounds like something out of *Wind in the Willows*.' Rachel said. 'What happened to Frank?' she asked.

'He grew up.'

He told her about Frank, child of an incongruous match, policeman and society girl. He told her how, when he grew into his teens, he had mixed with a set who toured the fashionable haunts of Kowloon and Hong Kong Island; how some of them had considered it amusing to introduce a policeman's son to drugs. Cannabis, cocaine, heroin. . . .'

'And your wife?'

'She blamed herself,' Price said. 'She went to live in Rome.'

'You stayed on to avenge his death?'

'To do my job,' Price said. 'Could you have saved Frank?'

'If he had wanted to be saved. . . .'

'God only saves those who want to be saved?'

Rachel stared at the salt flats outside Tai O. 'There are many questions I can't answer,' she said.

Maisie said in Cantonese: 'I didn't know the countryside was so green.'

She's our responsibility, Price thought. It was a long time since he had shared.

The town was divided by a seaway on which a flat-bottomed ferry propelled by two old women plied. The houses on the shore, some of them two-storied, were made from upturned boats cased in sheets of metal.

The taxi stopped at a soiled white house on the outskirts of the town. A group of young Chinese stood outside in a small garden cluttered with potted plants. As Maisie alighted they ran out to meet her.

They ushered her into the house as though she were a pop star. At the door she turned and waved. Price and Rachel waved back and she disappeared.

Price said: 'I love you, no shit,' and smiled.

'We'll come back,' she said. 'If you want to. . . .'

'We'll come back,' he said. And in the cab: 'Is she cured?'

'Do you want the sermon?'

'A summary.'

She told him that a complete cure could take up to a year. That, now that Maisie had been weaned off heroin without medical assistance, she would stay in Tai O for three months and, with the aid of helpers and the other residents, would find a new meaning to life. 'With God,' Rachel said.

'And then?'

'She can stay with us in the factory, find work inside or outside it. Help others as she was helped.'

'Just through God?'

'Through trust,' Rachel told him.

'Do you ever wonder about a God who cures the addicts who come to you but leaves others to die in the gutter?'

'Often,' she said.

'Do you lose any?'

'A few; we're not jailers. But we save most of them. And it's *their* faces I think of before I sleep at night.'

As the ferry approached the battlements of Hong Kong Island, as a wet breeze washed their faces, she said: 'Do you think it's wrong to doubt?'

116

He shook his head, stretched out one big hand and touched her cheek.

*   *   *

Two of the triads armed with axes, daggers and fighting chains waited in Statue Square, the Trafalgar Square of Hong Kong, while a third, the weatherman, sat three tables away from Price and Rachel in the revolving restaurant on the thirtieth floor of the Furama Hotel.

It was the time of the tiger, 2 pm. The square, divided by Chater Road, inched past. The dome of the old Supreme Court, a mushroom of colonial grace surviving opposite the Cenotaph. The battleship-grey, Star Trek colossus of the Hong Kong and Shanghai Bank, its floors, suspended from aluminium-sheathed columns, connected by sixty-two escalators and twenty-eight lifts. Next door, dwarfed, the Communists' Bank of China; behind that the Hilton.

Price, eating Japanese food from the buffet, pointed at the Bank of China. 'They couldn't remain like that losing face. They're building another one taller than the Hong Kong and Shanghai.'

The moving soft-carpeted restaurant was crowded with pointing tourists and businessmen. Price was vaguely aware of a Chinese in a crumpled fawn suit sitting close by; he was drinking mineral water and picking at his food. When a waiter spoke to him he dismissed him with an angry gesture that reminded Price of a triad hand signal.

The solid Bank of America structure crept past. The Prince of Wales Building, headquarters of the British military presence in the HMS Tamar compound. And the broad boat-scattered reaches of the harbour, stretching to Kowloon and the mainland three-quarters of a mile away.

'Cinemascope,' Rachel said. She drank her beer thirstily. 'I've never been here before.'

'Policemen shouldn't be seen in places like this. We get accused of corruption.'

He didn't know whether he felt sorry for Boyce or whether he despised him. Both. It was so easy in Hong Kong to take a bribe. A fortune compared with what you were earning. Corrupt bastards earned millions while you survived.

But you knew that when you joined. That was Hong Kong.

Was Boyce's crime getting caught? As simple as that? Price hoped not.

The Godber case in 1973–74 had supposedly purged the police of corruption. But no such purge was ever complete; not in any police force; set a thief to catch a thief. However Price believed that the core of the police was brutal honesty.

Across the water Kai Tak airport, Star House, the tiered shopping precincts of Ocean Terminal, Ocean Centre and Harbour City. Above them Lion Rock and China with clouds settling on her hills.

Why wasn't the Chinese in the fawn suit eating his food? He was playing with his chopsticks as though they were knitting needles.

Would I have succumbed if I had been offered one million Hong Kong dollars to ignore crime?

Never.

The knowledge warmed him.

She said: 'I wish I could help.'

'You could.'

'I can't; I told you.'

'To save a lot of kids?'

'It would be a betrayal.'

The waiter served coffee.

'One betrayal, the lives of thousands of children?'

'Your son?'

He said: 'If you change your mind. . . .' thinking that if I were in her place, if I accidentally learned from Kwan Tai about a shipment of heroin, if I knew that I could save so many young people, if this circumstance occurred then what is the significance of one betrayal?

She said: 'If Kwan Tai becomes a Christian thousands will follow him. In the end hundreds of thousands. . . . Isn't that better than locking them up?'

'There aren't any drug addicts in Christian societies?'

The Star Ferry . . . Post Office . . . Stock Exchange . . . Connaught Centre . . . Mandarin Hotel . . . Hong Kong Club. . . . They were back in Statue Square.

He said: 'Time to go.'

He noted that the Chinese in the fawn suit left before him.

* * *

From a red and gold room in the Mandarin Hotel Michael Lo stared through a pair of binoculars across the geometric pools and lawns of Statue Square.

He saw the triad in the fawn suit appear at a corner of the new and undistinguished pile that housed the Hong Kong Club and give a hand signal; two other members of 18G, one armed with a hatchet beneath a blue smock, the other with a knife beneath beggar's rags, walked briskly towards him. There was always a possibility that Price might take a cab or walk east along Connaught Road but, according to Boyce who was under investigation and wanted Price, his persecutor, dead, he always spoke to an old man dreaming in one of the rest areas whenever he was near the square.

Michael Lo hoped he remembered the old man today: he wanted him killed in the elegant plaza that was the heart of Hong Kong. A showpiece murder that would establish his credentials with both the Yellow Pang and the 18G rebels.

He saw Price round the corner. Brought him into fine focus in the binoculars. Features more alive than he remembered them as though forgotten purpose had pushed its way into his policeman's face. Blue blazer, despite the heat, striped tie, flannels . . . a programmed man. Stupid. Especially making a habit of meeting a tramp in Statue Square.

Michael Lo focussed on the triad in rags. A few paces behind Price. Hand reaching for the dagger with the ornate blade which he would leave in Price's body, hallmark of a triad execution; Michael Lo didn't want any lunatic or revenge-killer to get the credit for the assassination. If the triad with the dagger failed

119

then his partner carrying a hatchet, handle bound with cord, one edge of the blade razor-sharp, would split open Price's head, the weapon as unmistakably triad as the knife.

Now both the triad in rags and Price were together in the lenses.

*   *   *

Price waved to Rachel as she passed in a taxi, then sauntered into Statue Square looking for the old man who ten years ago had, like the dead street sleeper, saved his life.

He had been a hawker selling herbal cures. The leader of a gang investigated by Price had that day been jailed for seven years and, as two of his lieutenants jumped Price as he walked to his car off Chatham Road in Kowloon, he had shouted a warning.

Two days later, the hawker, having evaded police protection, had been beaten senseless; he had never truly regained his senses.

Price paused outside the Supreme Court building, an elegant anachronism crouching amid the high-rise and looked around. Today the only statue left in the square was that of Sir Thomas Jackson, manager of the Hong Kong and Shanghai Bank from 1876 to 1902, and it was near this monument that the old man could usually be found.

Price walked towards it. Past an Indian sketching on an easel, a short-sighted Chinese girl in a hurry burying her face in a lunch carton of noodles, a loitering Chinese in a blue smock, two Filipina girls walking hand in hand, an aged and angular European wearing long shorts lapping long socks and a pith helmet. . . .

He saw the old street hawker and waved.

The old man was on his feet shouting.

Ten years rewound.

Price fell to one side. The knife cut air. The killer in beggar's rags staggered forward. Price tripped him. He fell. On his feet, Price kicked him in the groin and jaw. He lay still.

They never struck alone.

Screams. Everyone except the European in the pith helmet backing away. Indian's easel collapsing. . . . Chinese girl's noodles spilling. . . .

Price swung around as the Chinese in the blue smock came at him with the hatchet. Price, ducked, side-stepped. The hatchet sliced the sleeve of his blazer and the flesh below. But his assailant was off balance. Price hit him on the side of the jaw with a Ving Tsun centre punch, heard the bone crack.

The blow spun his attacker round and the hatchet was coming at Price again, sunlight splintering on its blade. Grab and strike. But the strength was seeping from Price's wounded arm; red petals of blood appeared on the ground. Price knocked the hatchet blow aside and struck the Chinese in the armpit.

He wanted to go for his pistol but for a second he would be defenceless. They circled each other, two gladiators in the great arena of the Square. A helicopter clattered overhead; the siren of a police car squawked.

Shock him, Price thought. He wouldn't be expecting attack from a combatant with a wounded arm. Attack. The Chinese, face unnaturally angled by the broken jaw, held the hatchet with both hands swaying slightly.

Price launched a variation of *jeat sao*. Double palm thrust to the neck, up to the broken jaw.

The hatchet fell to the ground.

Price drew his gun.

But the shot wasn't his.

Beside the statue the Chinese in the fawn suit was aiming a pistol at Price. The bullet hit the hatchetman in the chest as he tried to stand up.

The man in the fawn suit turned and ran towards the Hong Kong and Shanghai Bank.

Price, blood dripping from one hand, ran through the parting crowds. Green tramcars were grinding along Des Voeux Road in front of the bank; two motor-cycle cops in dazzling yellow and orange vision jackets roared up.

The man in the fawn suit ran into the ground-floor plaza of the bank beneath a glass ceiling. Above the ceiling soared the great atrium lit by sunscoop mirrors, lined on either side by open-plan platforms of financial endeavour.

When Price reached the plaza the Chinese was half way up one of the escalators lifting customers to the third level of the bank, making robots of them.

Price dropped to his knee and aimed his pistol as the Chinese fired. The bullet spat chips of flooring at Price. There were two Chinese at the top of the escalator disappearing into the computerised heavens above. If I don't hit him now, Price thought, he'll vanish with them.

He squeezed the trigger. The Chinese fell and was carried gently to the high altar of Far Eastern finance.

*   *   *

Michael Lo slipped his binoculars into their case, let himself out of the red and gold room in the Mandarin, took an elevator to the ground floor and walked briskly along Connaught Road in the opposite direction to Statue Square.

CHAPTER 13

Hong Kong is horse-racing: Macau, forty miles away across the estuary of the Pearl River, is casinos. And in the hot summer days when there is no racing the compulsive gamblers of Hong Kong swarm into the tiny Portuguese enclave on mainland China – 6.1 square miles including two islands linked by bridges – by ferry, hydrofoil or jetfoil.

Michael Lo and Crystal Lam went by hydrofoil. On deck, green water surging past, he pointed out the verdant, hump-backed islands. The water turned brown and, with a sweep of his hand, he introduced her to Macau, City of the Name of God, Mecca of gambling in the Far East, its history inseparable from gold and opium smuggling, prostitution and, in 1949, when the gangsters fled from the new Communist regime in Peking, murder, blackmail, robbery and kidnapping.

Today, Michael Lo told Crystal Lam, the citizens living in Macau's teeming acres where old Portuguese-colonial resid-ences, Chinese shophouses, Christian churches and Buddhist and Taoist temples shoulder each other, were relatively law-abiding. And gambling was legal and almost respectable.

They booked into the Pousada de Sao Tiago, a fortress converted into an inn with water-walled corridors and guest rooms facing the People's Republic across a busy channel of brown water. They made love while children splashed in a blue pool on a terrace beneath their room and in the afternoon they toured the amalgam of Iberia and the Orient in a pedicab, the tricycle pedalled by a bristle-haired Chinese – the façade of the ruined church of St Paul's burned in 1835 during a typhoon, now

123

a gaunt theatrical prop at the head of a flight of granite steps; the rose-pink Governor's Office on the Praia Grande overlooking the Gateway to the Sea Mirror Bay; the memorial home of Sun Yat Sen, founder of the Chinese Republic.

In the evening they went gambling.

*   *   *

The concession for legal gambling in Macau is held by the Sociedade de Turismo e Diversoes de Macau. STDM, the Syndicate. Its palace is the 600-room, gold-tiled Hotel Lisboa, one Disneyesque wing crowned with a stone roulette wheel.

Michael Lo led Crystal Lam past the ground floor shops to a gilt and green entrance where plaster mermaids enticed the punters to the machines and tables.

He gave her 10,000 Hong Kong dollars – 1,300 dollars in Las Vegas – and told her to buy chips. He owed money in the Lisboa and it was possible, although unlikely if you were an 18G Red Pole, that the cashier would refuse to serve him. At least in Macau he was outside the influence of the Yellow Pang in whose illegal casinos in Hong Kong he had lost 4 million HK dollars.

'How many did you get?' he asked Crystal Lam, aloofly elegant in a dark blue cheong-sam.

'One.' She held up a mauve chip.

'You spent 10,000 dollars on one chip?' English came naturally to the two of them now.

Crystal said: 'You said you were a gambler. Isn't that what you wanted?'

'Roulette?'

She nodded. 'One number. It pays 35 to 1. Three hundred and fifty thousand dollars,' she informed Michael Lo.

'I thought you said you hadn't been here before.'

'I've been to Las Vegas. And I bought this in the lobby of the Lisboa.' She showed him a book *Gambling in Macau*. 'Or would you prefer me to play safe? Red or black, odds or evens?'

'One number,' Michael Lo said, the probability of winning receding, the possibility of pocketing $350,000 still slavering.

They threaded their way through the punters, humourless addicts and skittish tourists. A few Chinese nodded at them; Michael Lo smiled back until he discovered they were looking at Crystal Lam. A young Chinese in a white suit gave up his seat at the roulette table to her.

She turned to Michael Lo. 'What number?'

'Eight,' he said. 'Prosperity.'

She pushed the mauve chip forward. A breath of a sigh among the gamblers. Other chips followed Crystal Lam's, single number and combinations.

The croupier waited impassively. Then spun the single-zero wheel. The ivory ball danced.

Michael Lo bit the inside of his lip. She should have split the 10,000 and played the system; he was glad she hadn't.

The ball bounced into the eight.

And out.

Crystal Lam turned and smiled. 'Sorry,' she said. 'More chips?'

He gave her another 10,000. 'Ten in thousands,' he said, taking her place. She returned with ten green chips. He remembered at the last moment that Fu Lo Yung, casino baron of another era, had decided that green and white were lucky for the house, red for the player, hence there had never been red in any of his gambling houses.

Michael Lo, deciding on a Martingale, placed a green chip. The croupier shook one finger. Michael Lo felt a hand on his shoulder. A whisper in his ear: 'So sorry, Mr Lo, but we cannot accept any bets from you.'

Michael Lo froze. He said to Crystal Lam: 'Take my place.' He stood up and said softly to the stocky security officer: 'Go fuck your mother, you prick.'

'And yours, Mr Lo. But if you wish to settle your debts. . . .' He bowed and walked away.

Crystal Lam lost the ten chips in three spins of the wheel.

Michael Lo said: 'Let's go to another place.'

They took a taxi to the floating casino in the inner harbour at the end of the Avenue de Almeida Ribeiro, gaudy outside, bare and smelling of money inside.

On the way Crystal Lam asked: 'Why wouldn't they let you play?'

She shouldn't have asked, he thought – losing face is bad enough without decapitating the head. 'I'm sure you know,' he said. 'But don't worry, they'll pay for it.'

'I know you didn't want to make a scene in front of me,' Crystal Lam said and he forgave her.

In the floating casino, the Macau Palace, he decided to approach the cashier directly. He put down HK dollars and Macau patacas, and asked for $1,000 worth of chips.

The girl shook her head sadly. 'So sorry, Mr Lo.'

Michael Lo smiled fiercely at Crystal Lam. 'I know another place,' he told her. 'It's illegal, rough, not the place for you.'

'I'll be okay with you,' she said.

'Of course.'

'And they'll accept your bets in this place?'

'They don't care how much you owe. But you have to pay within two weeks at 1,000 per cent interest.'

He didn't tell her about the other advantage: it was run by a small Hong Kong triad under pressure from 18G fighting units: if he lost the debts would be wiped out if he eased the pressure.

The disadvantage: macho film stars were vulnerable to assault from ego-trip young toughs and the illegal gambling den was stiff with them.

They took another cab through the busy, flaring streets lined with cabins of family industry and commerce to the gambling den in the basement of a tenement.

'I don't think you should come in,' Michael Lo said.

She pushed him forward.

The basement was packed with smartly dressed gamblers barred from the Lisboa, the Floating Palace and the Casino Jai-Alai, coolies, crooks and bouncers. The bouncers looked at Michael Lo speculatively: good joss to kick the shit out of the Kung Fu star breaking everyone's bones on the cinema screens.

The games played on basic tables covered with green baize were black jack, roulette, fan tan, keno and poker in a room at the back of the basement guarded by a Chinese with a recent knife wound on his cheek sutured with stitches like spiders.

Michael Lo thought: what the hell am I doing here? The penalty of being a tiger – reckless and impatient. But a wonderful sense of humour; I will have to dredge deep to find it.˙

He bought $10,000 worth of grimy chips and sat in front of a girl with mauve lipstick dealing cards for blackjack. He concentrated. With four packs it was virtually impossible to memorise but with four tens and twelve picture cards per pack it was still possible to get some idea of groupings. His first cards totalled 15, odds favouring that, with a third card, he would exceed 21 and bust; he surrendered his cards, saving half his bet.

A few hands later he split two cards and, when the dealer was forced to stand on 17, picked up a stack of dollars on each, an 18 and a 19. He could hear his heart telling him he was onto a streak. Crystal Lam, beside him, placed her hand on his shoulder.

The girl with the mauve lipstick dealt. Michael Lo had the ace of clubs. The girl dealt herself a seven of hearts. The players placed their bets. Michael Lo bet $5,000.

A voice behind him said: 'I'll double that,' and put down ten 1,000-dollar chips.

Michael Lo swung round. 'You can't.'

'Sure as hell can.' He was Chinese, wearing white trousers and a blue silk shirt, but he spoke with an American accent. 'Macau rules. You heard of them, you being local?'

'Screw Macau rules,' said Michael Lo who knew that a spectator was entitled to play your hand if he increased the wager.

The stranger said to the girl dealer: 'Better call the management, pretty girl.'

The girl looked at Michael Lo inquiringly. He shrugged. 'Macau rules.'

She dealt the stranger the jack of diamonds. Blackjack.

She told the players in Cantonese, English and Portuguese that she was leaving the table.

Michael Lo stood up. 'You can't do that just because you're having a bad run.' He turned to the stranger. 'Macau rules, okay?'

The girl said: 'It's the end of my shift.'

The stranger said: 'That's a Macau rule.'

Trying to control his rage, Michael Lo said to Crystal Lam: 'Okay, time to go.'

They were met at the exit by the Red Pole of the Yellow Pang who said: 'You owe us $4 million. Someone must have forgotten to tell you we've taken over this cesspit.'

Michael Lo said in Cantonese: 'You'd better get out of the way, you piece of dog-shit.'

The Red Pole nodded at the guard with the stitched face wound.

Michael Lo said to Crystal Lam: 'You'd better go ahead.'

As she moved away players and guards closed on Michael Lo and the rival Red Pole.

The Red Pole said: 'We're reasonable, son of Kwan Tai. We know you can't have that amount of money with you. Just enough to lose quietly and pay for the whore,' pointing towards Crystal Lam. 'But you have owed us for a long time. True?'

'True that to bring a little honour to your society I played at some of your houses.'

The guard was pulling at the stitches on his cheek with his fingers.

'And you must start to pay. Now.' The Red Pole stretched out his hand. 'Whatever chips you have left. Whatever money you have left if the whore isn't looking after it for you. The balance within two weeks. Otherwise. . . .'

'What, foul mouth?'

'The whole of Hong Kong will know that the Red Pole of 18G failed to pay his debts to the Yellow Pang. And then no one in the 18G will grieve if you are cut into small pieces. Not even your father, Dragon Head.'

Michael Lo shouted. Jumped. A body turn. A flying kick. Down. Hands the bullets of my arms.

The Red Pole fell.

A voice: 'Just like his last movie.'

The stitched scar weaving in front of Michael Lo. His fingers parted it.

A back kick at an invisible opponent.

Spectators parting.

Then feet and hands coming in systematically. Blobs of pain. Arms swimming, pushing aside the pain. And then . . . I am being lifted.

A car. The smell of stale cigarette smoke and perfume.

Ayeeha!

'Don't worry.' Crystal Lam's voice. A touch of compassion in it.

A porch as big as the façade of the Church of St Paul's . . . urgent voices. . . . And then the line uttered in at least three of his films: 'Where am I?'

'China,' Crystal Lam told him.

*   *   *

'What I don't understand,' Crystal Lam said, sipping tea, 'is why you, Warrior of the 18G, can't get the money to pay your debts.'

'Confess that I lost it in Yellow Pang casinos?' Michael Lo, sitting in a garden on the Chinese side of the Portas do Cerco, the frontier arch, touched a bruise on his face bathed in tincture of arnica. 'That would be the ultimate humiliation.'

'Why did you gamble with them?'

'Where else does one gamble illegally in Hong Kong? Certainly not in an 18G casino; not a Warrior, not a Red Pole. And I am Chinese. . . .' He smiled at Crystal Lam sitting at a bamboo table opposite him. 'We have to gamble. And I thought I could take them for a fortune.'

'A system?'

'A feeling. . . .'

'A fortune-teller? The heavenly weight of your bones? The three characters of your name?'

'Something like that.' He made a joke of it, not wishing to confess that he had been guided by *Chou Kung's Book of Auspicious and Inauspicious Dreams*. 'After all *coffin* and *financial luck* sound very similar in our language.'

'Such sophistication,' she said. 'Such a cosmopolitan.'

Looking at Crystal Lam, black hair brushed austerely back from her brow, sitting outside the house where they had spent the night, Michael Lo thought: 'She is stealing my pride.'

He turned and gazed at a rainbow spearing a junk in the brown sea. He asked her: 'How did I cross the border without papers?'

'They know you, Michael Lo. They know you have papers.'

'And you?'

'I am Crystal Lam.'

'A taxi waiting outside the gambling house?'

'There are many taxis in Macau.'

'If diplomats in faraway places only knew how easy it is to cross the border. . . .' But was it?

'What will you do now?' she asked. The pull of her back-swept hair increased the aloof slant of her eyes; she had arrived here from the court of some ancient dynasty.

First he had to find the money: only then could he do battle with the Yellow Pang.

Her words hung between them, suspended coins. 'We can help you?'

We?

He and Crystal were strangers in an old silk tapestry. We?

'What do you mean?' hearing his own words.

She told him. The People's Republic was prepared to pay his debts in return for his allegiance. Wouldn't that be in the best interests of the 18G? An all-powerful alliance between the Communists and the ruling triads after 1997?

Delicately, with silver words, Crystal Lam outlined how such a union could be achieved without loss of face; sculpted an image of a triad leader who would be the power behind the nominal thrones of power in Hong Kong.

The junk moved away from the rainbow.

Michael Lo said: 'I've never known you, have I?'

'Does anyone know anyone? Do we trespass in each other's dreams?'

'It's a lot of money,' Michael Lo said, repossessing his voice.

130

'A promise of power is worth more.'

'You forget one thing: in 1997 Kwan Tai may still be the leader of the 18G.'

She laid her hand on his bruised arm. 'I think not,' she said.

*   *   *

Later Crystal Lam telephoned the headquarters of the New China News Agency in Hong Kong and spoke to Chen Chang, Lu Sun's assistant.

She told him to pass on a message: 'The tip to the Yellow Pang at the illegal casino worked: their Red Pole was there.'

'Anything else?' the voice of the pudgy assistant tight with resentment that he was taking orders from a woman.

'Tell Lu Sin the tiger is caged.'

CHAPTER 14

The 12th day of August in the seventh lunar month. Eight days till the Festival of the Hungry Ghosts, the date on which the biggest consignment of heroin ever smuggled into Hong Kong was due.

But would it get through? Sitting on the top deck of an old green tramcar on his way to a showdown with his son, Kwan Tai debated the misfortunes of the long hot summer.

In the past three weeks two more shipments of drugs – heroin, opium, cocaine and some cannabis – had been intercepted. The street price of a fix was astronomical, consequently the crime rate was high. But, according to the Chinese media, it might have peaked. And, according to an article in the *Far Eastern Economic Review*, the *Time* and *Newsweek* of the region, many addicts were being cured.

What had gone wrong? Kwan Tai, neatly dressed in grey trousers and white shirt for his meeting with his son, blamed two prime culprits – the Fight Crime Committee and Superintendent Harry Price. Accessories: Rachel Crown and his own son.

The battered street-car, one of the fleet of 162 that, since 1904, had trundled along the congested arteries of Hong Kong Island's heartland at speeds averaging 10 mph, stopped. Passengers embarked. Kwan Tai listened to them, accents varying according to the area. Hoklo, Chiu Chow, Shanghaiese. . . . Kwan Tai loved the old trams because they transported him to pre-Communist China.

To the solemn promises of his initiation when he had passed through the Hung Gate to the Circle of Heaven and Earth, to the

City of the Willows and finally to the Council Chamber where he had answered the 333 questions, been clothed in sackcloth and ashes, pledged fidelity to the triad vows with nine blades of grass, watched his blood from a pricked finger run with wine in a chalice.

Gods, such a noble ceremony, oaths burned on your soul: justice and sharing among members, help in hard times, absolute loyalty, death if you transgressed. . . . How could anyone fault such resolutions?

What *gweilos* criticised most about triads was drug trafficking. Kwan Tai had never properly understood their attitude because it was double-talk. Did they outlaw arms dealers when their products were made with the sole intention of killing? Did they prohibit alcohol? Did they prosecute the manufacturers of cigarettes even though tobacco killed hundreds of thousands more than drugs? Of course not; guns and booze and tobacco were big business. That was *gweilo* philosophy, hypocritical. They should live in the Walled City, in an overcrowded tenement, in a leaking shack on a hillside; then they might understand the happiness that white powder could bring. Temporary, perhaps, but the only happiness the addicts would ever know.

The tramcar moved away from a stop. Past the Soldiers and Sailors Home, a Park 'n shop. . . . So far, the Banker didn't appear to have brought much pressure on the crime fighters. Did he consider himself above the 18G oaths? Kwan Tai drummed stubby fingers on the seat in front of him. Piss on him and all his generations; perhaps the burning of his junk hadn't been a strong enough warning; perhaps his throat should be pricked with a myriad of swords. . . .

And what of that dogged current of air, Price? *Ayeea*, such persistence that I almost admire him. Millions of dollars worth of white powder in the hands of Chinese Customs because of his interference. And despite the flour fiasco he was still in power. Despite the shooting in Statue Square.

The Hong Kong and Shanghai Bank! Incomparable *fung shui*. A nobleman guarded by two sentinels, the Bank of China and the Chartered Bank, once taller than their charge; water in the ponds and fountains in front bringing prosperity. But not prosperity for the No. 49 shot dead on the escalator by Price. . . .

Which projected Michael Lo into Kwan Tai's reasoning. My son planned the assassination. Worse, he failed. The Yellow Pang would convene a festival to celebrate the loss of face.

A couple of Shanghaiese boarded the tram and sat in front of Kwan Tai. He listened to them. Anything to divert his thoughts from the meeting ahead.

Forty years ago the triads had ruled Shanghai. Ah, to have operated in those golden years. To have booked first-class tickets on a passenger ship; to have emerged from your cabin on the second day, taken over the ship at gunpoint and diverted it to an island in the East China Sea to loot it. Such glory, such loyalty to the Hung Family; torpedoed by the Japanese, sunk by the Communists.

His train of thought faltered and his son intruded again. Undoubtedly it was he who had ordered the killing of Red Eye Ng. Why? To assert himself as the new Red Pole? To impress the other members of the council he was inciting to rebel.

But he needn't have worried. My only son! Destined to take my place. Warrior, film star. Gods, you had everything. Too much? If only your mother, the Iron Butterfly, were still alive. Kwan Tai stared at the red, blue and white Cantonese signs protruding over the street. But she had died giving birth to Michael Lo's brother, and the brother had died with her.

What am I to do now? Kwan Tai wondered. Oath No. 6: *I shall never betray my sworn brothers.* . . . To do so was to incur the penalty of death. Far worse, surely, to betray your own father. But I cannot order the execution of my only son; surely the loyal members of the council would realise that. Unfortunately the evidence against his son supplied by Grass Sandal was damning.

Kwan Tai alighted from the tramcar in Hennessy Road and hailed a taxi. He told the driver to take him to the Royal Hong Kong Yacht Club. On the way it occurred to him that the fortunes of 18G had not been harmed irreparably by the shortage of heroin: other triad societies were equally affected, therefore 18G maintained its superiority.

What am I suggesting? That we can prosper without drug trafficking? For this irrational reasoning Kwan Tai blamed the influence of Rachel Crown.

Gods, what is happening to me?

From the yacht club he took a walla-walla boat propelled by a woman with a face seamed like cracked clay to his son's white gin palace moored in Causeway Bay.

*   *   *

The 12th day of August in the seventh lunar month. Also the Maiden's Festival.

Price, watching Maisie cut starved roses growing in a shady patch of the garden of the home on Lantau Island, thought she looked preoccupied.

Rachel asked her what was the matter.

'Nothing, Miss Clown,' she said.

'That's the trouble with English,' Rachel said to Price. 'It puts me in the circus.'

In one corner of the garden a Chinese youth who had been an addict was clipping a hedge still dripping from the night's rain; another was chopping wood, wasted muscles finding substance.

Price, sharing, worried about Maisie. He asked her: 'Are you happy, Maisie?'

Her smile was sunlight. 'Very happy, Mr Price.' She snipped a pink rose. 'Do you know about the Herdsman and the Weaver Girl?'

'Ah, so that's it,' Rachel said.

'That's what?'

'Today is the festival for lovers. The Weaver Girl was the daughter of the Sun and she married the Herdsman across the Milky Way. But she was so infatuated with her handsome young husband that she stopped working. The Sun got mad and parted them. But they're allowed to meet once a year. Today.'

'So why should that make Maisie unhappy?'

'She's not with her boyfriend, I guess.'

135

It hadn't occurred to Price that Maisie had one, merely a succession of one-night suitors in the topless bar in Wanchai.

Maisie, reverting to Cantonese, said shyly to Rachel: 'I should be honoured if you could do me a great favour. If you are anywhere near the Lovers' Meeting Rock could you ask a question for me?'

Rachel sighed. 'So now she wants me to take part in heathen practices.'

'I don't understand,' Price said.

'The Bowen Road Rock. Girls pray for husbands and fortune-tellers answer their questions. Married women ask if their husbands are being faithful.' She turned to Maisie. 'How can I go there when I'm a Christian?'

Maisie handed her a rose. 'You could go there and pray for me to your god.'

'Our God,' Rachel said. 'Where is your young man?'

'In prison,' Maisie said.

'For what?'

'He saw me leaving the bar with a British sailor and he attacked him.'

'First offence?'

'No,' Maisie said, staring at pink petals on the ground. 'Three other times, maybe four. He did not like me doing that work.'

'Then why did you do it?' Price asked.

'Chasing the Dragon. They injected me. I had to have Miss White. I had to have money. . . .'

Rachel asked: 'Does he want to marry you, this young man?'

'Maybe now I have left Wanchai.'

'When is he due to be released?'

'In one month's time,' Maisie said.

'When he's released, will you bring him to one of our meetings?'

Price said in English: 'Hard sell?'

Maisie said: 'I will ask him. . . . I don't know. . . . Today is very important.'

Rachel touched her shoulder. 'Don't worry, Maisie, I will go to the rock.'

In the taxi taking them back to Silvermine Bay Rachel said to Price: 'Why don't you come to one of our meetings?'

The breeze through the open window stirred her dark hair. How did she become so tanned? Price was visited by a vision of her sunbathing naked on a deserted beach. A missionary? Blasphemy. But the vision persisted. He wondered if she might seek the wisdom of a soothsayer at the rock on her own behalf.

'I'd like that,' he said.

*   *   *

'Why?' Kwan Tai asked his son.

'In the interests of the 18G,' his son told him. 'It is growing old in its ways.'

Like me? Kwan Tai wondered. What his son said was probably true but he wasn't convinced about his motives. His son was a tiger.

He paced the air-conditioned salon of the eighty-foot Broward with its pigeon-grey chairs and sofa and white, quilted ceiling. Through an open door he could see a cabin with a double bed and mirrors on the ceiling. Why would anyone want to watch themselves coupling?

He seated himself at the bar where his son was standing drinking brandy. What else? The status drink of the Hong Kong Chinese. His trend-conscious habits pleased Kwan Tai. Sad, though, that he never visited the tea store or the cell in the Walled City.

'You took the oaths,' Kwan Tai reminded him.

'Surely the greater glory of the society is more important than a recitation.'

Michael Lo, film star, wearing a cream suit and white, open-neck silk shirt, swilled brandy around his balloon glass. Kwan Tai looked at him and saw himself as a young man, fierce and strong with a wrestler's broad back. Except that I would have been wearing a vest and baggy trousers and my son is taller and straighter than I was.

He said: 'The recitation as you put it is part of the society's

137

glory. It is the very foundation of the Hung Family and it reminds us of our beginnings when we swore to overthrow the Manchus.'

'The Manchus. . . . We are not here, father, to re-fight the glorious history of the Three Harmonies Society.'

'You do not understand, my son. It is true that the Manchus have faded into the mists of time but they have been replaced by other threats. And the oaths of loyalty and fraternity are as true today as they were then.'

'If people insult or abuse you how should you react?'

'Suffer, endure and forgive,' Kwan Tai quoted.

'Ayeeha! What sort of philosophy is that?'

'You forget, that despite such gentle wisdom all Chinese are dedicated to overthrowing evil governments.' Such as the British colonialist government, he thought. And the Communists.

'Your history is a catalogue of contradictions.'

Kwan Tai said: 'Words are butterflies, observe their flight not their colours.'

'Holy shit,' Michael Lo said in English. He grinned and was a boy again. 'The old Dragon Head aphorisms. You know something? I used to write them down and memorise them and repeat them to impress the other kids.'

'Perhaps you should do so again,' Kwan Tai said, directing the conversation back to Cantonese. He found it difficult to sustain his anger.

Michael rolled brandy round his mouth. It doused his smile. He said in Cantonese: 'Father, have you thought about retirement?'

Ayeeha, so it had come to this! 'I have thought about it,' he said, 'for that is my privilege, but it is not a subject with which you should waste your time.'

'I fear that is not so, father. I am observing the flight of the butterfly. How long does a butterfly live? A few days?'

Kwan Tai gazed across the typhoon shelter harbouring the white gin palaces in which the rich Chinese besported themselves at weekends, pleasure junks and sampans. Oil made brilliant patterns, snakes and dragons, in the water. Beyond them the site where the noon-day gun was fired daily, and the big blocks lining Gloucester Road, the Excelsior Hotel, Riviera, Prospect, Miami Mansions, and what was said to be the longest sign in the world, CITIZEN. . . .

My territories, established and precisely bordered beyond those concrete walls, and the legacy I will hand over to my son. *When I decide the time has come!*

Kwan Tai paced the salon.

At last he spoke, his words stones.

'You wish me to retire now, my son?'

'The time is opportune. You would leave the council with grace and your achievements would be remembered for all time.'

'You must realise I cannot stand down now, *heya*?'

'Enlighten me.'

'I would be leaving the society in disarray. Humiliated.'

'I do not understand,' his son said coldly.

'The flour?'

'A victory.'

'Ah, such a victory. A fortune in white powder now in the hands of the Communists. And the current of air Price still in power. . . .'

'More heroin is on its way.'

Kwan Tai ignored him. 'And the attempted murder in Statue Square. . . . On your orders, my son?'

'It was not my fault –'

'Your responsibility! Three members dead, one delivered on a moving staircase into the hands of *gweilos*. Price still sitting at his desk.' Kwan Tai spat on the white carpet. 'You have brought ridicule upon the most revered society in the Hung Family.'

The balloon glass broke in Michael Lo's hand. Brandy spilled on the mahogany bar. Blood flowed down his fingers. He said: 'Someone has to make decisions.'

'Better no decisions than bad ones.'

'Chances have to be taken.'

'Chances are the loser's word for mistakes.'

139

His son wrapped a handkerchief round his hand.

And I thought only two enemies were pursuing me. Price and Rachel Crown. How could a man even consider that his son was stalking him?

'Who betrayed me?' his son asked. 'Grass Sandal?'

'You betrayed yourself,' Kwan Tai said.

'Was it not a sort of betrayal, allowing our society to become senile?'

Not old, senile now!

Kwan Tai said: 'Your actions will be reported to a full meeting of the council.'

'And their decision will be death. Is that what you want, father?'

'I will talk to them.'

'And deny those precious oaths?' His son poured himself more brandy in another glass. 'No, once the council has reached its decision there is only one penalty.'

'There is nothing else to be done,' Kwan Tai said softly.

'There is a lot that can be done.'

Ah, what it is to have a son born in the Year of the Tiger. Ho Chi-minh, Charles de Gaulle, General Eisenhower, Queen Elizabeth II who even now ruled Hong Kong . . . all tigers. Friends will come to help them in the hour of their need but they may be forced to spend money. . . . Could the rumours be true about his gambling? And at what time had he been born? At 11.33 am during the Hours of the Horse. Tiger and horse, two free-wheeling signs lacking responsibility. . . . Gods!

When Kwan Tai, bowed with his conclusions, didn't respond Michael Lo said: 'If I am leader, then the council cannot condemn me for what I have done for I shall be the policy maker. If you were to offer your resignation now and recommend me, your No. 1 son, your only son, then without doubt I would become the leader.'

'And if I do not believe that my time has come?'

'Then I will die. Or. . . .' He removed the handkerchief from his hand; the bleeding had stopped. '. . . I will be forced to take steps to make sure that you are no longer leader.'

'You haven't the support.'

'I wonder, Dragon Head. I wonder.' He drank his brandy. A butterfly fluttered into the salon.

'There is nothing more to be said,' Kwan Tai said.

'Think about what I have said, father. Let me know your decision before the Festival of the Hungry Ghosts.' A small boat drew alongside. 'And now if you will excuse me,' as Crystal Lam climbed on board.

Kwan Tai took the boat back to the shore. Then he went looking for the only person in whom he could confide.

*   *   *

On a balcony above a flight of stone steps leading from Hollywood Road stood an altar; above it an illuminated tray bearing replicas of gifts for the Seven Sisters, the maidens who were honoured because the festival fell on the seventh day of the seventh month. Below, a table bearing a roast pig and fruit, lipstick and cigarettes for the Sisters. At the other end of Hollywood Road stood an enclosure containing booths in which soothsayers foretold futures of female clients.

'A lot of them want to know if this is the last time they'll come here as maidens,' Rachel told Price. 'I haven't bothered. . . .'

Price felt awkward.

'Aren't you scared?' she asked.

'Should I be?'

'They tried to kill you once.'

'*They* have tried to kill me many times. That's twice the old man in the square has saved me.'

'And the street sleeper.'

'Poor bastard,' Price said. A cardboard tray embossed with combs and vanity mirrors was lit and went up in flames beside them. Firecrackers burst into gunfire; Price stopped himself from ducking. 'Did you do what Maisie asked?'

'I tried to make certain she would marry her boyfriend, sure.'

'You prayed to a heathen god?'

'I just prayed,' she said.

141

He said: 'I can tell you this, the Celestial Lovers make police work easier tonight. No one robs a girl when she parades her finery on the streets. It they do. . . .' Price drew one finger across his throat.

'And the next festival is the Hungry Ghosts.'

He told her about the premonition he had felt in Pokfulam above the terraces of graves. 'I'm getting superstitious.'

They walked out of the enclosure into the moonlit street.

'Why not? Another word for intuition. Religion is largely intuition.'

'And is intuition belief?' Another firecracker took him by surprise; he flinched. 'Can you tell me why we should believe?'

'Intuition,' she said, and: 'No, I can't,' and he put his arm round her shoulders and felt her warmth.

*   *   *

When Kwan Tai discovered that Rachel wasn't in the factory he retired to his tiny room in the Walled City, smoked a pipe and speculated about what advice she would have given him. None, probably, because she could hardly discuss a power struggle between father and son in a society that traded in narcotics.

His thoughts reverted to his reasoning on the tramcar. What if the 18G stopped selling heroin? Provided other societies were also deprived of supplies then it would retain its superiority.

He laid down his pipe and closed his eyes. His son, a little boy, came in from the alley. He was playing soldier, Nationalists versus Communists. He grew and there was a knife in his hand and it was plunging towards Kwan Tai's chest.

Kwan Tai awoke whimpering. He stretched out a hand and touched the *T'ung Shu*, the Chinese almanac. It was cold and shiny. He touched the black leather Bible Rachel had given him; it was warm. Hand resting on the Bible, he slept peacefully.

CHAPTER 15

Rome. In a small hotel off the Via Cavour a youngish woman who wore undistinguished clothes with style sat at a marble table beneath a glass dome rimed with dirt reading an old copy of the international *Herald Tribune*.

The tourists had departed for the Coliseum and the Vatican and she was alone save for a puppy testing its courage in front of an indolent tabby cat. The cat treated the puppy, black and white and pear-shaped, indulgently.

From time to time a sleek waiter wearing a grimy white jacket materialised in the lobby and gazed speculatively at the woman and her empty coffee cup. She surmised that, as she had rejected his offer to show her the Rome tourists didn't see, he had dismissed her as a Lesbian.

She turned a page of the newspaper. Stale news emasculated by the passing of time. Although sitting in this becalmed place that smelled of geraniums it was easy to forget that time existed. She glanced at her wristwatch: he was late.

The puppy, mustering an apprentice growl, dabbed at one of the cat's paws; the cat hissed half-heartedly.

But, of course, he invariably made a point of being late to assert himself. He had probably walked twice round the block to make sure he wasn't early.

When, finally, he arrived she was absorbed with old news. He apologised; she hoped he wouldn't make a joke about his dilatoriness; once his jokes and puns had been endearing, part of his self-deprecatory honesty; now she recognised that honesty as an invitation to bolster the complexes of growing old.

No jokes. He ordered coffee from the waiter and said: 'The trouble with you is you're predictable.'

'Because I was on time?'

'That's symptomatic.'

'As a matter of fact I was early. Is that worse?'

He staged a smile, touched his thinning hair and pulled in the slight bulge above his tailored jeans, and she thought how absurd it was that an Englishman should want to be mistaken for an Italian, and she wondered what she had ever seen in him and why nine months ago she had consented to live with him.

He pursed his lips to sip his coffee. The cat licked its paws and blinked at the puppy replanning tactics.

Hong Kong. The words jumped from the page of the *Herald Tribune*. Two paragraphs. Police had swooped on a junk at Aberdeen – a small town on the south-west coast of Hong Kong Island, the paper explained – in the hope of seizing a record haul of heroin. Instead they had found flour. The operation had been planned by a Superintendent Harry Price.

The woman stood up.

Her lover said: 'Where are you going?' and then, tapping his mouth with his forefinger: 'Of course, sorry. . . .'

'As a matter of fact,' Jane Price said, 'I'm going to Hong Kong.'

The puppy sprang. The cat dabbed lethargically and the puppy's nose began to bleed.

CHAPTER 16

When? Where? How?

The consignment had to be soon and it had to be substantial. Probably the biggest ever smuggled into Hong Kong.

Price eavesdropped across the territory but his sources were fickle. Who could blame them? Red Eye Ng and the street sleeper both murdered.

The forces of law and order weren't co-operative either. Poor, bloody Boyce under investigation on the eve of retirement. A one-man vendetta by Price. Narcotics and Customs excluded from the last operation. The shooting in Statue Square. . . .

You're bad joss, Harry Price. He read it in their faces: whenever he joined colleagues for a drink they were on the point of leaving.

The Commissioner spoke to him at a reception at Government House for members of the judiciary from Bangkok. It was evening and the big chamber with its L-shaped alcove was stiff with judges, lawyers, police officers and the stalwarts of Hong Kong Society.

Outside, the lawns and azalea beds beneath the tower, erected incongruously in the middle of the decent old nineteenth century colonial mansion by the Japanese during World War II, were a silk print.

The Commissioner guided Price to an unoccupied patch of blue-grey Tai Ping carpet. He pulled at one tufted eyebrow, sipped his gin and tonic and finally said: 'Bad business in Statue Square.'

145

'It could have been worse,' Price said. 'I could have been killed.'

'Bad publicity. Makes Hong Kong sound like Chicago.' He fingered the knot of his red and blue striped tie. 'Draws attention to this one-man crusade of yours.'

'What should I have done, sir? Run for it?'

'Perhaps,' the Commissioner said, hunting for words, 'you shouldn't have got yourself in that position in the first place.'

'With respect, I can't stay at home playing patience.' Price took another glass of whisky from a waiter's tray; it was tepid.

'You can stop playing the Lone Ranger. You are still in charge of Organised and Serious Crime because everyone has the deepest sympathy for your circumstances. But you can't go on like this.'

'Like what, sir?'

The Governor passed by and smiled at the Commissioner. He was in his mid-fifties with grey hair and a young face and canny eyes and an inscrutability born of service in Peking; it was his brief to begin the integration of Hong Kong with China without a Boxer Rebellion. He can't have enjoyed the shoot-out in Statue Square, Price thought.

The Commissioner said: 'It's common knowledge that you're putting out feelers.'

'My job, sir. We've got a heroin famine on our hands: there must be a big shipment any day now.'

The Commissioner prodded the soggy slice of lemon floating in his drink. Then he said: 'You make it sound as if you're looking forward to another consignment. Hasn't it occurred to you that we're doing very well at the moment? That we don't want another spectacular foul-up?'

'You'll never beat the narcotics in Hong Kong until you beat the triads.'

'One particular triad?'

'Kwan Tai killed my son, sir.'

Price noticed the 18G's banker talking to an American financier. He seemed to have lost some of his gloss. Who had burned his junk?

146

The Commissioner lowered his voice. 'There's been more pressure to relieve you of your duties. That's the only reason you've still got the job.'

'Why bother to mention it, sir?'

'Because if you continue to pursue this . . . this lonely path of yours . . . then you will have to take extended leave.' The Commissioner stared across the gardens at the lights multiplying in the dusk. 'I wouldn't want you to think it was because I had been. . . .'

'Got at?'

'Exactly.' The Commissioner nibbled his slice of lemon. 'Bad business about Boyce. . . .'

'One tends to forget that policemen are human. They have the authority to discipline frailty: it doesn't mean they're not frail themselves.'

'It must have been very hard for you to report him.'

Conventional logic no longer surprised Price. 'No, sir. If he had been on his death-bed I would have reported him. You see, once we become policemen we don't have many values of our own left – we're guardians of other people's. What we do have left is honour. Maybe that is all we do have left. If one policeman betrays that honour then he is more despicable than any villain he pursues. I had to report Boyce,' Price said, not knowing whether the Commissioner understood, knowing that he resented him for turning over a stone and revealing qualities that he, too, despised.

The Commissioner said: 'You should never have been a policeman, Harry.' He placed his empty glass on a table. 'I wonder how many of us really wanted to be. Or how many people in this room wanted to be what they are.' He patted Price on the shoulder. 'I wanted to be a guardsman in front of Buckingham Palace. You?'

'I forget.'

'We all try to.' The Commissioner smiled at a lawyer in a pin-stripe and said: 'I'll be right with you, Tony,' and to Price: 'Don't make me insist on that extended leave, Harry.'

147

Price, seeing Frank on the lawns with him on Azalea Day a long time ago, didn't reply.

*   *   *

He found Sandilands in Bottoms Up, a plush night-spot, topless and touristy, on Hankow Road, Kowloon, managed by a former showgirl at London's Windmill Theatre.

He was sitting with a group of Australians and Americans at one of the circular bars encompassing a chatty black barmaid with magnificent breasts. The men, accompanied by wives and girlfriends, were theatrically indifferent to the mammaries swinging a few feet away from them.

What will the Communists make of this? Price wondered.

He signalled to Sandilands who, unaccompanied, was appraising the ebony bosom with healthy interest. It was the first time Price had noticed anything sensual in the sandy-haired detective's attitudes.

Sandilands finished his beer, shook his head expressively and joined Price outside. Powdered rain was falling, coaxing reflections from shops and clubs onto the shining streets. They caught a cab to Temple Street Market and walked past the stalls which supposedly catered for men's requirements, pornographic books of Chinese girls with spreadeagled thighs among them.

They sat at a table beneath a canopy lit by butane gas lamps opposite a mahjong hall and drank turtle soup.

Price said: 'So, what do you hear?'

'In Kowloon? Nothing. I'm blown here; you know that.'

'Elsewhere,' Price said, watching a pickpocket plying his trade a few feet in front of a Chinese policeman in plain-clothes. The night was alive with rain-soaked whispers and the click of mahjong tiles.

'Not much. Sometimes I wonder what the hell I am hearing.'

'I don't understand,' Price said.

The Chinese detective stopped the pickpocket extracting a wallet from a woman's handbag and arrested him.

'I hear them in the New Territories and on the islands.'

'Heard what for Christ's sake?'
'Two words,' Sandilands said. 'Boys –'
'Or Boyce?'
'And ghosts.'

*　　　*　　　*

Kwan Tai drove to the factory the following day.

He saw addicts whom he had mentally consigned to the grave sweeping, painting, hammering. Their health and their enthusiasm astonished him. Fleet Foot Yan, Hard Knuckle Xu . . . they addressed him as though he were a brother instead of the Dragon Head of the 18G.

He was greeted by a pale agitated European girl who said: 'I don't know if Miss Crown can see you; she has a lot on her agenda.'

Kwan Tai, wearing his fawn jacket for the occasion, said: 'She will see me.'

'I will ask,' the girl said, showing him to a seat in the corridor outside the office. Beside the chair stood a carton of grapes; Kwan Tai picked one; it was plastic. What am I doing here? Are my brains even older than my eyesight?

Rachel said: 'Welcome, Kwan Tai, a day to remember,' and to the girl: 'Run along and get us some tea, Lilian.'

In the office she said: 'I always hoped but I was never sure whether you'd come.' She wore pink, a skirt and a top and when she stretched her arms above her he could see a stretch of tanned flesh between the two.

Kwan Tai, sitting opposite, said: 'I came to offer you advice,' because he couldn't admit that he had come to seek it.

'I am honoured,' she said in Cantonese.

A pause hung between them. 'The dates of your prayer meetings, you must choose them more carefully. Never the fourth, that is death.'

'Ah, numbers. Do you really believe our destiny can be controlled by them?'

For this he had come prepared. 'Of course. Figures, dates,

149

what appear to be coincidences. Take the late President Kennedy. . . .'

The girl returned bringing tea and worry with her. Tea! Kwan Tai looked with horror at the two greyish bags lying at the bottom of the cups.

Rachel apologised. 'We have a very tight budget. An English missionary brought the tea bags.'

'But they're filled with powder.'

Rachel poured boiling water from a chipped brown teapot onto the cups. Where was the ceremony, the adjudications? The tea bags when fished out of the cups reminded him of used condoms.

He pushed aside his cup. 'Another time, I left my thirst behind.'

She sipped her tea, giving every semblance of enjoying it. 'What about Kennedy?' she asked him.

'Do you know when he was elected?'

She frowned. 'Nineteen sixty?'

'Correct, your memory does you credit. And Lincoln?' And when she hesitated: 'I will enlighten you. Eighteen sixty.'

'So?'

'Did you know both presidents were assassinated on the sixth day of the week of your calendar, Friday?'

She didn't. 'What does this prove, Kwan Tai? Two coincidences. . . .'

'Coincidence is a word invented to dismiss destiny.'

'And that is all?'

Kwan Tai shook his head, concentrating on what he had memorised that morning. 'Lincoln's successor was named Johnson. Am I right?'

She admitted he was, adding: 'And so, of course, was Kennedy's.'

'Andrew Johnson,' Kwan Tai said, thinking hard, 'was born in 1808.'

'And Lyndon Johnson was born in 1908?'

'Correct. That potion,' pointing at the cup in her hand, 'has not addled your wits. And Lincoln's assassin?'

150

'Booth,' she said.

'Born?'

'I have no idea.'

'Eighteen thirty-nine.'

'And I suppose Oswald was born in 1939?'

'Just so. Do you not agree that such patterns are more than coincidence, more than chance?'

'Sometimes,' Rachel said, placing her cup on an unmatching saucer, 'it is better to neither believe nor disbelieve.'

Kwan Tai accepted the concession gracefully. 'There are other similarities.'

'I don't doubt it.'

'Both the assassins were assassinated before they were tried. . . .' Now, in the ascendancy, he could discuss his son.

She listened attentively, sipping her noxious brew. When he had finished she said: 'I cannot advise you, Dragon Head. He is your son. But I can make a suggestion.'

Kwan Tai inclined his head.

'We can pray.'

'To your God?' It cannot do any harm, he thought. The Bible had brought him comfort; not its content, its touch.

In the makeshift chapel, kneeling in front of packing cases covered with table-cloths, Rachel prayed with tongues. At first Kwan Tai felt embarrassed but when he heard his son's name the feeling passed. And when she prayed to the Lord Jesus Christ to heal the rift between father and son he found his lips moving and his eyes were drawn to Christ nailed to the brass cross on the altar.

'Father and son,' she said as they walked across the factory floor. 'A recurring theme in The Bible. *Have we not all one father? Hath not one God created us?* Malachi,' she added.

Had she looked that up before they met? Just as I memorised the likenesses between the deaths of Lincoln and Kennedy? No, she hadn't known I was coming. He picked up a sprig of plastic peach blossom and acknowledged the greeting of a young Chinese whitewashing a wall who had been a member of 18G, theoretically still was.

151

They reached the open door. Children played in the dust outside; he could smell rain and he longed for the autumn when the sunshine was sweet and dry.

Her words dispelled the sunny visions. ' . . . shortage of drugs. And you are in a position to keep it that way.'

'I don't understand,' said Kwan Tai who did.

'You are the leader of the most powerful triad in Hong Kong.'

Not according to my son, he remembered. 'Are you suggesting that the 18G smuggles drugs?'

She led him into the sunlight as a green and white jet lowered itself towards the airport. 'Everyone knows the triads move heroin into Hong Kong.'

'Everyone?'

'Have the fortunes of 18G been seriously affected by the shortage of white powder?'

'A difficult question to answer, Miss Crown, when I have not agreed that our society trades in such a commodity.'

'Then has a fictitious triad been affected?' The sunlight found flecks of gold in her eyes.

Kwan Tai chose his tones of Cantonese with care. 'It is possible that an imaginary triad may have discovered that it has not been as disastrous as they feared. That their investments from previous sales now reap considerable dividends.'

Although the Banker's attitudes were deplorable he still handled 18G funds with expertise.

'That being so,' Rachel Crown said, 'wouldn't it make good sense for this mythical society to stop importing white powder?'

So that was it. 'A trade, Miss Crown? Prayers for my son in exchange for a promise?'

He was disappointed; then he recalled that he had been wondering what would happen if the 18G abandoned drug trafficking, simultaneously increased their stake in prostitution, pornography, gambling, loan sharking and protection. Or was that an old man thinking? Not so old, watching the movement of Rachel Crown's breasts beneath the pink cotton.

152

'If you made such a decision other triads might follow.'

'I will think about what you have said,' Kwan Tai said because the prayers for his son must not be jeopardised.

She put an arm round his shoulders. 'Obviously there will be a big consignment soon.'

'For this imaginary society? It is extremely likely.' She smelled of peach blossom and he glanced at the plastic sprig in his hand.

'And it could be . . . diverted?'

'It could be.' He moved away from her because the perfume was muddling his reasoning.

She said: 'Go home with a light heart, Kwan Tai, God has heard your prayers.'

Blackmail!

'*Your* prayers, Miss Crown.'

'Ours,' she said. 'And now that you have found the faith others will follow your example.'

'Are you suggesting that you have converted me to your faith?'

'Only you can answer that.'

Ayeeha! 'I only want the wound bleeding between my son and me to be healed.'

'And you believed that God might heal it. Doesn't that mean that you believed?'

He stared at her appalled.

She said: 'We have prayer meeting next week. Will you come, Kwan Tai?'

'What day?' he asked. The Chinese calendar could be relied upon to provide an excuse.

'In our calendar August the twentieth.'

'I am deeply sorry,' squeezing the relief from his voice. 'That is the Festival of the Hungry Ghosts.'

He bowed and picked his way through the children. When he was past them he turned and said: 'By the way, Miss Crown, did you know that Lincoln's secretary was named Kennedy and Kennedy's secretary was named Lincoln?'

CHAPTER 17

Compared with other glittering cities the streets of Hong Hong are relatively safe. Not on the night of August 15. Not at the junction of Mody Road and the golden mile of Nathan Road in Kowloon.

The air was humid, stars blurred. Stores selling opal and jade, computers and clocks, satin and silk, gold and ivory beckoned tourists; hawkers and shoeshine boys and club touts cajoled them. And the tourists ebbed and flowed from the big chain hotels, Sheraton, Holiday, Hyàtt, and the old and elegant Peninsula with its fleet of Rolls Royce Silver Shadow IIs.

Among these visitors were Mr Harold 'Ginger' Wesley and his wife, sheep farmers from Roxburgh on New Zealand's South Island. They had never been abroad before and Ginger was fulfilling a promise to his wife, Alma, that one day they would venture overseas. They were in their seventies, both with bright white hair and skins matured by the open-air and they were determined not to be overawed by a pushy city. They had dined extravagantly, taken coffee among the gold and cream columns of the Peninsula lobby and emerged into the busy streets to buy gifts for their grandchildren.

Ginger Wesley kept his money in a belt beneath his shirt; Alma clasped her handbag tightly even though it contained little money. 'We musn't spoil the kids,' said Alma, keeping a sharp lookout for pickpockets, but Ginger, patting his money-belt, said: 'What the hell. Don't want to hear them saying, "Good riddance to the mean old bastard" on my death-bed.'

Alma stopped outside a jeweller's and pointed at a Rolex Oyster.

'Know something, Ginger,' she said. 'I've always wanted one of those.'

'You hang suspended in the Pacific staring at humpback whales?'

She stared at him. 'Too much brandy with your coffee?'

'An advertisement,' Ginger explained. 'This woman, a marine biologist, wears a Rolex.'

'I could take up marine biology. . . .'

'Sorry, old girl, I can't run to it.'

She squeezed his arm. 'Don't worry, you've bought me memories.' And then: 'You know something else? There's a lot of life here, a lot of bustle, but somehow it's not as noisy as I expected. Quiet in fact.'

It was at that moment, 10.38, that the shooting started.

*   *   *

The five Chinese, members of a small breakaway triad society, wore white cloth masks and bullet-proof vests and carried pistols – Lugers, Berettas and a Smith & Wesson.

They piled out of a laundry van and, parting the crowds with their guns, ran towards a store glittering with clocks, watches and jewellery.

One armed with the Smith & Wesson stood guard outside. Another waved the sales staff into a corner with a Luger. The other three savaged a display case.

As their hammers bounced off the reinforced glass two red taxis carrying British and Chinese police, alerted by lookouts posted in the golden mile Holiday Inn and the Hyatt, moved in.

The first shot was fired by one of the gangsters. Into the lock of the showcase containing jewellery while his two accomplices shovelled Rolex Oysters, Longines, Omegas, Patek Philippes, Tissots, Piagets from other cases into a sack.

One of the taxis, tyres squealing, stopped outside the store. As police leaped out the lookout opened up with his Smith &

Wesson, puncturing a tyre, frosting the rear window and wounding two policemen.

Pedestrians dived. Ginger Wesley pressed his wife against a steel window shutter beneath a sign GEMS. 'Quiet?' he asked.

A superintendent shouted through a hailer: 'Throw down your guns. Come out hands behind your heads. You're covered.'

They came out shooting. Windows shattered. A woman screamed, a child cried. The second taxi arrived. Police on foot dressed as tourists, carrying guns instead of cameras, began firing.

'Quiet?' Ginger Wesley asked again, shielding his wife's trembling body.

Shooting indiscriminately, the gangsters hurled themselves into the laundry van, the last one carrying the sack of watches. As he jumped in watches spilled onto the pavement.

Ginger Wesley gazed at them thoughtfully.

The van took off down Mody Road and was abandoned in Peace Avenue where the gang hijacked a cab to a building site at Sha Tin, then stole a car and disappeared among the duck farms, fish ponds and temples of the New Territories.

Later Ginger Wesley climbed into bed beside his wife who had taken a sedative in their room in the Peninsula.

She said sleepily: 'If you say "Quiet" once more to me I'll scream,' but instead he kissed her eyes, closing them, and laid the Oyster Rolex made with steel and 18 carat gold on the bedside table where she would see it first thing in the morning.

*   *   *

While the shoot-out was taking place eight members of the Yellow Pang who, to create a diversion, had tipped off the police about the robbery marched into a clip-joint protected by the 18G.

Their brooding middle-aged Red Pole flashed a triad dagger at the handful of early customers and told them to get out. '*And you*,' to the twittering girls cupping their small bare breasts with their hands.

When they had all gone he addressed the manager, a thin Shanghaiese with a welcome smile printed on his hollow features. The Yellow Pang, he informed him, were going to protect the premises from the evil influences that had recently infiltrated Kowloon night life.

'You heard the shooting down the street?'

The manager admitted that he had heard some such noise.

'You will never be threatened by such hooligan elements when we are looking after your interests.'

The manager fingered the hollows in his cheeks as though looking in them for answers and informed the Red Pole that, really, he had no worries because he was paying protection to the 18G.

'Then why were we allowed to enter your premises?'

'Because you wish us no harm?' the manager suggested with little hope.

The Red Pole placed his hands together in a prayer-like gesture. 'Yes,' he said, 'and no,' moving behind the bar and dropping onto the floor a bottle of *luk soi*, green water, the drink the bar girls ordered when customers such as the sailors from the American Warship USS *Towers* who had been in the bar earlier in the evening entertained them.

'And no?'

'Surely that is self-evident. Why would we offer to protect you if we wished you harm? But,' and here the Red Pole sliced the lapel of the manager's tuxedo with his dagger, 'it is surely idiotic to suggest that, if you are being protected, we of a different society should be allowed to enter your premises. Without even a challenge,' he added with unaffected surprise.

The manager agreed that it was certainly surprising. But, remembering the legend of the 18G, the most powerful of all triads who had spear-headed the Chinese Nationalist cause into Hong Kong, suggested that protection must surely be imminent.

The Red Pole said he hoped so for the manager's sake because, if it didn't materialise, and if he still declined the Yellow Pang's offer of protection, he would be forced to sever the

157

tendons of the manager's shoulder blades with a hatchet, thus making his arms as impotent as a stalk without balls.

'You have pressed the button behind the bar?' he asked.

The manager said he had.

'Then where are your protectors?'

'At the shooting, perhaps?'

'Dereliction of duty,' the Red Pole said, slitting the watered silk of the other lapel of the manager's tuxedo. 'The 18G are a spent force. Their leader, Kwan Tai, has lost direction, his officers are in disarray. To seek protection from the 18G is to summon a toothless tiger. But have no fear, we will take over the duties so shamefully neglected by the 18G.'

'But that will create trouble,' the manager said.

'Without a doubt, but you will not get hurt.' The Red Pole picked up a hatchet and touched the blade with his thumb. 'And we are not expensive, a mere $10,000 a month.'

The manager rotated a finger round one hollow cheek. 'Very well, I will consider your offer.'

'And 15,000 now,' the Red Pole said swinging the hatchet in small, pendulum movements.

'I haven't –'

The Red Pole nodded to a 49 standing at the bar. He broke open the cash register with a hatchet and took out 15,000 in yellow and red bank-notes.

'Thank you,' the Red Pole said to the manager. 'You are very wise. Have you heard,' massaging the side of the hatchet blade with the tips of his fingers,' when the next consignment of 18G white powder is due?'

The manager shook his head, wincing as the hatchet parted the lapels of his tuxedo, drawing blood beneath his white shirt.

'Come, you must have entertained many of their 49s here. What did they say after they had drunk the good brandy you keep hidden beneath the bar?'

'I have heard vague talk about the Hungry Ghosts.'

The Red Pole handed his hatchet to a 49. 'See that you don't join them,' he said and led his men out of the clip-joint.

That evening they took over a pub, a disco and a seedy club

158

where, just before dawn, ancient harlots offered decrepit sex to clients too drunk to discriminate; all deep in 18G territory. Ghosts, under duress, materialised in each of them.

Finally they sliced and beat up two 18G members with brandy breaths wandering down Granville Road. From bloodied lips: 'Ghosts. . . .'

Four days away.

*   *   *

Observed, with minimal interest, by Crystal Lam, Michael Lo once again fought with a ferocity that hadn't been envisaged by the director or the scriptwriters. Barehand outside a temple guarded by two stone lions against two opponents, one armed with a sword, the other with a cudgel.

Long shadow boxing. Sweep of the hand, jump, kick. His foot hit the neck of his oponent who fell, sword clattering beneath a lion's lichen-furred paw.

'Michael.' He heard the director's warning cry. Ignored it. Turned to face the cudgel, the weapon which made the Monkey King invincible.

His opponent became the watchdog at the casino in Macau, Price, the Red Pole who the previous night had invaded 18G territory, won the first battle. *Ayeeha*, I have to fight back.

A foot sweep took the cudgel fighter's legs from under him. An instant follow-through but the fighter, a teenager with flat dedicated features, was on his feet. The cameras followed him.

A simultaneous block and counter.

We must have a council of war, a meeting of rebels, today.

He cried out, kicking backwards, feeling the impact of his foot against kneecap. A crippling blow.

No mistake smuggling the heroin this time. Revitalise the society's purpose.

The young fighter was leaping, brandishing his cudgel. He wore thong bracelets on his wrists and a plume of red feathers fluttered from the tip of the cudgel.

159

Michael Lo ducked as the cudgel swept over him, feathers brushing his forehead.

Attack, defend, counter. He tensed himself.

But what if Kwan Tai mismanaged the collection of the drugs on the night of the Hungry Ghosts? There was even talk among members that he no longer cared about narcotics.

The cudgel fighter became Kwan Tai.

The cudgel hit Michael Lo on the side of the head knocking him senseless.

*   *   *

In the train taking him from Kowloon to Canton Lu Sun considered the information imparted by Crystal Lam in the Wan Lai Restaurant in Shanghai Street where bird fanciers gathered. She had spoken admirably – crisp, articulate and devious. With her eyebrows shaved beneath the tips into disdainful angles, her polished hair pulled into a coil, her smooth brow and high-collared blue jacket, she beckoned him into a past which was increasingly overtaking the present.

In between sips of Kwan Yin green tea she told him in Mandarin that Michael Lo was now irrevocably committed to the Communist cause. 'We have paid his gambling debts and if this was ever revealed he would lose so much face that he would be laughed out of the 18G.'

Lu Sun nodded wisely, glancing at the canary he had just bought in the bird market in Hong Lok Street which he hoped to mate with his pet on Hong Kong Island. The canary sang occasionally but seemed subdued. He drank red tea made from an inferior leaf to that sold by Kwan Tai.

Crystal Lam, her appearance so severe that no one recognised her, elaborated. Michael Lo had experienced a succession of humiliations; to maintain stature he had to produce brilliancies.

'Such as?' Lu Sun opened the door of the bamboo cage and poured seed into the feeding bowl; the canary ignored it, sang a few sorrowful notes and fell silent.

'Rout the Yellow Pang,' Crystal Lam said.

'Of course. Excellent.' Lu Sun favoured her with one of the benign smiles that had smoothed so many crises in his life. 'We would then have the combined power of the two most powerful societies in Hong Kong behind us. And?'

'Make sure the next shipment of heroin reaches the streets of Hong Kong and make sure he takes the credit for it.'

'You are wise, Crystal Lam. That would be a great face saver.' *Even though under the Communists he would be shot in the back of the head for such a crime.* 'And?'

'He must take over leadership of the 18G.' Her ingenuity knew no bounds. 'Only then can we be assured of triad support.'

'Is he strong enough to take over from Kwan Tai?'

'He is gaining strength by the day.'

'Really? I never suspected that he was unduly weak.'

'Nor did he.' It was then that Crystal Lam surprised Lu Sun. 'But I have taught him that aggression is merely a disguise for weakness. Now that he has sighted humility he is sighting resolution.'

But I have taught him. . . . Lu Sun glanced at her. Sensuality dissipating the hauteur. Gods, he thought, she loves him in her way.

After the meeting Lu Sun, who lived alone, took the canary across the water on the Star Ferry and introduced it at a distance to its mate in his apartment in Happy Valley near his office. The birds scuttered up and down their respective perches and an inquisitive and worried silence enveloped the two cages.

Then Lu Sun, who had been worried about the fragility of his bones and the parchment quality of the skin on his hands, went to a herbalist on Bonham Strand to correct the balance between the Yin, the negative female force in his body, and the Yang, the male positive, the two forces from which the universe had been forged. He suspected that an imbalance had caused his inner world to become too dry.

The herbalist examined his hands, felt his bones, took his pulse, scrutinised his face, confirmed Lu Sun's theory that there was too much fire in his body and, tapping yellow teeth with his forefinger, considered the glass jars assembled behind him: sea-horses, pulverised tiger bones and rhino horn, red ginseng from North Korea, wild ginseng from the mountains in the north of China, roots, grasses, lichen, seeds, petals, barks, husks of insects. After he had prescribed a potion Lu Sun, who believed himself to be a hypochondriac – only a true hypochondriac can diagnose hypochondria – also bought pearl powder for his skin and monkey bezoar powder for his cough, telling the herbalist that his purchases were for a friend.

Then, summoned to Canton to meet the Overseas Intelligence director in charge of the Hong Kong Operation who had travelled from the Fragrant Hills west of Peking, he recrossed the water and caught the 12.55 train from Kowloon.

The train, No. 92, transported him into the past where he liked to dwell. Paddy fields, water buffalo, green fans of lotus leaves, villages becalmed in time, all framed by the lace curtains on the windows of the gently-swaying, blue-grey coach. Back to the time before contradictions. How could the Chinese with their religions and superstitions and veneration of their ancestors really believe in godless Communism? How could Peking, the City of Kings – now Beijing, City of the People – ever collaborate with barbarians in Moscow?

The Chinese he pitied most were those who had been con-scripted into the Cultural Revolution. How could young people who had been taught to revere Mao suddenly reject his memory? It was a mockery of their fervent and strident youth. And what would they make of the new liberalisation? As soon as it was introduced students rioted and had to be suppressed. Such irony.

And you, Lu Sun, what is your justification for representing all these contradictions in one of the last outposts of colonial rule? He watched a Hakka in a broad black hat berating a water buffalo. Because, like my life, Communism is only a few threads in a tapestry: I represent Cathay, the ancients and the ancestors, which transcends change.

Lu Sun closed his eyes as the train burrowed through a tunnel. Mao Tse-tung, Chiang Kai-shek and Sun Yat Sen acknowledged him as he regressed through dynasties, Ch'ing – the Manchus, the pure Mongolians who had ruled for more than 250 years –, Ming, Yuan, Chin . . . back to the Five August Emperors and the Three August. . . . Lu Sun bowed before an emperor; a gong echoed through the Fragrant Hills; Kwan Tai smiled benevolently from his throne. . . .

'If you wish to eat food is now being served in the dining car.' The attendant wearing grey skirt, white blouse, and maroon tie smiled at him.

He ate duck and noodles and drank tea in the diner lit with tiny coloured lights while around him tourists from America, Australia and Britain sampled sweet red wine from Peking. Soon, if I win over the triads, I will be strolling past the Hall of Annual Prayers in the Temple of Heaven . . . ironic that to do so I have to destroy a man who also holds aloft venerable principles like banners, Kwan Tai.

Three hours and four minutes after leaving Kowloon the train pulled into Canton. From the station Lu Sun took a cab south through the centre of Canton or Guangzhou, City of the Rams or City of the Rice Ears – founded according to legend by five gods riding rams each with a grain of rice in its ear –, a metropolis of 7 million souls, each of them riding his bicycle this hot August afternoon through streets lined with sturdy buildings like old banks, apartment blocks bracketed with balconies, parks and temples and new luxury hotels which were amalgams of Hilton, Sheraton and Hyatt.

The taxi dropped him at the White Swan on the island of Shamian where foreigners once lived in the city. It was palatial – shaped like a swan, with an indoor waterfall, a thousand air-conditioned rooms, bank, post office, pool, shopping mall and a gym full of weight machines and small, muscle-pulsing men –, built to accommodate burgeoning Sino-West trade. The past shipwrecked on the island was more to Lu Sun's taste. The Opium Wars when the British barbarians sold opium to the Chinese in exchange for silver and tea. . . .

He waited for Kang Li in his room on the 34th floor overlooking the broad waters of the Pearl River. Barges idled past, ferries ploughed back and forth; on the far bank lights glimmered in the past. . . . Gods, am I already senile? This one last assignment then I, too, can settle in the mists. For Kwan Tai and me the final act. One way or the other.

A ring on the bell and Kang Li, heavy-lidded with brandy-flushed cheeks and tough grey hair, came in, sat on a pink upholstered chair beside the television and surveyed the room sardonically. In Kang Li's mind every habitation was compared with Block 3 of Shanghai Prison where, during the Cultural Revolution, he had spent three years. He seemed to enjoy disparaging the trappings of luxury which he took every opportunity to explore.

'So, Lu Sun, what about a drop of brandy to fuel our discussions?' he said in Mandarin.

Lu Sun who had come prepared placed a bottle of Courvoisier and two glasses on the coffee table and poured two measures, the larger for Kang Li. He sipped his; Kang Li tossed his back and sighed; as he did so his cheeks became more suffused; he was, in fact, a congested sort of man, everything heavy and contused except his ears which were small and fragile, petals adhering to the side of his head. He poured himself another slug of brandy and stared at it.

He said: 'I have read your reports. So has the minister. So have members of the Politbureau. Everyone is pleased with your ideas even though you are a little slow in implementing them.'

Ah, so that was it: someone in Peking – Kang Li? – wants quick results to further their own interests. 'Curious you should say that, Kang Li, when I have had messages from Beijing congratulating me on the dispatch with which I have carried out orders.'

'Indeed?' He didn't, of course, make the mistake of asking who had sent the messages. 'I am pleased for you, Lu Sun, but I wonder if you appreciate the importance of your assignment. With the triads on our side the transition will be as smooth as good brandy down a thirsty throat.' He drank Courvoisier. 'Imagine a New York in which the Mafia worked for the City Council instead of against it. . . .'

Lu Sun who had never been to New York said: 'I am sure I don't have to point out, Kang Li, that such a miracle has not even been glimpsed since the first Italian set foot in the New World, and I have been negotiating for only a few months.'

'Negotiating? Scheming would be a better description.' Kang Li leaned across the table and switched on the television. The Bill Crosby Show beamed from Hong Kong. He changed channels. A committee at Peking airport welcoming a delegation from Albania. How could anyone be so delighted to see anyone else?

Kang Li switched it off. 'Do you know what our treat was in Shanghai Jail?'

Lu Sun, sighing inwardly, shook his head.

'Table tennis once every two months. Up at 7 am, congee for breakfast, three hours of ideology, rice and vegetables for lunch, a few hours reading the *People's Daily* or playing chess, one visitor a month, hard labour in chains if you transgressed. Death sentence postponed for two years to see if you had learned your ideological lessons. If you hadn't, a knife in the larynx to save bullets.'

'So you learned your ideological lessons?'

'On the contrary, the Chairman of the Party died. . . . And Kwan Tai, will he ever change his ideological opinions?'

'You know he won't,' Lu Sun said, surprised. 'A Nationalist who brought the 18G to Hong Kong to escape the Communists?'

'The question,' Kang Li said, 'was academic. According to your reports everything depends on his son.'

'Not everything,' Lu Sun said guardedly. Over-elaborate manoeuvring bored him and boredom was a breeding ground for mistakes.

'You have an alternative plan?'

'Many,' Lu Sun lied. 'But let us concern ourselves with Michael Lo. We have paid his gambling debts and he is infatuated with Crystal Lam. He is ours.'

Suddenly Lu Sun wanted to get out of the room which had become an interrogation cell. To roam the streets of the city which, a thousand years ago, had been famed for the evening glow of Shimen, morning after rain on the Haishan Mountain, autumn scenery on the Pearl River, clouds over Juhu Lake, the misty rain of Datong. . . .

'So he is ours. What now?'

'It is in my reports.'

'I want to hear it from your lips, Lu Sun. Your words are gossamer threads of intrigue.'

'Very well.' Lu Sun poured himself another brandy. 'He is disgraced. The only ways he can regain respect are by humiliating the Yellow Pang who have moved into 18G territory in Kowloon, by superintending the shipment of heroin into Hong Kong and by taking over the 18G. When he has accomplished these three objectives he will be in a position to co-operate with us.'

'A very big *when*, Lu Sun.'

'I don't think so,' Lu Sun said, lies oiled by the brandy. 'He is the Red Pole, the Warrior. He has many members of the 18G behind him; he knows when the heroin is due.'

'How do you know that?' Kang Li asked.

'I know,' Lu Sun said.

'Crystal Lam?'

'You, Kang Li, are an impresario. You should not concern yourself with the choreography of the play.'

The Director of Overseas Intelligence changed tack. 'Am I right in assuming that the overthrow of the Yellow Pang is timed to coincide with the arrival of the heroin?'

'You would have to ask Michael Lo that.'

'I am asking you.'

'Then I shall have to ask Michael Lo.'

'Very well.' Kang Li tipped more brandy into his glass; Lu Sun wondered if the Bill Crosby Show was over; he liked to watch American and British comedy shows while his canary – two, now – sang in his living room. 'One thing does bother me,' Kang Li said. 'What happens if Kwan Tai overrules his son? If he has more support than you credit him with. He is, after all, a much respected elder. Like you, Lu Sun.'

The possibility had occurred to Lu Sun many times. What tormented him was that, in a way, he hoped Kwan Tai would triumph over his son. But in a practical sense no. Not for the sake

166

of Cathay, not for the time when I settle in the mists. He told Kang Li that it was an improbable eventuality. The walls of the room closed upon him. He breathed quickly. Asthma? What a treacherous malady hypochondria was.

'Because,' Kang Li said, words discharged in capsules of brandy-heat, 'if it appears that Kwan Tai is poised to defeat his son there is only one possible solution. Don't you agree, Lu Sun?' And when Lu Sun didn't reply immediately: 'He will have to be killed.'

'By us?'

'My dear old friend, you are losing your touch. By us? How could you of all people envisage anything so clumsy? No, he will have to be killed by his son.'

The following day at 11.15 Lu Sun caught Train No. 94 to Hong Kong. But instead of the past the train seemed to be transporting him into an uncertain future.

CHAPTER 18

The Aw Boon Haw Gardens owe their existence to a cream, Tiger Balm, for which a catalogue of medical cures is claimed. The manufacturer, Mr Aw Boon Haw, made millions from his balm and in 1935 landscaped the gardens on a steep hill to the north-east of Hong Kong Island above Causeway Bay.

The gardens are a joy; they are also a sermon because Mr Aw Boon Haw devised them as a warning to transgressors to seek salvation before it is too late; before, that is, they fall victim to some malady beyond the recuperative powers of even Tiger Balm.

His exhortations are preserved in a congregation of pagodas and statues drawn from Buddhist and Taoist fables. Dragon, Phoenix, Unicorn, Crane and Roc representing strength, goodness, virtue, longevity and the shining future; the Five Buddhas of Wisdom – thought, pursuit of enlightenment, learning, achievement of enlightenment, acceptance of nirvana; two dragons fighting over a pearl – don't meddle in other people's affairs; the ten courts of hell – the ultimate destination of transgressors who don't repent; Su Wu, an official during the Han Dynasty who, because he refused to change his faith, was imprisoned for nineteen years on a diet of icicles . . . the magnificent Tiger Pagoda which, more than fifty years ago, cost Mr Aw Boon Haw a million Hong Kong dollars.

Price waited for the informant, whose name he had discovered after a raid on Boyce's apartment, beside the Laughing Buddha, the kindest of all the statues. There had been other names in the grey Knowledge exercise book but none with the three crosses merited by Chen Lip.

Price had run a computer check on Chen. Aged forty-three, earning 2,000 Hong Kong dollars a month at a ball-point pen factory on the third floor of a penitentiary-style block in Aberdeen, paying $500 a month for a small apartment, seven days' paid holiday a year. An 18G triad and a drug addict. Price hoped the Laughing Buddha could spare some of his philanthropy for Chen Lip.

He looked around. There were only a few people in the gardens, a couple of families staring at the dragons fighting and one or two solitary men cowered in the damp heat. A park, Price thought, could be the loneliest place in the world. When Chen Lip approached he barely noticed him such was his frailty; he wore long shorts and a string vest and his fragile bones looked as though they might pierce his parchment skin; but his eyes and his chip-tooth smile were bright and Price assumed he had just given himself a fix.

He claimed he had just left a rice wine party and told Price about the ghosts who had visited it, spirits of the scholar, fighter and begger who, 4,000 years ago, had been murdered to draw their blood to perfect China's first wine. He described the philosophical influence of the scholar when he and his guests had started to drink *Siu Hing*; the aggressive effect of the fighter half way through the party; the debilitating presence of the beggar towards the end of the boozing.

As they walked round the Tiger Pagoda, Price followed up Chen's lead. 'Perhaps the ghosts at your party will be appeased in three day's time.'

'Perhaps many people will be appeased.' Chin Lip smiled brightly.

'That is what I have heard, Chen Lip.' They passed the Eight Immortals. 'What puzzles me is where and when the white powder will be delivered.'

'It is indeed puzzling,' Chen Lip agreed. 'Such puzzles are very expensive.'

Exorbitant if he was main-lining. Price glanced at the stick-like arms but there were no puncture marks. Either he was chasing the dragon on a massive scale or he was injecting into the thighs and groin. Whichever, he was close to death.

'*Where* could be worth 500 dollars,' Price told him. '*When* another 500.' Two weeks' wages.

'What worries me,' Chen said, 'is that if I were to solve this puzzle for you then many people who crave the company of Miss White would be disappointed.'

'But if they had sufficient money they would still be able to buy her companionship.'

Chen said: 'One thousand dollars to suggest *where* she will be delivered. One thousand for *when*.'

A month's wages to escape cramps, vomiting, sweating, paroxysms. But money in his pocket would be a death sentence. Or a merciful release? Catch Kwan Tai and his son in the act of delivering and I may save thousands of lives.

'Do you have the answer to the puzzle with you now?' Price asked the living skeleton walking beside him.

'You give me 500 dollars now and I will have the answer tomorrow. I will meet you here, beside the Laughing Buddha, and you will have 1,500 dollars with you.'

'How do I know you won't spend the 500 and forget to come back?'

Chen pulled Price's shirtsleeve with chicken-bone fingers.

'Mr Boyce was always very good to me. But now he has lost face, *heya*? So he no longer gives me any money. I will work for you the same way I worked for Mr Boyce. Tomorrow' – Chen Lip winked hideously – 'will be one big day for you, Mr Price.'

Price handed him five 100-dollar notes. 'If you don't turn up you know what will happen?'

'I know.' He crossed his wrists as though they were handcuffed.

'Same time,' Price said and watched him walk away unsteadily and saw him for a moment as a schoolboy quick with life. When Chen had parted with the information, Price decided, he would arrange with Narcotics to move him to a rehabilitation centre and knew even as he made the decision that Chen was beyond any cure on this earth.

He glanced at the statue beside him. Kwan Shi Yin, the Goddess of Mercy who 'hears the cries of the world'.

*   *   *

In his echoing apartment that evening Price studied the programme for the festival to appease the spirits of the dead which, having been released from Hades, roamed the world for a lunar month.

In the morning a puppet show was staged on one of two moored junks, on the second a service was held and a roast pig, pink dumplings and fruit were offered to the departed.

At midday an effigy of Yen Lo, Ruler of the Nether Regions, was taken on board on this junk, strung with lanterns, while a team of women were putting the finishing touches to a fleet of model junks and steamships to be launched during a cruise round the great harbour dividing Kowloon from Hong Kong Island.

Firecrackers exploded, drums beat, cymbals clashed and, with chanting priests on board, the junk set sail leaving in its wake brightly-coloured paper clothing for the drowned and banknotes drawn on the Bank of Hell – also accepted in Heaven – to finance the ghosts.

Price picked up a banknote and examined it. Blue on one side, red and green on the other. No. 482159, value five million Hong Kong dollars.

The junk made scheduled stops around the coastline and the model boats loaded with tea, rice and oil were launched. As darkness descended another service was held on the other junk anchored off Kowloon before an altar bearing two artificial lotus blossoms and a table with a gold statue of Buddha on it.

At 8.30 a priest wearing white and scarlet vestments, watched by passengers on other vessels crowded round the two junks, prayed on the fo'c'sle for the dead in hell.

One and a half hours later lotus blossoms fashioned from red

171

paper were fuelled with oil and given to women standing in the
bows of neighbouring vessels who lit them and launched them
onto the dark waters. If a woman caught a blossom still alight
then she would become pregnant.

The festival finished with a bonfire in a metal basket strung
between the two junks and the earthly manifestations of Yen Lo
and his henchmen, their spirits appeased, were burned.

But where was the heroin going to be picked up in the first
place? Price poured himself a Scotch and spread a map on the
dining table. The junk that was to tour the harbour was to be
launched on the morning of the festival from a boat-building
yard on the banks of the Pearl River estuary in mainland China.
So presumably the drugs would be picked up somewhere in the
estuary.

Price shrugged: it didn't really matter; he had no intention
of boarding the junk at sea – the heroin would be jettisoned,
another fiasco. What concerned him was where the cargo
would be delivered. God willing, Chen Lip would provide the
answer.

Boys? He frowned remembering the conversation with Sandilands. No, it must have been Boyce.

He sailed his finger down the estuary, skirting islands, until it
reached Kowloon. He anchored there and sipped his whisky.
Then he crossed the harbour to Sulphur Channel, made several
more stops, returned to Kowloon at dusk. . . .

He saw tiny oil lamps floating on the water, heard the priests'
prayers. And heard a voice from Frank's bedroom. 'Can I have a
drink of water?'

He closed his eyes, gripped the edge of the table.

He watered the indoor plants, returned to the map and the
quayside at Kowloon. A one-man operation? Impossible. But
who else was there now that Boyce was finished? He still had
trusted friends in Organised Crime, a few in Customs, a couple
in Narcotics. . . . But Boyce had been trusted. No, this had to be
solo.

You were a good copper once, Harry Price. What you are
contemplating now is reckless, irresponsible. If you fail Hong

Kong will be gorged with heroin, lit with temporary euphoria followed by despair.

He imagined the cargo being unloaded while an innocent priest performed one of the ceremonies. Saw Kwan Tai and his son.

Kwan Tai. . . .

' . . . drink of water. I'm so thirsty.'

Price opened the bedroom door.

The emptiness was palpable. How small the empty bed was.

He shut the door.

The map.

The front door bell shocked him.

He peered through the Judas Eye.

Boyce.

'I had to come,' Boyce said.

'To plead?'

Boyce sat in an easy chair, touched his pugilist's eyebrow. 'I helped you when you first came to Hong Kong.'

'I thought you were an honest cop. I thought I was learning a policeman's honesty through you.'

'What makes you think a policeman is so different from anyone else? We just do a job,' Boyce said, North Country accent even stronger than usual.

'More,' Price said. 'Much more. We make sure everyone else can do a decent job.' He wished he could find the pulse of truth. Were policemen, lawyers, judges really any different? Why should they pass judgement? Because they had been sworn in? That surely doesn't make us any less fallible to temptation. Why should we pass judgement on others?

The magistrate was born lucky. Money, position, privilege. . . . Why should he damn the prisoner in the dock?

Didn't the prisoner have as much right to invoke the weaknesses of Mankind as the judge, the magistrate, the copper on the case. . . ?

He said: 'You destroyed what I believed in.'

'Don't bullshit me, Harry, you were never a copper.'

'Destroyed what I tried to believe in which is worse.'

173

'Keep your beliefs. That's why I'm here.'

'I don't understand,' Price said.

'I can help you.'

'With friends like you I don't need enemies.'

'Half smart. Have you ever wondered what divine right gives us the right to impose what we like to call justice onto others?'

Price who had been wondering just that said: 'Maybe a conclusion over the centuries about what is right and wrong.'

'Concluded by the privileged. You know summat, Harry, I sometimes wish I'd been born the son of a farmer. Grown up with cattle and money and security. Maybe then I'd be sitting on't bench passing judgement on the poor bastards who were the cattle. . . . Did you ever wonder, Harry, what right they had to pass judgement?'

'I always knew what was right and what was wrong,' said Price, realising that Boyce was voicing his own questions.

'So did they. . . . Maybe they harboured terrible thoughts but had the means to contain them.'

'You should have been a lawyer not a copper,' Price said.

'I should have been a villain, Harry. Am a villain. So what's the difference? You know, what's the fucking difference?'

'Set a thief to catch a thief?'

'Just don't say, "Someone's got to do it."'

'There's justice in the minds of kids,' Price said. 'We've got to remember that. Keep reminding ourselves of what we once believed. . . .'

'What we were taught to believe. By adults. Take a look in the dock one of these days, Harry. Look at the kids you've just put there. They didn't have the chances you did. Does that make them guilty?'

'Some people are born bad,' Price said.

'Their fault?'

'Maybe not. But it's our job to protect the innocent against them.'

'So you're born guilty or not guilty. You don't have much say in it. Or do you think that's bullshit? That's what they always say in't movies these days when the scriptwriter has written himself

174

into hole. Bullshit. I heard one bullshit and two assholes on television last night.'

Price said carefully: 'I was brought up to know what was right and what was wrong. I was taught to protect the former, prosecute the latter.'

'Bullshit,' Boyce said.

'The trouble with decency is that is sounds . . . decent.'

'Right,' Boyce said.

'Which is a crying shame.'

'Correct.'

Price watched water dripping from the leaves of a rubber plant. Jane would have over-watered it.

He said: 'If your kids are molested who do you send for?'

'The police,' Boyce said.

'If there's a riot and innocent people are beaten up who do you send for?'

'The cops.'

'If your house is burgled?'

'The fuzz.'

'If your wife is raped?'

'This is getting boring,' Boyce said. 'Haven't you got a beer?'

'Remember that time a Chinese cop climbed onto a balcony ten stories high to save a would-be suicide?'

'I remember. He fell. They scraped him off pavement.'

'And the suicide climbed back into his apartment.'

'Okay, okay. *I think your policemen are wonderful.* Have you finished defending yourself?'

Price said: 'I once saw a sergeant defend a woman and two kids against a mob looking for her husband. He was beaten almost to death.'

'I think. . . .'

'It was you,' Price said fetching a can of Tooheys' from the fridge. 'Why have you come here?'

Boyce poured the beer into a glass and said: 'A deal.' His pugilist's features looked fragile as though the blows he had taken in the past had resurfaced.

'What kind of a deal would that be, Charlie?' Price, glass of whisky in his hand, stood at the window looking down at a pasture of jungle-thick bamboo and undergrowth lit by lights from the apartments; during the day butterflies fluttered through it like petals of blossom in the breeze.

'I know when the next consignment is due.'

'So do I,' Price said.

'Exact time? Location? How it's going to be off-loaded?'

'I know when it's due,' Price said. 'By tomorrow morning I'll know the rest.'

'Chen Lip?'

'It doesn't matter who,' Price said, shaken.

'He told me he'd seen you.'

'That was loyal of him,' Price said.

'You were lucky,' Boyce said. 'What he was going to tell you was all bullshit.'

'*Was?*', knowing.

'He's dead,' Boyce said. 'One last fix. Too much. He's in the morgue. Did you pay him?'

Price felt the sweat on his skin, ice-cold the way it was supposed to be with junkies in withdrawal. 'Why do you want to help me? I thought you tipped off villains not cops.'

'I said a deal, Harry.'

'You want me to save you? Perjure myself?'

'You're the main witness against me. Without you there isn't a case.'

Price sat opposite Boyce. 'Why did you do it, Charlie?'

'An inspector after all those years. Beaten up, knifed, kicked half to death. . . . I was owed, Harry. The cottage on't moors, the pigeons. . . .'

'Your pension would have taken care of those.'

Boyce gazed into the froth on his beer as though searching for truth. 'And I owed money.'

'Gambling?'

'Aye. Happy Valley and triad casinos. The old lady deserved better than retirement on't pittance.' Boyce leaned forward. 'You need me, Harry. One man can't pull this one off.'

It shouldn't be one man, Price acknowledged. '*Kwan Tai, I*

arrest you for the murder of my son.' Dereliction of duty? Are we all corruptible?

He said: 'If you hadn't tipped off the 18G I would have confiscated that entire shipment.'

'What you really mean, Harry, is you would have nicked Kwan Tai. End of fucking crusade. Right?'

Price placed his glass carefully on the coffee table. 'What time, Charlie? Where?'

*   *   *

The next interruption was the telephone.

Rachel Crown said: 'Maisie's disappeared.'

*   *   *

The water taxi, a decrepit motorised sampan, dropped Price and Rachel at Silvermine Bay on the island of Lantau at 10.45 pm. They hired a cab to take them to Tai O.

The occupants of the hostel weren't unduly disturbed by Maisie's disappearance: she wasn't the first addict who had failed to kick Miss White out of their lives. And they were more concerned with the new arrivals seeking help during the heroin famine.

Price questioned the group leader, a Chinese waiter who had been chasing the dragon on the towering Mei Foo Sun Chuen housing estate in the New Territories. Apparently Maisie had boarded the 1.45 pm bus to Silvermine Bay the previous day. Had she been seen on the 2.45 ferry to Hong Kong Island? The group leader didn't know.

He showed Price the dormitory where Maisie slept in a bed partitioned by flowered curtains. The bed was neatly made. On the wall above was a print of Christ on the Cross. Furniture consisted of a rattan-seat chair and an amateurishly varnished chest of drawers.

Price opened one. A trace of powder. He tasted it. Talc. A copy of *Sisters* magazine. A packet of hairpins. A scrap of paper

177

with his telephone number scrawled on it. A lucky jade charm. Scattered glass beads. All that was left of Maisie.

'It happens,' said the group leader who was young with a premature frown stamped on his forehead.

'Could she have been abducted?'

'She packed.'

'Others might have packed for her.'

'No signs of a struggle.'

'You don't struggle with a knife at your throat,' Price said.

The waiter shrugged. It happens. He spoke in shrugs. His indifference irritated Price. 'Don't you care?'

'Of course I care. But you don't understand: when one of us runs away we fear for ourselves.'

'Does this often happen?' Price asked Rachel who had come into the dormitory.

'Occasionally. But I didn't think Maisie would make a break: someone must have got to her.'

We shared her, Price thought.

He said to the leader: 'Did she confide in anyone? Would anyone have an idea why she might have disappeared?'

'We all confide in each other.'

'One in particular? And please don't shrug.'

Rachel touched Price's hand. 'He's trying; you don't know what he's been through. He sees himself running away, returning to the dragon.'

The leader said he had seen Maisie talking beneath the banyan tree in the garden with a girl named Lindy Sham, a former prostitute.

Lindy Sham wasn't a girl. She was middle-aged, plump, maternal. She told Price she had no idea why Maisie should have absconded. Price didn't believe her. He had interrogated so many prisoners and witnesses that evasions and half-truths hung in the air.

Perhaps it was because he was a policeman; Lindy Sham must have known many.

He said gently: 'Are you protecting someone, Lindy?'

'Gods, why should I do that?' She smiled, gap-toothed, at

178

Price. She was guarded but not hostile or half-smart or frightened. Her attitude intrigued Price.

'We only want to help Maisie,' he told her.

'I know that otherwise Miss Crown would not favour you with her company.'

'You really have no idea why Maisie left?'

Lindy Sham shook her head, compressing her smile as though a secret might escape through the gap in her teeth.

Price telephoned police headquarters and told a duty officer to circulate a description of Maisie. He didn't hold out much hope; it was usually stupidity or homing instinct or an informant's tip that netted a fugitive in Hong Kong.

It was too late to return to Hong Kong Island. Rachel slept in Maisie's bed: Price lay down on a mattress in another dormitory in the overcrowded hostel.

He closed his eyes. Black holes fringed with light framed Boyce, then Maisie. How could he sleep? Then it was daylight and Rachel was standing above him and Maisie was beside her. 'Guess what,' Rachel said, 'she's just gotten married.'

*   *   *

They called first at Price's apartment.

Rachel fried eggs and bacon and made coffee while he showered and shaved. With the corner of a towel he wiped steam from the mirror on the wall cabinet. The blurred face that returned his look was bold and devious.

He remembered the conversation on the ferry bringing them back from Lantau with the commuters and Rachel's disappointment that Maisie hadn't trusted her.

'Would you have allowed her to marry a jailbird?' he had asked.

'Of course. But in our chapel in the factory.'

'She didn't know that. She was scared you wouldn't let her.'

'We can still have a ceremony. A Service of Blessing. And he can visit her until she's completely cured.'

'Couldn't he stay on Lantau with her?'

179

'There isn't room. One bed-space is one life.' A rain-smelling breeze teased her hair; mist clung to the heights of Hong Kong, making it grey-haired and old. 'You make me sound a calculating bitch,' she said. And then: 'Are you so straight, Harry?'

'I'm honest with myself.' What sort of answer was that?

'You're waiting for the next consignment of heroin, aren't you?'

'So is every policeman in Hong Kong.'

'Do you want the heroin or Kwan Tai?'

'Both,' he said.

'Supposing I persuade Kwan Tai to abandon the heroin once it's been landed.'

'I admire your optimism,' Price said. 'I'm a realist.'

'He prayed in the chapel the other day.'

'You're not suggesting he's a convert?'

'He prayed,' Rachel said.

'To hedge his bets.'

She turned on him. 'Know something? I reckon Kwan Tai is straighter than you. You don't give a damn about the suffering that cargo will bring to Hong Kong: all you care about is revenge.'

Price turned his head away from the glib face in the mirror.

After breakfast Rachel showered. When she came out of the bathroom she was wearing his blue towelling robe. She walked round the apartment, opened the door to Frank's room.

When she turned round the sharing had returned to her face and, as he reached for her, the echoes receded from the apartment and were lost.

CHAPTER 19

Thirty-five thousand feet above the Saudi Arabian desert Jane Price, on her way to Hong Kong from Rome on a Cathay Pacific 747, ordered a glass of champagne.

To Jane the smile of the Chinese stewardess in red skirt and red-patterned blouse seemed more spontaneous than the smiles of European hostesses, as though the girl knew she was returning to her birthplace for the first time since her son died.

The smile lit tableaux. The cinemascope view of the churning harbour and serene hills from the lounge of the Regent Hotel . . . the waterfront fruit store where they sold carambolas from Singapore, guavas and papayas from Thailand and durians with an aromatic smell so vile that they were banned in some public places . . . the arrogant geese employed as watchdogs outside her parents' home . . . the fountains in the glass-roofed Landmark shopping plaza, their jets controlled by sound levels . . . the fans on the blue ceiling of St John's Cathedral riffling colonial sanctity. . . .

How long had she been away? Three, four years? Then it had seemed impossible that she and Harry could ever live together again, the death of Frank a wound that could never heal. But, although the scar remained, it had healed – except when she saw teenagers with their parents.

She sipped her champagne in the Marco Polo Business section of the jumbo jet, opened her handbag and took out the ivory figure of a naked woman that Harry had given to her before they were married, a Chinese antique that demure women had used to show their doctors where their ailments were located. She

181

had never loved him with abandon but she had admired his resolve in a profession that he should never have entered. The admiration had fused with affection and warmth, had encompassed them.

She replaced the ivory antique, the colour of old teeth, in her bag and stared at the bubbles spiralling in her champagne. Across the aisle a young Chinese folded his salmon-pink *Financial Times*, removed his spectacles and, looking suddenly vulnerable, closed his eyes and appeared to sleep instantly.

Would she go back to him? Presumptuous to assume that he would want her; but she sensed he would; already he was more real than the tailor's dummy who had driven her to the airport at Rome. She decided to book into a hotel to adjust before contacting him. It would be about the time of the Festival of the Hungry Ghosts; time to lay our own ghost to rest.

CHAPTER 20

From the circular bed on the yacht Michael Lo stared at Crystal Lam and himself in the mirror on the ceiling; he was aroused beneath the sheets but she didn't seem to be. If any of the girls from the past had been so dilatory he would have taken them forcibly and then kicked them off the boat. He adjusted the sheet so that he could see her breasts in the mirror.

She touched one absently with the trailing fingers of her hand and said: 'So the time has come.'

'Tomorrow,' he said. 'But there is plenty of time for pleasure today.' She had taken the combs from her hair and she seemed more gentle. An illusion.

'Your time,' she said. 'Your opportunity. In the Year of the Tiger.'

He touched her breasts; she pushed his hand away.

'It's all taken care of,' he told her.

'Tell me.'

'I have already told you.'

'Tell me again. I want to share your triumph tomorrow, to be with you in spirit.'

'As you know the Yellow Pang has discovered that the heroin will arrive with the festival junk tomorrow. We have traitors, running dogs, in our midst who will die when the Hungry Ghosts have been appeased.'

'You believe in this ceremony?'

'Only fools disbelieve. Which doesn't mean to say I believe.'

'A cautious view,' Crystal Lam observed.

Michael Lo's groin ached for her. He said: 'We have some little

183

horses in our midst who have been well briefed. They haven't denied to the Yellow Pang that the Hungry Ghosts will deliver the drugs tomorrow: they have elaborated.'

'Giving the wrong location?'

'The middle of Kowloon Bay at four. During the hours of the Tiger. When I was born. Claws and Teeth. Wild moods. . . .' His hand strayed beneath the sheets.

'An ambush?' As though she didn't already know, as though she craved the reiterated excitement.

'Their boat will be sunk before it reaches the junk. Their pride will be swallowed by the waters of the South China Sea. And the junk will sail on to Yaumatei to appease their wandering souls.'

'And you will do a deal with the Yellow Pang?'

'Deal? We shall take them over, draw their teeth.'

'So the two most powerful triads in Hong Kong will be one under your leadership?'

Michael Lo paused: leadership hadn't figured in the previous briefings about tomorrow's operation. He said: 'And the heroin, of course, will be unloaded as planned.'

She covered her breasts with the sheet. 'Supposing the police know about the Hungry Ghosts.'

'They don't know,' Michael Lo said.

'You sound very sure.'

'We have little horses in the police; they haven't heard a whisper.'

'But the Yellow Pang have.'

'All members of the Hung family. No one would inform the police, the enemy.'

'Price?'

'He more than anyone.'

'He knew about the shipment at Aberdeen,' Crystal Lam said.

'And we knew he knew. Flour, remember?'

Water slapped the hull of the yacht; black-eyed kites looking for *lap sap*, garbage, flew past; a gun fired – noon.

Crystal Lam said: 'He knew through Boyce.'

'And he reported Boyce for corruption. Boyce isn't going to do him any favours.'

'A deal?'

'Price withdraws the charges if Boyce gives him details about the shipment?'

'To quote one of my worst films – you catch on fast,' Crystal Lam said.

Michael Lo was no longer aroused. 'It's possible that Boyce does know the details.'

'You'd better find out,' Crystal Lam said.

'Even so it's only Price, the Lone Ranger. He won't tell anyone else.'

'You must still find out,' Crystal Lam said. 'If he has then you know what to do. Even if he hasn't. . . .' She pulled back the sheets. 'But a few moments now won't make any difference,' as her hair brushed his belly.

As he dressed she said: 'You didn't answer me just now.'

'About what?' Knowing.

'The leadership of the 18G.'

'Kwan Tai is still nominally Dragon Head.'

'Nominally is good enough?'

'The members will follow me.'

'Not all of them,' Crystal Lam said. 'And you can't afford to have a split.'

'So what are you suggesting?' thinking: Gods, don't let her say it.

'You are the Tiger,' she said. 'Claws and teeth.'

*   *   *

That afternoon Michael Lo caught the ferry to the island of Cheung Chau to meet the rebel committee in the apartment overlooking the small harbour crowded with boat people's homes. Five members . . . but how many were totally loyal to him? How many were merely waiting to see who won the power struggle between father and son? The robust, shaven-headed Grass Sandal certainly; quite possibly he was totally committed to Kwan Tai – he was the right age. But after tomorrow I will rule. . . .

He accepted a glass of brandy from the Vanguard and sat at the black table starred with mother-of-pearl. But what if Kwan Tai resists me? If he opposes me. . . . Crystal Lam's implications writhed like the smoke from the joss stick. A knife, a hatchet . . . my father?

He said: 'Of late we have given an impression of weakness. An impression, no more. Tomorrow that impression will be erased forever.'

He unrolled a nautical map of Kowloon Harbour and spread it on the table. With one finger he indicated the vantage point from which 18G members would ambush the Yellow Pang. He was a true Red Pole, a Warrior. Kwan Tai would be proud of me, he thought, and was scared.

'But what if Kwan Tai opposes this plan?' asked White Fan who, as usual, talked in questions.

'Why should he?' asked Michael Lo.

'Why indeed,' Grass Sandal said, 'if he knows nothing of it.'

Michael Lo stared at the goldfish ogling him. Then said: 'Grass Sandal, do not become a rebel within rebels. We all know why we are here – to re-establish the might of the 18G. And we all know that to achieve this we must question the authority of the old guard. If the elders do not understand that the Yellow Pang must be overthrown then they must go.' He pointed his finger at Grass Sandal. 'And that includes you.'

Grass Sandal pushed the stubble on his scalp forward so that a frown appeared on his forehead. 'That is what I wanted to hear,' he said, the lie hanging in the smoke of the joss stick. 'Initiative, resolution.'

And your ancestors! Michael Lo thought.

The Vanguard pulled at the hairs growing from one of the two moles on his face. 'Does Kwan Tai know of this plan? Does it have his support?'

Michael Lo spoke the truth. 'He knows about the plan. Whether it has his support I do not know. We shall find out tomorrow, won't we, Grass Sandal?'

The goldfish blew a bubble.

That evening Michael Lo, Warrior, went looking for Boyce.

He found him in the oval shaped bar of the Foreign Correspondents' Club on Hong Kong Island where journalists and businessmen talked and drank with application. In one corner the news of the day beamed by satellite repeated itself on a television video beside a teletype wire machine machine-gunning bulletins.

Boyce was isolated at the bar beside a tall journalist who looked like a buccaneer who had dallied in Savile Row, a chunky Australian executive of an international news agency in a dark blue safari suit, a girl feature writer, also Australian, from the *South China Morning Post* whose gentle questions were deceptively acute, and the plumply commanding figure of a freelance authority on China. They were discussing an article in the *Far Eastern Economic Review* about the shortage of heroin. Good or bad? They were uncharacteristically in agreement: good in a future that was unforseeable, bad in today's climate in which crime and suffering were increasing. Michael Lo, film star, nodded at them and sat at the bar a few feet from Boyce and ordered a brandy.

The detective looked drained, punished features sagging, jowls perfunctorily shaved, wisp of cotton wool sprouting from a cut on his chin, whisky tongue thick in his mouth as he ordered another drink from the Chinese barman.

Michael Lo wondered why, as he wasn't a member, he was being served. Had probably claimed that he was waiting for some worthy who did belong. Me? A doubtful proposition in view of the fact that Boyce had been accused of collaborating with the 18G and every policeman in the territory knows I am their Red Pole. Unless Boyce now knew that the case against him had collapsed. . . .

Boyce peered at him with boozy concentration and said: 'Great to see you, Mike. How's the grunt and groan business?'

So he isn't afraid of being seen with me, Michael Lo thought. He said: 'Can't complain. I hear you've been having a rough time recently.'

'You should know.'

Michael Lo glanced anxiously around the bar; he hadn't anticipated that Boyce would be so drunk. But no one took any notice of them. Shreds of the adjoining conversation reached him. 'Bound to be another consignment soon. . . . Pakistan destroying the opium crop. . . . So what? One door closes, another opens. . . .'

A young detective superintendent, a member, came in, spotted Boyce and walked to the other side of the bar.

Michael Lo said softly: 'Can you spare a few moments? Outside?' And even more softly: 'We are very grateful. . . .' He settled both their bills and strode out of the club to the corner of the street where every few minutes the traffic lights released an attack force of red taxis.

Boyce joined him a few moments later. He smelled of liquor and sweat. He disgusted Michael Lo. They walked round the corner.

'How grateful?' Boyce said.

'We're sorry you've been suspended. That bastard Price. . . .' He glanced at Boyce; there was no reaction but the rheumy eyes pleaded. 'We're going to compensate you,' Michael Lo said.

'How much?'

'Twenty thousand Hong Kong.'

'Okay, hand it over.'

'Here? Don't be stupid.'

'Where?'

'Cat Street.' Michael Lo gave him an address. 'Now.'

Then he walked briskly back into the FCC so that he would have an alibi as the sharpened umbrella-spoke slid between Boyce's ribs into his heart.

*   *   *

Lu Sun lingered in his office that evening long after the sun had spent itself and Hong Kong had unclasped its jewels. Tonight his beliefs felt as fragile as his bones and his skin which the herbalist had failed to revitalise; perhaps the imbalance of Yin and Yang had reached his brain.

He picked up the decoded cable from Kang Li in Peking. It was disagreeably to the point: if Michael Lo refused to kill his father then Lu Sun would have to appoint another assassin. But Kwan Tai was one of the few Chinese in Hong Kong whom Lu Sun respected; he saw their spirits, entwined, rising from the same crucible of ancient convictions. Ordering his death would be partial suicide. ´

Hypocrite! Did you torment yourself thus when you allowed yourself to believe that Michael Lo would commit patricide?

In case it contained a nuance of hope Lu Sun played back the recording of his conversation with Crystal Lam in his office earlier that day.

A few pleasantries, then:

'So, Crystal Lam, what is the mood of your lover?'

'Amenable, Lu Sun.'

'How amenable?'

He remembered detecting a trace of a smile on her contained features and thinking: *Gods, I was right. In her way she does love him.*

'He has set a trap for the Yellow Pang tomorrow.'

'But surely they know that the heroin is arriving with the Hungry Ghosts?'

'But not when, Lu San. Not where. Michael' – the smile had been mouled with secret hollows – 'has misled them.'

'So he *is* poised to take over the Yellow Pang?'

And he recalled hoping that she would reply: 'And the 18G.'

Instead: 'That goes without saying.'

Ayeeha! A pause. The cassette whirred. Then:

'And the 18G?'

Lu Sun stopped the tape. After the meeting with Kang Li in Canton he had suggested to Crystal Lam that she might implant a suggestion of murder into Michael Lo's consciousness. Perhaps after sexual fulfilment? Her reply had been non-committal, certainly not negative.

He composed himself to try and identify a trace of hope and pressed PLAY.

'If Kwan Tai resigns.'

If!

'Does Michael Lo believe he will?'

'It is a possibility.'

'I need more than possibilities, Crystal Lam.'

'You need miracles, Lu Sun. We are discussing the relationship between a son and his father.'

A slight cough on the tape. Drumming fingers on the desk. A knock on the door. 'Later,' his voice said. Then: 'We are discussing the future of Hong Kong, Crystal Lam. We are discussing the future of the People's Republic. We are discussing your future.'

And mine, he remembered thinking.

Another pause. Teacup on saucer. Scrape of a match, exhalation of cigarette smoke.

Crystal Lam: 'I have implanted your suggestion. But subtly. . . .'

'After. . . .'

'Sex, yes. But perhaps it should have been before.'

The smile had assumed another, ruminative angle.

'So what do you deduce, Crystal Lam?'

'It remains to be seen whether the brain accepts or rejects the implant.'

He pressed OFF. There had been nothing more constructive; both he and she had known that the chances of a son killing his father, especially during the Festival of the Hungry Ghosts, was as remote as the stars.

Reluctantly Lu Sun rejected conjecture and summoned his podgy apologist, Chen Chan.

He came in carrying a copy of the Canton party newspaper, the *Southern Daily*. He had probably inferred from an article some obscure pointer to 1997, or westernisation, that not even the author had intended to convey. And wants to impart it to me.

Lu Sun pre-empted him. 'Are you still in training, Chen Chan?'

'Training?' He stopped in the act of opening the newspaper; Lu Sun saw that several paragraphs had been marked with yellow highlighter.

'Did you not learn *wushu* at Shaolin, Number One Monastery Under Heaven? Did you not specialise in broadsword and scimitar?'

'I did but –'

'I have a job for you,' Lu Sun said.

*   *   *

In his room inside the Walled City Kwan Tai agonised. Tomorrow his son planned to rout the Yellow Pang and he rejoiced in his tiger daring. 'A wise son maketh a glad father' – *Proverbs*.

But he should have consulted me *before* devising such an audacious scheme. Does he still want me to retire before my time? Worse, does he plan to depose me if I refuse? He accuses me of lack of initiative but what future does the 18G have if the spirit of all the 36 oaths is scorned?

Kwan Tai had consulted Grass Sandal but the Messenger had merely answered: 'Your son speaks in riddles,' thereby intensifying his torment. Kwan Tai lit his pipe but it brought him no comfort.

Earlier he had sought answers in his copy of *T'ung Shu*, the Chinese almanac, juggling with the 28 constellations, numbers, dates, dreams, the strokes in his name, palmistry, physiognomy. . . . But no combination had proved auspicious.

He had prayed to the Goddess of Mercy in the small temple behind the street stalls outside the Walled City; he had prayed to Rachel Crown's God. And afterwards he had been visited by an extraordinary notion – that on both occasions he had been praying to the same deity.

But the possibility had kindled another worry that had become the focus of his dilemma: he had told Rachel Crown that the next consignment of white powder could be lost after it had been delivered and she had replied. . . . What were her words?. . . . 'Go home with a light heart, God has heard your prayers.'

Did that mean that if he didn't keep his side of the bargain her god – and his, for that matter, if his recent portent were true – would not heal the wound bleeding between him and his son?

Kwan Tai placed one hand on The Bible, the other on *T'Ung Shu*. And the answer presented itself: he would anonymously tip off Price that the heroin was arriving tomorrow with the Hungry Ghosts. Price would once again act alone and we will be waiting for him.

Kwan Tai hurried out of the Walled City to a telephone booth. Behind him teeth grinned in the windows of the dentists' shops.

CHAPTER 21

The new motorised junk chosen to appease the Hungry Ghosts of Hong Kong set sail from the boatyard on the east bank of the Pearl River estuary on mainland China at dawn.

Ten minutes later it paused in the mist beside a green islet to pick up a floating cargo that would appease the living ghosts – the territory's 100,000 drug addicts.

The heroin, Nos 3 and 4 grades – picked up without the knowledge of the organisers of the festival – was contained in five batches, five to neutralise No. 4, death, five being sacred – the segments of the earth, north, south, east, west and centre, the immortal five who flew to Canton with grains of rice in their mouths. . . .

As the mist began to lift thunder grumbled in the distance. A typhoon was approaching; Signal 1 warning that it was within 400 nautical miles of Hong Kong had already been hoisted; if No. 3, anticipating gusts between 22 and 60 knots, was hoisted, shipping would take to the typhoon shelters and some ferries would be cancelled.

The Chinese crew of the junk listened apprehensively on the radio: No. 8 warning and the operation would be abandoned, fortunes lost.

But the broad waters of the estuary were only tufted by a breeze and there were more cargo boats, junks and sampans than waves. On both banks buffaloes tethered to the lotus quiet of the early morning stood motionless in the paddy fields.

To the starboard Macau. Ahead the pirate peaks of Lantau, Broken Head, still swathed in mist.

193

The skipper, a tall, inward-looking Chinese from the north, near the disputed border with Russia, gave the engine full throttle and spun the wheel with an authority he did not feel; it was only the third time he had navigated the estuary and it would be the last when he was paid for delivering the heroin. Then he would return north away from the scheming toads of Canton.

The junk passed the flanks of Lantau, the complex of Sea Ranch to the port, and to starboard Cheung Chau, the smell from its fish-processing factory salting the breeze from the South China Sea. The skipper wrinkled his nose, turned his head away and saw the sharp prow of a grey and black police patrol boat pushing aside the water.

Its number was 89. Eight prosperity; nine enough. Enough prosperity. . . . For them or us? the skipper wondered as an imperious voice ordered them to heave to.

The skipper said to his second-in-command, a skinny Chuang from the south-west: 'Let us pray that the foul-mouths are seeking illegal immigrants.'

'Miss White is an illegal immigrant,' said the Chuang who possessed a sense of humour that was sometimes misplaced.

The boarding party consisted of a Chinese uniformed inspector of marine police and a sergeant. The inspector, young and brisk and polished, announced: 'We are going to search your ship.'

Should he spring the trap-door and jettison the weighted cargo or brazen it out? Ditch it and you bid farewell to a new home on the banks of the Amur, the skipper reasoned. After all, the white powder was disguised well enough.

'Consider yourselves to be my guests,' he said.

'You could make it easier for us,' said the inspector in his neat voice.

The skipper waited.

'Any illegal immigrants on board?'

'I would be a fool if I had,' the captain said, staring at the skinny Chuang.

'Deep Bay is full of fools. Some may have strayed into the estuary.'

'I am not Cantonese,' said the skipper with dignity, instantly regretting the observation because in all probability the inspector was.

'Nor I,' said the inspector, elaborating in Hakka and then, when he had spent himself: 'But we must have a look around.'

The search was perfunctory. Stowaways was what the inspector was looking for. He saluted and departed.

Said the Chuang: 'Perhaps Miss White is Hakka.'

The junk pushed ahead. Sunshine Island, Green Island. . . . Jets on the western flight approach began to settle above them. . . . Hong Kong Island to the starboard . . . ahead, Stone Cutter's Island, beyond it Kowloon. Ferries and lighters, hydrofoils and jetfoils, old freighters and sampans. . . .

The breeze grew sinews. The skipper of the junk thought it smelled dangerous.

The junk reached the moorings to the west of Kowloon at 10.08; then the Hungry Ghosts came on board.

*   *   *

Price, sitting in the office of a jade exporter on the third floor of a weathered waterside block near the typhoon shelter on the east shoreline of Kowloon, watched the two junks through field-glasses.

Lanterns in honour of Chiang Hau, the god who cares for the inhabitants of Hades, moved in the breeze in front of the vessels; a marine police launch busied itself among the crowds of small boats pushing forward; from one junk came the wailing of priests in black, crimson and gold robes intoning in front of the three pyramids of food topped by hands fashioned from rice; from the second the cries of children watching a puppet show.

Price moved a lavender jade model of Tin Hau, the Taoist Queen of Heaven, fine-focussed the field-glasses and saw Michael Lo, dressed as a coolie, board the recently-arrived junk.

So it was on!

195

He put down the field-glasses and paced the office littered with jade figurines, yellow, black and red, but mostly green. He stopped in front of a baleful dragon and checked the pistol in his shoulder holster.

The raid would take place here. Just after dark. After the new junk had returned from its tour of the harbour. As the ceremonies were reaching their climax, drums, cymbals, lanterns. As the heroin was being unloaded.

Boyce's intelligence had been confirmed on the telephone the previous night by an informant. Male, Chinese. But where was Boyce?

Even with Boyce backing him up with an Armalite from the jade export office, the operation would be perilous. Without the support of a devastating burst from the automatic rifle it would be . . . stupid?

Kwan Tai caught in possession. Michael Lo, his son, with him. Frank, my son. Price gripped the butt of the pistol inside his jacket. It was warm.

*   *   *

Michael Lo conferred with the skipper of the new junk in the cabin which smelled of new wood and varnish and incense.

'Are you sure about the crew?' he asked.

'Of course.' The skipper was a crude northerner, monosyllabic to the point of boorishness.

'Him?' Michael Lo pointed at a sullen Cantonese watching the puppet show on deck.

'You should know, *Warrior*, he is a member of your branch of the Hung family,' the skipper said in appalling Mandarin.

'I cannot know every member of such a vast congregation. Where did he join you?'

'At the boatyard,' the skipper said. 'Highly recommended.'

'And the other two?'

'Perhaps,' the skipper said, 'you need some courage.' He opened a cupboard and took out a bottle of brandy and two glasses.

The brandy burned Michael Lo's stomach. He said: 'And the crew that was supposed to sail the junk round the harbour?'

'They dispersed. They didn't argue.' The skipper placed a Smith & Wesson on the table between the two glasses.

Guns . . . although it was the Chinese who had invented gunpowder Kwan Tai, like all the elders of the societies, detested them and this was one of the few of his father's viewpoints with which Michael Lo agreed. Death should be an extension of murderous intent, a kick, a chop, a cut, a puncture. A severance of life, not an explosion. Regretfully guns would have to be used later. Guns that made the Smith & Wesson look like a toy.

He had arranged to pick up Kwan Tai on the waterfront at dusk for the climax of the operation. But by that time I will have smashed the Yellow Pang. Surely then he will have to stand down. If not. . . . Michael Lo remembered the messages in Crystal Lam's voice; her tones had reminded him of silk thread cutting through flesh.

He drank more brandy and said: 'Your men know what to expect?'

'This isn't one of your movies, Michael Lo.'

Piss on all your generations, Michael Lo thought. When this is over I will cut your tongue from your foul mouth and replace it with your prick.

'The ambush,' Michael Lo said pleasantly. 'They know about that?'

'Of course.'

'And *they* don't know anything?' pointing at the priests on the other junk.

'Nothing, Michael Lo. They are only bit players. You are the star, are you not?'

*   *   *

At 10.25 an anonymous tip-off was received on the Fight Crime Committee's anti-triad hotline, 5 – 277887. 'Time?' asked the excited duty officer.

'Nightfall,' said the caller and rang off.

*   *   *

By mid-afternoon the typhoon a hundred miles away in the South China Sea had turned its back on Hong Kong and the breeze funnelling through the islands had dropped.

At 4 pm the new junk anchored in the middle of Kowloon Bay beside a rusting cargo ship that had become a fixture there and dropped a yellow buoy as a floating gravestone, a blizzard of brightly-coloured paper, a model junk and a model steamboat and an incalculable fortune in Bank of Hell scrip. The toy ships headed for the mainland, paper and banknotes followed inscrutable currents. The water was as untroubled as the blue-grey sky.

From the cabin of the junk Michael Lo viewed the cargo boat. It was Liberian-registered and named *Evita*. Its grey hull was bruised and rust-streaked, its bridge and decks as desolate as an abandoned wharf.

According to Michael Lo's information the attack force of Yellow Pang would emerge from the far side of the melancholy vessel in a Green Beret water-jet patrol boat capable of 24 knots, one of the many American relics of the Vietnam war that had lodged in Hong Kong. Their plan: to snatch the buoy which they believed was packed with heroin and escape without firing a shot because the 18G wouldn't be able to fire from a floating altar for the dead. For the 18G the ultimate loss of face. . . .

The river patrol boat rounded the stern of *Evita* just as the junk's anchor was being raised. There were six Yellow Pang on board the low-slung vessel. They all wore casual clothes, fishermen out for a day's sport. The Red Pole carried a boathook. Celebrants on the junk waved as, sharp prows pushing aside wings of spray, the patrol boat neared the yellow buoy.

The boathook snared the buoy. A knife flashed, rope parted. The Red Pole held the buoy aloft grinning.

Michael Lo allowed them to knife open the buoy and find it empty before signalling, one hand raised, sacred five fingers parted.

The three 18G opened up with their Armalites from the rail of *Evita*. The fishermen threshed and died and, as a lobbed hand-grenade exploded in the patrol boat, joined the Hungry Ghosts.

The living were lifted from *Evita* by a helicopter piloted by an aviator who, for HK 25,000 dollars an hour, never questioned the nature of a charter, and flown, south of the western flight approach, to an abandoned monastery deep in the green peaks of Lantau.

As police launches and rescue craft converged the skipper of the junk swung the wheel and took his terrified passengers back to the moorings off Kowloon waterfront at Yaumatei.

*   *   *

The junk and its elder sister were magnets. Around them, like iron filings, smaller junks, lighters and sampans, gathered.

Kwan Tai reached the new junk just before dusk by stepping from one attendant boat to another. The skipper greeted him laconically.

'So nothing has changed?' Kwan Tai asked, pointing at the more venerable vessel where the evening services were to be held.

'Why should it? The Hungry Ghosts showed their wrath in Kowloon Bay. The need to appease them is even greater than before.' His words were slippery, cynical.

'Where is my son?'

'Maybe his make-up needs repairing for the last scene.'

Kwan Tai tightened his muscles beneath his faded blue shirt. 'Maybe you, too, should prepare for your last scene.'

The skipper who belonged to a triad with distant connections with the 18G adjusted his tone. 'He's on the other junk.'

Kwan Tai peered across a narrow avenue of water. The elder sister was resplendent – altar screened by the smoke from joss sticks, tables dressed in red and white, priests in blue and gold vestments. After dark as lanterns burned, the chief priest would plead from the fo'c'sle with the Prince of Darkness for the wandering souls.

199

Of his son there was no sign.

The skipper said: 'Perhaps, Dragon Head,' a hint of humility in his tone, 'you could pay me now and then I will not intrude in your triumph.'

'You will be paid,' Kwan Tai told him, 'when Miss White has been safely delivered.' *And then will I divert the heroin?* He didn't answer the question.

He leaned against the rail. On the other side of the deck a sullen-looking member of the crew coiled a rope, glancing at him from time to time. Kwan Tai felt uneasy, as though unseen eyes were observing him from the floating houses, shops, school, barbers. . . .

Surely no one, apart from the Yellow Pang who acting on false information, had been routed, and Price, who was being kept under surveillance by two 18G 49s, could know about the delivery.

The sky paled. The crowds on Ferry Street and the blocks separating Nathan Road from the waterside began to take on nocturnal substance. A wolfish time of day.

Kwan Tai peered at a sampan from which two crones were selling dried fish. A musclar coolie squatted beside them; he had been staring at the junk but he lowered his head when Kwan Tai looked at the sampan.

On a small junk heavy with boat people another Chinese stood alone as though he had the plague. What was so different about him? Smock, too clean, legs and arms well muscled but lacking the corded toughness of the labourer. . . .

Police?

But I only tipped off Price and he is on the waterfront, alone, vulnerable, the lone warrior whose crusade will take him to his death which is, perhaps, what he desires. To the grave of his son.

Where is my son?

The warm fish-smelling breeze that had sprung up once again since the junk returned to Yaumatei changed its odour. Kwan Tai sniffed, frowned. The evening was toothed with mysteries.

200

Then he had it – the smell of custard tarts from the bakeries on Man Cheong Street.

*   *   *

No Boyce.

But policemen everywhere. Disguised as coolies, lightermen, boat vendors. . . .

And this was going to be a one-man triumph, Price thought bitterly. The end of a vendetta, vengeance.

The sampan paddled by a Chinese policewoman neared the two junks. Drums and cymbals and the cries of the living calling the dead.

Price, crouching behind bolts of red and green dress material in the prow of the sampan, peered at the floating altars. At the rail of the older of the two he saw Michael Lo, plastic red buoy in his hand.

So he had switched junks.

He fired a shot. Two policemen disguised as coolies boarded the junk and, pushing past the priests, jumped Michael Lo.

The buoy, weighted by an anchor attached to a rope, fell as Price dived into the tepid water. The rope uncurled and Price felt the anchor slide past him. He surfaced beside the buoy.

From the old junk screams. Shots from the newer vessel. Then the savage voice of the Armalite as Sandilands opened up from the jade exporter's office where Boyce should have been.

More shots. Sobbing. The silence after gunfire that isn't silence at all.

Price hauled himself onto the sampan and, with saw-edge scissors used to cut the bolts of material, savaged the buoy. Inside nestled a transparent bag of white powder.

Price pierced it, tasted the powder. Heroin. But scarcely a record haul. A pittance in fact. Boyce, you bastard. Price's hands began to tremble and his chest ached.

In the window of the jade exporter's he noticed a silhouette. Sandilands. The word ballooned from the past: 'Boys –'

And his own voice: 'Or Boyce.'

201

OR BUOYS.

He grabbed the policewoman's radio handset.

*   *   *

Hearing the shots, Kwan Tai jumped from the new junk and leapt from sampan to sampan, stepping stones to the gunfire. Chen Chan, Lu Sun's assistant, who had joined the crew at the boatyard on the banks of the Pearl estuary dropped the coil of rope, pulled the broadsword from beneath a tarpaulin and went after him.

He reached him on the fourth sampan. Kwan Tai, seeing the eyes of the vendors looking behind him, swung round, ducking. The sword cut air above his head.

He tried to balance himself on the small rocking boat. Another slice from the broad blade. It would have taken my head off, he thought. But what sort of man is this? An Ox, patient and tireless? And I am a Dragon!

It is almost always the unarmed fighter who gets the upper hand.

At sixty-two years of age? as he swayed from a thrust from the tip of the sword. But you are Dragon Head. And you are young and it is *not* yet your time. . . .

Saliva ran in his mouth; old skills danced in his skull; sap flowed in his muscles.

Watch their eyes.

Guarded, dutiful, self-righteous eyes. . . .

Ayeeha! This Ox was *wushu.* Jump, kick, thrust, slice. . . . The wrestling that Kwan Tai had learned as a boy overcame these feats of balance and athleticism because, although it appeared cumbersome by comparison, it was founded on inate graces.

Come on, Ox. How old are you? An old Ox.

Chen Chan feinted and cut and was surprised that the sturdy veteran in front of him still possessed a head.

The sampan joggled.

Kwan Tai waited for the next lunge, the one that would take the Ox off-balance.

He saw eyes on the boats crowded around them.

202

No more shots.

My son, are you safe?

And it came, the lunge from Chen Chan's fighting arm, and it drew blood and then it was past, taking with it a slice of Kwan Tai's shoulder and Chen Chan was off balance, righting himself, and Kwan Tai was closing in and his arms were round the Ox's chest and the Ox's ribs were cracking, splintering and then Kwan Tai thought: 'But I don't want to kill this man, this Ox,' and he jerked his shoulders and the sword was in the water, cutting the depths, and the Ox was on the deck of the sampan bleeding from the mouth and Dragon Head was on his way across the bows of the small boats to the old junk where, on the deck, he found his son bleeding from a wound in the chest inflicted by a bullet from an Armalite rifle.

*   *   *

Three of them outside intensive care in the hospital where Michael Lo lay listening to the calls from his ancestors.

Rachel Crown, Crystal Lam and Kwan Tai.

The surgeon said: 'We are doing everything we can,' as surgeons do.

Hope?

The surgeon made beggar's hands. 'The bullet is still there,' tapping his chest. 'It depends. . . . He is strong.'

'He is weak,' Crystal Lam said. 'And sometimes that is stronger than strength.'

Kwan Tai stared at this woman who spoke in contradictions and said: 'He will survive, he is a Red Pole, son of Dragon Head,' and she said in English: 'That is shit, and I don't mean any disrespect, but I love him too.'

Weakness, strength?

Rachel said to Kwan Tai: 'I want you to come with me,' and when he asked why: 'To pray.'

We are doing everything we can. Hopeless was what the surgeon was saying.

Such a pity, Michael Lo, film star, that you never learned

humility. Kwan Tai touched his thick eyebrows with the tips of his fingers so that the palms of his hands covered his eyes.

Such a pity that to you the 39 oaths were merely echoes from your youth.

He went back into intensive care. His son's eyes were closed, his breathing slight, his body fed with tubes.

Just the one son.

He touched his hand.

Then he went with Rachel Crown, leaving Crystal Lam alone in the corridor.

She led him to a private room furnished with a bed and a table and an easy chair and together they kneeled beside the bed and prayed in tongues to Rachel Crown's God.

CHAPTER 22

Boys, Boyce, buoys. . . . 'I was stupid,' Price said. 'They were off-loading the heroin in buoys at every stop the junk made on its tour of the harbour.'

Rachel, walking down the hill to Price's apartment from the bus-stop where he had met her, held his hand.

'Did the marine police get them all?'

'Just about. It was dark but they found most of them still floating because the triads didn't want to collect them in daylight. A couple of deliveries were intercepted on shore.'

'Did Kwan Tai know the heroin was being distributed?'

'That's important to you, isn't it.'

She said it was.

'He only knew about the last delivery,' Price told her. 'He thought the entire consignment was being delivered in Kowloon, at Yaumatei. His son was smarter.'

'Are you going to arrest him?'

'No case to answer,' Price said, glancing at a cab parked on the other side of the street; the passenger in the back seat was facing the other way. 'We didn't catch him red-handed; he was just an observer and no triad will testify against him. Death from five thunderbolts if they do.'

'I wonder if he intended to get rid of the heroin once it was landed.'

'I suggest he did better.' Price squeezed her hand. 'I received an anonymous 'phone call. . . .'

'Kwan Tai?'

Price didn't believe that Kwan Tai had been motivated by the interests of justice: much more likely that he had been hedging his bets – trying to appease Rachel's God knowing that the 18G could easily take care of a solitary crusader.

He said: 'You seem to have got through to him,' which in a way was true.

'The end of the vendetta?'

'The beginning of the crusade,' he said.

'But not alone?'

'Alone? I've never seen so many cops. . . .'

'Who tipped them off, I wonder.'

'I think you know,' he said and kissed her cheek.

*   *   *

Observing the kiss, Jane Price tapped the taxi driver on the shoulder and told him to drive down the hill away from the apartment that had once been her home.

*   *   *

In Victoria Park, as the day began to assemble, Lu Sun unwrapped his thoughts and contemplated them. So Kwan Tai had survived. He agonised and rejoiced. A man of the past, like me. But there is still a lot of time between now and 1997. By then you and I will be much older and that is not an unpleasant prospect. In the cage hanging from the hibiscus the canary began to sing and then its notes were doubled and, looking through the bars, Lu Sun saw that, for the first time, the canary he had bought in Kowloon was joining in the dawn song.

*   *   *

Rachel put down the 'phone in Price's apartment. She said: 'Michael Lo's going to be all right.'

Price asked: 'Should I be overjoyed?'

'He's going to live,' Rachel said, 'because Kwan Tai prayed to God.'

* * *

In the small temple outside the Walled City Kwan Tai offered thanks to the Goddess of Mercy for answering his prayers. Then he adjourned to a soothsayer to see what the future held for himself and his son.